The Prophecy
Daughters of the People, Book 1

LUCY VARNA

The Prophecy

Daughters of the People, Book 1

LUCY VARNA

Bone Diggers Press
www.bonediggerspress.com

For Bailey
The first Daughter

First edition © 2014. Second edition © 2015 C.D. Watson. All Rights Reserved.

Cover design © L.J. Anderson, Mayhem Cover Creations.

Published by Bone Diggers Press, Clayton, Georgia.

ISBN 978-0-9907730-7-8

TITLES BY LUCY VARNA

THE DAUGHTERS OF THE PEOPLE SERIES
Book 1: *The Prophecy*
Book 2: *Light's Bane*
Book 3: *The Enemy Within*
Book 3.5: *Tempered*
Book 4: *In All Things, Balance*

THE SONS OF THE PEOPLE SERIES
Book 1: *Say Yes*

THE CULLOWHEE HERITAGE SERIES
Book 1: *A Higher Purpose*
Book 2: *A Wicked Love*

Notes from the Fab Four

Notes on the People compiled by Tom Fairfax, Phil Walters, George Howe, and James Terhune, known at the IECS unofficially as the Fab Four.

Aenkanien. A tattoo inked into the left-hand shoulder blade of a Son who becomes the husband of a Daughter. Once approval has been granted by the mothers of both parties and the tattoo is in place, a formal marriage ceremony is unnecessary; the two are considered married in the eyes of the People, though many couples choose to undergo a civil or, less frequently, traditional ceremony.

Amaetien. The tattoo Sons receive on their sixteenth birthday (the day they become men under the traditions and laws of the People) to indicate their maternal lineage. Usually inked onto the upper left arm, the *amaetien* is a symbol of the mother's eternal protection and devotion, and a warning to any who would harm the Son.

Ankana. Woman. Also refers to the Woman with No Face.

Council of Seven. The People's ruling body, consisting of seven women, one representing the line of each of the Seven Sisters.

Daughter. A direct descendant of one of the Seven Sisters, Daughters may be either immortal (if they have not yet broken their own curse) or mortal (if they have broken their own curse or are the daughter of a mortal Daughter).

Eknon. Student.

Eternal Order. A supposedly mythical group devoted to undermining the ultimate goal of the People, to break the curse of immortality for every Daughter through the fulfillment of the Prophecy of Light.

High Guard. Seven Daughters devoted to eradicating the Eternal Order. A highly secret and deadly group.

Institute of Early Cultural Studies (IECS). Located in Tellowee, Georgia, USA, the IECS is the main historical research branch of the People and serves as a repository for much of its history.

Kaetyrm. Sister, usually used in a formal situation, though not always.

Maetyrm. Mother, usually used as a term of respect for an elder Daughter and not necessarily as a reference to one's own mother. Teachers, for example, are referred to as Maetyrm.

People, The. The name used by the descendants of the Seven Sisters to describe themselves. The People include all immortal and mortal Daughters, Sons, and the mortal descendants of all submitted Daughters to the second degree (i.e. through the grandchildren of Daughters who have submitted their wills and become mortal). Other descendants are not counted among the numbers of the People.

Prophecy of Light. Issued by an unknown person at some distant point in the past, the Prophecy of Light portends a way for the curse of immortality to be lifted from all of the People, and not solely the Daughters who submit their wills and become mortal. (See the Daughters of the People website.)

Seven Sisters. The progenitors of the modern People. The seven women, all sisters, avenged the deaths of their parents by killing the men of the People (the original band) and were cursed by the god An to live immortal lives without the ability to bear sons. The curse was tempered by the goddess Ki, who decreed that the curse could be broken by each one if she would submit her will, in whatever way (except sexually), to the man she loved. (See the Legend of Beginnings on the Daughters of the People website.)

Shadow Enemy. The traditional enemy of the People.

Son. Usually refers to the child of a Daughter who has broken the curse and become mortal, but may also reference the child of a Son or another male descendant of a Daughter.

Tellowee, Georgia, USA. One of the centers of the People, located in rural northeast Georgia.

PROLOGUE

Circa 7,500 B.C.E.

A HARD MOON shone down upon four hands worth of seasonal shelters. Kiya, eldest daughter of the First Seer in her union with the Warrior Chief, leaned her spear against a boulder and settled into her shift of the watch on top of a flat stretch of dirt. She squinted at the moon, so round and full above her. Its light was as pure as anything she'd ever seen. Maybe this would be the night the Lady Ki would grant her a vision, the way Mother always said She would. Kiya's bleeding time had come upon her two moons past. She was a woman now and ready to fulfill her duty to the gods, but without that first vision, she was relegated to the watch, a position anybody with two eyes and working ears could fill. Would she ever be able to begin her training as the People's next Seer or would the Lady find another of her sisters more worthy?

A pebble bounded across the rocks behind her and Kiya sighed. "Come out, Abragni. I know you're there."

Kiya's youngest sister crawled out of the shadows and sat down an arm's span away. "How come you always know it's me?"

"Because you're the noisiest of the Seven." Kiya held her arm out, beckoning Abragni closer. "You should be sleeping. We break camp tomorrow. Who knows how long it'll take us to reach the next one."

Abragni leaned her head against Kiya's scrawny chest and snuggled into her sister's embrace. "Marnan keeps poking me and Bagda won't make her stop."

"I'll speak to them."

"They won't listen to you either."

"Then I'll speak to Mother."

"Speak to the Lady, Kiya. *She'll* make them stop."

Kiya pressed her lips together. How could she tell her sweet sister that the Lady refused to share the future, guarding it as closely as Father did the People's safety? "I'll pray to An. How's that?"

Abragni's voice dropped to a whisper. "But He's grumpy."

"And He hears all," Kiya teased. "Here, little one. Rest your head on my leg. I'll protect you."

"I know you will." Abragni yawned and curled up on the ground beside Kiya, one hand on Kiya's leg under her head. "Forever and ever."

"Forever and ever," Kiya echoed.

The moon moved steadily across the sky, sliding through the stars along its nightly path. Kiya smoothed her hand over Abragni's dark hair, soothing her sister into sleep. The camp was still and quiet, the fires banked, the People resting with their families. Weariness crept over her. She shook it away, sharpening her gaze, tuning her ears to the slightest noise.

The guard wouldn't have been necessary if they weren't camped so close to another settlement, a walled city half a day's journey away. Father had refused to share his reasoning, but there had been rumors, ugly whispers among the women that their men grew tired of the People's nomadic life and wished to join their fortunes to those dwelling behind the high walls.

Nonsense, of course. The People were happy and hale, their children hearty, and though they had no wall to protect them from predators and war, they did well enough.

A shadow flitted across the encampment. Kiya sucked in a

quick breath and scanned the valley floor around the People's shelters. The shadow moved again, shifting from one side of the camp to the other, zigzagging toward the tent on the far side where Mother and Father rested with Kiya's five other sisters.

Another shadow joined the first and a third, and Kiya's heart thudded hard in her chest. She pressed one hand over her sister's mouth and shook her awake with the other. Abragni's wide, dark eyes blinked open. Kiya leaned down and whispered, "Something's wrong. We need to wake everybody. Can you help me?"

Abragni nodded slowly.

Kiya removed her hand and grabbed her spear. "If we get separated, make your way to the edge of the waters next to the cave Ganenda likes to hide in and wait for me there."

"I will," Abragni whispered. "You won't leave me there, will you?"

"I'd never do that."

They made their way around the perimeter of the camp, searching for the other men and women who were supposed to be on watch, and found no one. With each step, Kiya's chest grew a little tighter, her skin a little more prickly. She grasped Abragni's hand and urged her forward. They were halfway between the last watch position and the encampment when a scream rent the air, shattering the night's quiet.

Kiya's breath froze in her throat. "Mother."

Abragni's face crumpled. A tear slid down her round cheek. "I'm scared, Kiya."

Me, too. Kiya swallowed her fear and knelt in front of her sister. "Go to the cave now, little one. I'll wake our sisters and meet you there. Stick to the shadows."

Abragni sniffed and swiped the back of her hand across her face, smearing dirt through the tears. "I hate the shadows."

"Don't. You've nothing to fear among them. Now go."

Abragni slipped away and Kiya stood, spear in hand. An unnatural hush settled over the People's shelters. Nothing

3

moved. She sniffed, testing the air, and found no scent that shouldn't be there.

Kiya approached Mother and Father's shelter cautiously. Her footsteps were silent as she moved over the hard earth and her eyes never still. Three spear lengths away, a soft sob drifted to her and a female voice spoke, the words too faint for Kiya to make out. She eased up to the back of the shelter and dropped to her haunches in the sparse shadows lingering there. The voice came again, scarcely louder than it had been, and Kiya strained her ears, hoping to discern meaning in the quietly spoken words.

No, the voice was still too soft.

She crept around the edge of the shelter toward the opening and halted. In the clearing between the shelters, a handful of men stood over two limp forms lying prone on the ground.

"It's done, then," a man said, and Kiya's eyes widened. That had sounded like Dunan, Belara's man.

"A shame they had to be killed." That voice belonged to Tem'n, a young warrior just into his manhood, barely two seasons older than Kiya. "Especially the Seer. Her visions were useful."

An odd pressure filled her chest. *The Seer.* Her mother, the revered conduit between the People and the gods. Could she truly be dead?

"Are the women bound?"

Kiya frowned. She couldn't place that voice. It had to be a male of the People. Who else would be in their camp at night?

"It's been done," Dunan said. "We're missing two, the eldest and youngest of the Seven."

"The Seven?" the unfamiliar man said.

"The Seer's daughters," Tem'n said. "Five are inside. They're strong girls, brave. They'll make good slaves."

Kiya's heart skipped a beat. Kind Tem'n had never had a cross word to say to any woman, and now he wished to enslave her and her sisters? Such a life would be intolerable for any among the People. They were free, roaming where they willed, their only limits their need for food, shelter, and protection from the wild beasts and other people. How could anybody wish to deprive her and her sisters of that freedom, and why?

The men moved away, their conversation dwindling into murmurs too low for Kiya to understand. She waited and watched, biding her time. The men disappeared into a shelter on the far side of the camp. The moon's light dimmed, throwing the area around her into shadow. She glanced up. A cloud, a large, dark one, fully covered the bright moon. It would give her just enough time.

She crawled forward as quietly as she could along the hard-packed earth, her eyes scanning the darkness, and stopped beside the two still forms. Mother's eyes stared blindly into the sky. Something dark covered one side of her head, her life force, surely. Beside her, Father rested on his stomach. Kiya edged her fingers along the back of his head and encountered a dent the size of her fist among the sticky strands of his dark hair.

A whimper alerted her to another person's presence. Kiya crouched low, scanning the encampment. It came again, and this time she pinpointed it precisely. The whimpers were coming from her, from her own mouth. She bit into the side of her hand and closed her eyes, and a storm of sorrow whirled through her. Mother and Father, dead. The women of the People bound by their men. Five of her sisters enslaved, and one alone in the dark.

And she, barely fourteen seasons, had no guidance, no voice in her heart, no vision sent by the Lady illuminating the path Kiya must take.

Tears leaked down her face over her hand. She sat there for long moments, rocking slowly to and fro, her heart pounding and her breaths uneven. She couldn't do anything about Mother and Father. Their spirits were long gone now, lost to the Seven as surely as if they'd been taken by An. There were too many men to free all the women, too many for one lone woman to counter, but she could at least try to free her sisters.

She released her hand and ignored the throb of teeth marks

imprinted into the skin. Her spear. She'd need that if the men had left a guard. She grasped it firmly and inched across the ground toward Mother and Father's shelter.

A sliver of light peeked out from under the edge of the opening flap, barely enough to see by. Kiya shifted onto her haunches beside the flap and lifted it aside a scant hand's breadth. A fire crackled in the center, its edges delineated by stacked stones. Her sisters huddled together on the far side, their eyes wide. Kiya squinted and eased upright slightly. Their hands were in front of them, maybe bound, maybe not.

A solitary man passed between them and the fire. Thin, white scars marred his sun-darkened skin, formed under the claws of the animals the People hunted, and under the hands of their enemies. Kiya dropped the flap and put her back to the shelter. Young Mol'k, one the fiercest warriors among the People. He was brutal and hard, and so skilled, none could take him, not even the great beasts. She pressed trembling fingers over her mouth and breathed a prayer to the Lady. She'd never been to battle before, never faced man or beast except in practice, but her sisters were in there, relegated to a fate as harsh as death. How could she leave them?

Kiya inhaled through her nose and exhaled through her mouth, again and again in slow draws, willing her heart to calm and her mind to clear. Mol'k had her sisters. They needed to be freed. Kiya was the only one left to help them. Whatever she must do, so it must be.

She stood slowly and gripped her spear, then slid into the shelter. In a single glance, she took in her sisters' frightened faces, their hands and feet bound in front of them, and the man standing between her and them.

Mol'k turned, facing her. His lower body was clad in leather breeches, his feet were bare under the hem, and the muscles of his upper body rippled as he moved. "We've been looking for you, Kiya."

"I was on watch." She rolled her shoulders. "Why are my

sisters bound?"

His eyes glittered in the firelight. A small smile twisted his lips. "I think you know why."

"Maybe."

"You should join them."

Kiya bared her teeth. "I think not."

He laughed and edged around the fire toward her, hands held out to his sides. "I always liked your spirit. Come quietly, little one, and I'll make sure your sisters go to good men."

"Will you?" she murmured. "And what of me?"

His smile widened. "I've already claimed you."

"Have you?"

"No one will challenge me. Who would dare?" He inched his way forward, drawing ever closer, and Kiya's hand tightened around the shaft of the spear. He wiggled his fingers. "Give me the spear, little one. Think of your sisters. Think of the life you could have with me. I'll protect you and the children we make, this I swear."

Behind him, Lilleni shook her head slowly, barely moving it from side to side.

Kiya focused on Mol'k, on his size and strength, on his unwavering smile. She lowered the spear and loosened her grip. "You're a good man, Mol'k."

"Kiya, no!" Eleni cried, and Bagda rammed her shoulder into her sister's arm.

"Father respected you," Kiya continued, and gathered her courage for what must be done. "If I give myself to you, can you guarantee my sisters' safety?"

Ganenda lowered her head, hiding the tears streaming down her face, her shoulders heaving in silent sobs. Kiya's sisters leaned their heads together, Bagda with her dark, steady eyes on Kiya. She lifted her hand, flashing a stone-bladed knife, and Kiya jerked her attention to Mol'k.

"I'll do everything I can." He stepped forward, closing distance between them, and held a hand out. "Give me the spear,

Kiya. Let me help you."

"I'll give you the spear in exchange for a kiss. I've never..." She cleared her throat and shoved down the nerves biting her insides. "I've never lain with a man."

"I know." Mol'k placed a hand on the spear's shaft behind the point, pushing it to the side, and slid a hard arm around her waist. "A kiss, then, so you'll know I can be more than the hardened warrior your father trusted."

Kiya bowed her head. "Did you kill him?"

"I had no hand in that, little one, nor in your mother's death." He brushed his cheek along her temple and lowered his voice. "I went to her after your first bleeding time and asked for you."

Her heart leapt into her throat. "What of Rila?"

"Barren. She wishes to return to her people at the next gathering. I've already freed her." Mol'k's sigh feathered across Kiya's skin. "Your mother asked me to wait for you, said I'd know when the time was right to claim you, and when I saw her body on the ground..."

"She's dead."

"I know."

"Do my sisters know?"

"They suspect." He laughed, soft and short. "The Seer said even after I claimed you, you'd make me wait to have you. I can't believe she was so wrong."

"She never was," Kiya said softly. And wouldn't be this time. She had only to delay. Surely the six of them together could take down this one warrior, even with his strength and cunning. She dropped her hold on the spear and gripped his narrow hips. "You promised me a kiss."

Mol'k tossed the spear aside and cupped her face. His mouth lowered to hers, claiming her gently, and she forced herself to relax under his unfamiliar touch. A little longer. Bagda had to've freed herself by now. She had to be working on freeing their sisters.

Mol'k's hand slid down her face and cupped her nape, holding her close to him as his mouth moved across hers. A scuff sounded behind him and he jerked back, breaking the kiss.

Kiya wrapped her arms around his lean torso and stood on tiptoe. "Teach me how to please you."

"I will, Kiya," he murmured. "We'll please each other."

His hands tightened on her skin and his mouth met hers, hard and demanding, and Kiya pressed into him, desperate to buy more time for her sisters. A little longer. A little more.

A thud shuddered through him and his hold loosened. He swayed and crumpled to the ground, taking Kiya with him, and she bit back a sob as they fell into the dirt. Soft hands tugged her away from him into the embrace of her sisters.

She pushed herself away from them and knelt beside Mol'k, running her hands over the lump one of her sisters had knocked into his head. He groaned and stirred, and she backed away.

"We have to hurry," she whispered. "Abragni's waiting for us by Ganenda's cave."

Bagda lifted Kiya's spear and jerked her head at Mol'k. "What of him?"

Kiya stood. "Leave him."

"He'll come after us," Lilleni murmured.

Kiya shook her head. "Mother told him he'd have to wait to claim me. He won't go against her vision."

She shushed their questions and ushered them out of the shelter one by one. They traveled on quiet feet to the edge of the water, accompanied by the moon's cold light. Abragni was waiting for them, huddled inside the cave's entrance, her tiny body shivering, her face streaked with tears. Kiya lifted the youngest into her arms, holding her close, and told her sisters what she'd observed, of Mother and Father's deaths, of the men's treachery, and of the vision Mol'k had shared. They sat in silence for long moments, listening to the water lapping against the shore and the breeze blowing through the brush.

Lilleni lifted her face to the moon. "What will we do, Kiya?"

"We wait. We learn. We prepare." Kiya stood and stared down at her sisters, meeting their gazes one by one. "And when the time is right, we strike, avenging the wrongs done to the People tonight. Tomorrow, we seek shelter away from those who harmed Mother and Father. For now, we rest. Get some sleep, my sisters. We have a long journey ahead of us."

"Blessed be Ki," Eleni said.

"Blessed be Ki," Kiya murmured.

The soft cry echoed through the cave's interior, bouncing against its stone walls, embedded there as surely as if it had been carved. From that night on, the Seven Sisters hardened their hearts, and they never, ever forgot the fate delivered upon them by the envy of men.

ONE

The present

MAYA BELLEGARDE stepped off the private jet and breathed in the sweet air of late spring, bracing herself against the heat boiling up from the tarmac. The flight from the States to Stockholm hadn't been bad. Long, but not bad, and it had given her plenty of time to think.

Dani Nehring halted beside her, yawned, and pulled her body into a bone-popping stretch. "So, Swedish men or Swedish food?"

Maya didn't bother with exasperation. The younger Daughter was irrepressible, her sunny personality a reflection of her bright looks. Dani's blonde curls, crystal green eyes, and easy-going smile drew stares wherever she went. In many ways, she was an ideal companion, optimistic and always quick on the uptake, and maybe that was her biggest flaw. Very little came between her and a good joke, the bigger the better. Maya had learned early on to never drop her guard around Dani, unless she wanted to fall victim to a good-natured prank.

A trim woman approached from the hangar, her ebony hair pulled into a high ponytail, her pale face set in an impassive gaze. She was an inch taller than Maya's own five foot seven inch frame, slender and graceful, her body fit beneath a loose white cotton shirt and olive green cargo pants. The woman bowed and her ponytail swung forward, brushing the ends over one shoulder.

Maya returned the bow. "How have you been, Indigo?"

Indigo's sapphire eyes glinted in the bright sunlight. "Very well, Maetyrm. How was your flight?"

"Largely uneventful, even with Dani cracking jokes from takeoff to landing."

"Hey, now," Dani said, and Maya shot her a quick grin.

A slight smile tilted Indigo's serious features into soft humor. "I've already made arrangements for your stay. Two rooms inland close to Sandby borg and a late model Volvo sedan, exactly as Director Upton requested."

"And the dig?"

"As soon as you've settled into your cabins."

"So, no men, then?" Dani asked.

Maya rolled her eyes skyward. "Business before pleasure."

Dani grinned and flipped her blonde curls back. "I have to brush up on my Swedish first, anyway."

As soon as the luggage was loaded, Indigo slid into the driver's seat of the Volvo. Maya slipped into the back, leaving a chattering Dani to the front. During the drive southeast from Stockholm, Maya tuned one ear to Indigo and Dani's conversation as they shared gossip old and new, and focused on their destination, an archaeological dig at Sandby borg, the site of a fifth century land fort that had been abandoned after a brutal massacre.

When Indigo had contacted Rebecca Upton, head of the Institute for Early Cultural Studies, to report a promising gravesite at the borg, Maya had volunteered to visit and examine the skeleton and any artifacts. She'd tried not to get her hopes up. Over the years, she'd visited a lot of archaeological sites only to come away disappointed. This one was different, though. There was something here, something the People could use. She could feel it in her bones, and a Daughter's instincts never lied.

THEY CROSSED ÖLAND BRIDGE, a six kilometer road connecting Öland Island to the Swedish mainland. Maya brought her attention back to the conversation as Indigo pointed out landmarks in the small villages they passed through. They took the perimeter highway north, then a series of smaller roads inland. Within twenty minutes, a small group of rental cabins appeared on the side of the road. Indigo pulled up beside one and parked.

Dani stepped out of the rental and wrinkled her slim, straight nose. "I thought Sweden was, like, old. This looks like downtown back home."

"Not everybody can live in medieval castles, Dani," Indigo said.

They checked in at the main cabin, dropped their luggage off in their separate units, and freshened up in Maya's room. The cabins weren't air conditioned. The June heat had driven the interior temperatures to a nearly unbearable level, in spite of the efforts of a single desktop fan placed in each room.

Dani tugged the neckline of her t-shirt away from her chest. "Man, tonight's gonna be miserable. How do you stand it?"

Indigo smiled, flashing dimples. "We have air conditioning."

"Spoiled," Maya said.

Dani groaned. "You're not gonna tell us one of those 'good ol' days' tales, are you?"

"Maybe later, if you're really bored," Maya said drily. "If it makes you feel better, you'll be spending part of the night watching the camp instead of here sweltering in the heat."

"She may not need to be at the dig tonight." Indigo dropped onto the edge of the room's only bed. "Looters have hit a couple of nearby digs, so we've been taking turns staying on site at night. It's my turn tonight."

Maya nodded. "Still, I may have Dani do a little recon after dark."

"She can keep me company, then."

"Sure," Dani said. "Soon as I have a good look-see."

The dig was a short drive from the cabin. Indigo slowed on approach, allowing plenty of time for Maya and Dani to study the outer ring of Sandby borg's ruins. The crumbling foundations of ancient walls rose from the grass, a long-unneeded protection for the interior buildings. A handful of tents covered tables stacked with tools, plastic and cardboard storage boxes, and computers. A trailer was located on the opposite end of the site, near a small storage shed. Only a handful of people were on site, some engaged in fine digging, others apparently sorting and cataloguing. One young woman sat alone about fifty yards from the main dig in an open, rectangular pit, her bent head and shoulders visible above the earth.

Indigo brought the Volvo to a halt in the graveled parking area next to a handful of other vehicles. The three women got out, and Maya and Dani followed Indigo into the main part of the dig toward the tents. As they approached, two men looked up from their work at one of the tables, one ancient and stooped, the other on the upside of middle age.

The older man retrieved a wooden cane from its resting place against the table and leaned into it as he faced the women. "Indigo, my dear," he said, his English heavily accented, his sagging features animated under a mop of silver hair. "You've brought us quite the treat today."

"Dr. Lindberg, this is Dr. Maya Bellegarde from the Institute for Early Cultural Studies and her assistant, Daniella Nehring. They're here to examine the anomalous burial."

"Of course. I remember. So much excitement here now. The days run together." Dr. Lindberg gestured to the younger man by his side. "This is my colleague, Dr. James Terhune. I brought him in to consult on that burial."

"Pleased to meet you." James grasped Maya's hand, his own calloused and firm. The warmth of their grip spread up Maya's arm. Her heart skipped and her skin tightened, and a delicious flutter of nerves tingled in her abdomen.

The heat generated by the simple touch intrigued her. She

studied James from beneath lowered lashes, assessing him carefully. He was taller than her by about four inches, slim and athletic. Intense chocolate brown eyes peered at her out of a thin face with high cheekbones, an aristocratic nose, and a mouth that wasn't quite wide enough to overpower his other features. He hadn't shaved in a day or so and his rich brown hair was slightly unkempt. The ends brushed over the collar of an untucked, blue cotton shirt worn over jeans and hiking boots. His hand slid away from hers, creating a warm friction along her palm, and her stomach jumped.

"Likewise." Maya tucked her hands into the pockets of her cargo pants, curling her fingers around the heat lingering on her palm. "We're anxious to see the site."

Dr. Lindberg pointed the end of his cane toward the grave. "Come, then. James and I shall escort you. Indigo, would you be a dear and set up refreshments for our guests?"

"Certainly, Dr. Lindberg."

"Supper tonight," Maya said.

Indigo nodded and bowed. "Yes, Maetyrm. Dani, gentlemen." She pivoted and strode toward the trailer, her movements efficient and precise.

Dr. Lindberg smiled fondly after Indigo. "Such a good girl, always so helpful. Very bright, too."

"I've found her to be so myself," Maya agreed mildly. The *girl* he'd just sent on errands was twice his age, though Maya had a feeling that wouldn't matter one whit to Dr. Lindberg, even if she could tell him. His fondness would undoubtedly color his opinion and he'd still think of Indigo as a young woman and not the century-and-a-half years old warrior she was.

Dani tucked her hand into the crook of Dr. Lindberg's elbow. "Well, now that the competition's out of the way, I can flirt with the handsomest man here."

Dr. Lindberg laughed and patted her hand with gnarled fingers. "Tell that to my wife, please. She thinks I've become crotchety in my old age."

15

As the unlikely pair strolled across the site, Maya fell into step beside Dr. Terhune. They walked for a few moments in silence, listening to the cadence of the conversation between Dani and Dr. Lindberg.

"I read your paper on female divinities in sedentary hunter-gather bands. Fascinating perspective." James stuffed his fingers into the front pockets of his jeans. "Now that I've met you, though, I can't believe somebody as young as you are could write something like that. The research alone must've taken years and you..."

Maya glanced at him. "I what?"

He cleared his throat, his gaze focused on the couple in front of them. "You barely look old enough to be out of college."

"Just what every woman wants to hear."

He smiled and the corners of his eyes crinkled along faint laugh lines. Their arms brushed as they walked, shooting a spark of warmth down Maya's arm.

"You take the IECS' *Journal*, then?" she asked.

"Who doesn't?" He hesitated, cleared his throat again. "I applied for a pass to the IECS Archives a few years back. They turned me down flat."

Maya pursed her lips together. So he wanted access to the Archives, did he? And just when the People needed him to be there. "I'm sure Director Upton could be persuaded to grant you a pass if you're still interested. I'd be happy to put in a good word for you."

"Just like that, no strings attached, for a man you just met?"

"Oh, there are always strings, and we have just met, but your reputation precedes you. You're part of the reason we're here."

"Do tell." His mouth twitched into a crooked grin, flashing white, even teeth. "Is that my professional reputation or the reputation I gained in my misspent youth?"

She laughed. "We're hoping to lure you to the IECS to work with a new collection we've acquired."

"So, my professional reputation, then."

"It's a good one."

Maya slowed to a stop. Ahead of them, Dani and Dr. Lindberg had reached the pit, and whatever was in it must've been something. Dani loped away from it, crossing the open ground quickly, and bounced to a stop in front of Maya and James, her green eyes sparkling. "Maetyrm, you have *got* to see this." She spun and bounded back to the pit.

James eyed Dani's receding figure. "Does she always bounce like that?"

Maya sighed. "I'm afraid so."

They approached the pit at a quicker pace. The young woman Maya had spotted earlier was hunched over a sketchpad next to a single skeleton turned partially on its side. Over time, dirt had filled in the space between the bones, holding the remains in place, allowing the archaeological team to examine it *in situ.* Wisps of what could've been fabric clung to some of the bones. Aside from an armband encircling the humerus of the top-facing arm, the only other items resting near the body were the remains of a long, fire-hardened wooden spear with a rusted metal point, still partially submerged in the dirt.

Maya inhaled deeply, willing her racing heart to calm. "Female?"

Dani tilted her head in a slight nod.

"Quite exciting. Burials from that time period are very rare. Immolation." Dr. Lindberg leaned against his cane, both hands pressing into its top. "Pyres were very popular in the fifth century. Good for the soul, but bad for archaeologists, eh?"

"Have you definitively dated the burial?" Maya asked.

"Still waiting for the lab to settle that." James shifted into a wide-legged stance and crossed his arms over his chest. "Some of the artifacts appear to be centuries older than others. It's made dating the burial itself a little tricky, but the team here believes she was buried at the same time as the massacre."

A tendril of excitement wound through Maya. Dani caught her eye and inclined her head toward the skeleton, her eyebrows raised.

"Dr. Lindberg, would you mind if I took a closer look?" Maya asked.

"Certainly not." A gentle smile lifted Dr. Lindberg's expression. "We welcome your good opinion."

The sketch artist gathered her material and climbed out of the pit, heading toward the main encampment. "Be back when you're done."

"Thanks." Maya maneuvered herself carefully into the pit and examined the skeleton's upper torso as she picked her way around the remains. "Strange that this one body was buried when the others were left laying where they fell."

"She must have been quite significant," Dr. Lindberg said. "Perhaps a courier or a diplomat of some sort."

Maya paused in mid-step. "What makes you say that?"

"That's the reason I'm here." James waggled his eyebrows. "Late last week, the team found a small stash of documents sealed in a metal box that was buried with our mysterious female."

Indigo had reported that cylinder seals had been found with the body, possibly worn as jewelry, but not documents. Maya filtered through her knowledge of Iron Age Scandinavia. "Documents, in northern Europe during the fifth century? Maybe Roman in origin?"

"Only one." James' smile exuded the same excitement clawing at Maya. "But it wasn't produced in northern Europe, best I can tell. There were at least three languages written on a variety of media buried here. Some pictographs as well." His smile stretched into the grin of an academic with a rare treasure on his hands. "One item was a small clay tablet written in Linear A."

Maya blinked, clamping her jaws together against a disbelieving gape. "No."

"Oh, yes." He rocked forward onto the balls of his feet and back again. "So far, we've uncovered the clay tablet, animal skin, papyrus, half a dozen cylinder seals. Some of it just fragments, but still."

She sucked in a breath. The smell of freshly turned dirt seeped through her, comforting in its familiarity. "A regular library, then."

Dani cleared her throat. "Maetyrm, *the armband.*"

Maya knelt in the dirt beside the skeleton, carefully balancing herself above it. The armband glittered dully in the late afternoon sunlight, and a small chill went up Maya's spine. It was crafted of hammered copper, greening with age and exposure to the elements and the dirt it had been buried in. In the dimming light, she could just make out a symbol stamped into it, a single eye staring at her from across at least fifteen centuries. It was a symbol she knew well and it raised her hopes higher than she'd ever allowed them to soar.

She stood and brushed her hands off against the loose cotton of her cargo pants. Dani's grin held smug satisfaction, an emotion Maya could hardly deny the younger Daughter. It was welling up in her own chest, even as she tried to tamp it down. Hope could do funny things to a Daughter, and here was hope in its highest form, a possible clue to the lost prophecy contained in one of the most ancient symbols of the People, a symbol associated specifically with that prophecy.

Maya glanced from Dr. Lindberg's weathered face to James' smiling one. "Take me to the artifacts," she said, and crawled out of the pit.

THREE HOURS LATER, Maya stood in front of the bathroom's mirror towel-drying her hair. As soon as they'd arrived back from the dig, still burning with excitement, she and Dani had retreated to their separate rooms to clean up. Jet lag would kick in soon, but for now, adrenaline kept them going.

Moisture fogged the mirror. Maya swiped a hand towel over it and cleared a space big enough to work, preparing for the night ahead. She smoothed an anti-frizz product through her hair. The tightly coiled curls relaxed slightly then sprang into shape. As a young woman, she'd wished for any kind of hair other than the slightly coarse, kinky brown headful she'd inherited from her mother. Long silky hair like Indigo's or wavy curls like Dani's. Anything. Nostalgia plucked at her. Young girls always wanted to be different, no matter the era.

Maya leaned forward and applied eyeliner to her almond shaped eyes, then brushed mascara over the thick, black lashes. She'd inherited those features from her mother, along with the high, arching eyebrows, the wide, full lips, and pixie face. The aristocratic nose came from her father and seemed out of place covered by her *café au lait* skin. A sharp pang hit her, regret mingling with sorrow. She'd had them for such a short time. What she wouldn't give to have known them better.

She paused, gazing at herself in the mirror. Her mind rarely drifted to her parents. They were both long dead and, except for the night of their brutal murders, she remembered very little about them. Sometimes a smell reminded her of her mother's embrace or she'd hear her father's voice in the timbre of another man's. Their kindness, their love; those were the things she'd clung to during the long, lonely years of her childhood.

She shook the memories away and checked her watch, set to local time as soon as they landed. After a quick mental calculation of the time difference between Sweden and the IECS, she called Director Upton. The director's receptionist answered on the second ring, then patched Maya through.

"Maya." The voice was smooth, cultured, and well-modulated. Rebecca Upton appeared to be in her early fifties, but she was much, much older, and had the political and business savvy to prove it. Maya closed her eyes and imagined the director as she usually was in the middle of the afternoon on a workday, wearing a tailored power suit, bold but tasteful, with spike-heeled shoes in a matching color, and just the right touch of accessories. Her ash blonde hair would be twisted into a chignon, not a strand out of place, and her delicate features would be artfully enhanced with barely-there makeup.

To the world, Rebecca Upton was a successful business woman who ran the Institute for Early Cultural Studies with the precision and strategy of a battlefield general. Few knew that she was in reality a centuries-old warrior and had once literally been the equivalent of a battlefield general. Few among the Daughters were as canny, or as powerful.

"Director Upton." Maya wandered to the lone window and flicked the curtains closed as she briefly outlined the status of their trip and relayed the information they'd gathered on the dig: The condition of the other skeletons, unmoved after the massacre; the discovery of jewelry and other artifacts, also left by the marauders; and the threat of looting that had pushed Lund University, one of the dig's sponsors, to take protective measures.

"What about the burial Indigo reported?" Director Upton asked.

"More than promising, Director. The skeleton was female. She was buried with a spear and a small cache of writing."

The creak of a chair drifted over the line. "Fragments?"

"Primarily, some in remarkable condition. Dr. Terhune believes at least three separate written languages are represented, but there could be more."

"I'd like to see those myself, if it can be arranged."

"I'll discuss that with Dr. Lindberg tonight."

"Do that." The chair creaked again. "And Dr. Terhune?"

Maya paused, considered. "I can think of no one better suited to deal with these artifacts."

"You'll make the arrangements?"

"Tonight, if possible."

"I'll look forward to seeing you in a few days, then."

"One more thing, Director." Maya inhaled a deep, steadying breath. "The skeleton was wearing the symbol of Marnan."

"The eye." The director breathed the word out, her voice soft and reverent. "I never thought we'd find it again."

"None of us did."

"Finally, we have hope." Rebecca laughed, the wondrous, brilliant laugh of someone discovering light after years of living in darkness. "After all this time."

"Yes, Director, I believe we do."

"There's no question then that this is a Daughter." Another sigh, a slight creak. "Make the arrangements, Maya. I'll contact the Council of Seven immediately. They'll want a full report on your return."

They ended the call not long after. Maya checked her watch again, wished briefly that Dierdre wasn't in school right then, and promised herself a call to her youngest daughter after supper. Business before pleasure, she reminded herself, and left her room in search of Dani.

TWO

JAMES TERHUNE sat at the bar of a hotel in Borgholm where the dig crew had gathered after Maya had treated them all to a meal. He sipped a local brew and watched Dani charm Olaf Lindberg's wife, Helene. The young woman had latched on to the elderly couple at dinner and appeared to be delighted with their company. The three shared a love of old movies, something they'd discovered when Dani had shared a childhood wish to *be* Audrey Hepburn when she grew up.

Strange young woman, that one. James couldn't quite put his finger on what was off about her. On the surface, she appeared to be a typical blonde co-ed, friendly, vapid, and working toward a Mrs. degree. After observing her for a while, though, he realized that the ditzy act was just that. Dani blended in wherever she went, as at ease chatting with the students as she was discussing classic film stars with the Lindbergs. She was astute, observant, and a lot more intelligent than he'd first thought, and that surprised him. Usually, he was a better judge of character.

His gaze drifted to Maya, deep in conversation with Dr. Lindberg. Now, *there* was a mystery and another woman he suspected possessed hidden depths. Maya Bellegarde appeared to be no older than Dani, yet she commanded the respect of the other woman with an ease hinting at a far greater depth of experience. Where Dani was a sunflower basking in the warmth

23

of the light, Maya was reserved and occasionally somber. During dinner, she'd maneuvered the conversation with little effort, directing it from topic to topic in order, it seemed, to achieve a specific goal without saying much herself. He suspected that goal had something to do with the anomalous burial, but her manipulation was so subtle, sometimes he thought he'd imagined it.

He also suspected he was attracted to her, and that touched off an emotion he couldn't quite pinpoint. Concern? Dismay? He shrugged it off. She was an attractive woman. Ergo, it wasn't unusual for him, a red-blooded man in his prime, to be attracted to her.

Maya smiled at Dr. Lindberg, drawing the older man out. She didn't flirt and charm as Dani might. Instead, she met Olaf on an intellectual level. That intellect was damn appealing, especially when coupled with serene features and a compact, athletic body. Apparently, he was drawn to women who wore their power well. Who knew?

Since his divorce two years before, he'd hidden himself away from the dating world. His and his wife's parting had been amicable, or amicable enough. He and Linda had both wanted to protect their daughter, Amelia, the center of their world, or so he'd thought. When Linda had told him she wanted a divorce, he'd been stunned. In her view, they were two moons on different orbital trajectories independently circling a planet named Amelia.

He'd thought they were a family and she'd thought they were a planetary system. That's what he got for marrying an astrophysicist.

He wasn't ready to go through that again. Hell, he wasn't even ready to date yet. Thankfully, none of his friends were stupid enough to try setting him up on a blind date, or any date for that matter. Between work and Amelia, he'd managed to fill his free time and ignore the loneliness that had moved into his apartment with him.

He frowned down at his glass. One beer and he was as morose as a man deep in his cups. If that's all it took to push him into that kind of contemplation, he really needed to get out more.

"May I join you?"

James glanced up. Maya stood beside him, hands in the pockets of loose cargo pants, one eyebrow arched.

"Sure," he said.

She perched on a stool beside him and waved away the bartender, then swiveled, facing the room. The noise of the crowd ebbed and flowed around them. Laughter rang out, drawing his eye to the Lindbergs' table. Dani rose and pulled Helene up from her chair, tilting her head toward the stage, speaking softly to the older woman. Finally, Helene smiled shyly and nodded, and the two women threaded their way across the bar to a karaoke machine. They chose a song and a moment later, the opening measures of an old doo-wop rang through the bar. The two hopped up on the small stage, Dani leading the way, and began to sing, hamming it up for the crowd egging them on.

"She's something else." James pointed toward the stage. "Your assistant."

Maya's lips twitched into a small smile. "Yes, she is."

"You've known her a while?"

"Since she was a little girl."

"So, the two of you grew up together."

Her smile widened. "Not exactly."

He sipped his beer, eyeing that smile. "What exactly, then?"

"She was my student for a while, a long time ago."

He huffed out a laugh. "You can't be more than a year or two older than her, not nearly old enough to be her teacher."

"You're very kind." She dipped her head toward him, her eyes sparkling. They were almond shaped and an odd golden brown in the low light of the bar. "But I'm a good deal older than I appear."

"You know, men don't really care about a woman's age."

"I know," she said, grinning. "That's why we torment you with it."

He laughed and his earlier mood slipped away. "So, you were her teacher, then. And Indigo? Did you teach her, too?"

Maya nodded. "She was an excellent student, as was Dani."

"Is that why they call you... What was the word they used?"

"Maetyrm."

He tried the word out, letting the syllables roll across his tongue as he analyzed them. "A Latin derivative?"

Maya turned her gaze to Dani and Helene's extravagant bows. "Not quite."

He couldn't tell if she was ignoring him or simply didn't want to answer the question. "What does it mean?"

She hesitated, smiled as Dani raised her hands in a cheer while she bounced back to the Lindbergs' table. "It's a term of respect, usually meaning mother or even revered mother. At the school, it's reserved for teachers. And yes, I'm certain it isn't a Latin derivative."

His brow furrowed as he mentally sifted through the roots of the many languages he'd studied, searching for a match.

"It's not from a language you've ever studied."

Her voice startled him. "What, are you a mind-reader now?"

She laughed and her golden-brown eyes glimmered. "You're one of the world's foremost experts on archaic languages. I'd expect you to pick apart an unfamiliar word and trace it back to its origins."

He slid back on the stool, nonplussed. "Am I that easy to read?"

"Your occupation is. If you weren't curious about word origins, I doubt you'd be such a success in your chosen field."

He lifted his glass in a simple salute. "You've got me there."

"Speaking of which." Maya scooted around on her stool, facing him. "Were you serious about researching at the IECS?"

"Absolutely."

Her eyes met his, and his heart jumped in his chest. Damn attraction.

"Dr. Lindberg will probably release the artifacts from the burial to the IECS for conservation. We have facilities there that can't be matched in Sweden."

"To deal with the writing fragments?" The noise in the bar escalated. Without thinking, he leaned closer to Maya. "Will they be allowed out of the country?"

"We'll eventually be returning them to Sweden, so yes, I believe so."

"What if they're not released to the IECS?"

"Then we'll find another way to handle the matter."

He studied her, admiring her steady gaze and calm composure. "Do I want to know how?"

"Only if you want a detailed account of wrangling with politicians."

James mulled that over. If politicians were involved, he really didn't want to know. Her, though, he wanted to know more about, and he damn sure wanted to figure out how to get a crack at the IECS' Archives. "What does my interest in the Archives have to do with the Sandby borg artifacts?"

"We want you to come work for the IECS on a temporary basis, deciphering and translating the documents found in the anomalous burial. If you have time after that to work with our other collections, all the better." She tilted her head to one side and her lips twitched into a knowing smile. "Of course, you'll have plenty of free time to work on any special projects you might bring with you."

What an offer. The very thing he'd been working toward on his own, handed to him on a silver platter. It couldn't be that easy. "What's the catch?"

"No catch. You'll receive on-site housing and a salary while you're there. We won't claim any of your work product other than any translations you make for items held in our possession. It's a beautiful work environment."

"It feels like there should be a catch."

"No catch," she insisted. "You'll have your own office and a separate laboratory, full access to a library, the dining hall, and the gym. The campus is lovely and has miles of running, biking, and horse-riding trails, camping and picnic areas. We do have schools on-site, so teachers, students, and even other staff members may drop by on occasion to chat with you."

"I knew there was a catch."

She laughed, full-throated, beautiful, and a wave of heat washed over him. Damn attraction.

"Set office hours and you'll be fine," she assured him.

"It sounds idyllic."

"In a lot of ways, it is, but not all. Summer in Georgia makes Sweden feel like Antarctica. Humidity is always a problem and the mosquitoes are relentless."

"Another catch."

"I'll make sure you have plenty of bug repellent."

He grinned. When was the last time he'd had a conversation this interesting? Hell, when was the last time he'd had anything close to an interesting conversation with a woman?

His grin faded. That woman was giving him an opportunity to follow a dream, of going to the IECS and working with those artifacts, of having the chance to pursue his own research in the archives there. Either opportunity alone was worth the hassle of finding somebody to sublet his apartment and take over his classes. It was so difficult to gain access to the IECS' holdings, this might be his only shot. If he passed it up, could he live with himself afterwards?

Then again, a move like that would be hard on Amelia. Linda loved their daughter, but sometimes, she got distracted to the point of neglect. That wasn't a problem when he was a stone's throw away, but if he moved several states south, how would his daughter fare?

He released a slow breath. "I'll have to think about it."

"I expected as much."

"You're taking that awfully well. I expected you to argue or, I don't know, cajole."

She smiled in that enigmatic way she had, as if she knew something he didn't and wasn't about to share. "Everything will work out exactly the way it should."

Dani bounced up to them, her step light in spite of the late hour. "I'm heading back to the site now."

"Indigo said it was her turn to stand guard tonight," Maya explained. "Dani's keeping her company for a while."

"Let me guess," James said. "You went to school together."

Dani cocked her head to the side. "Nope. We're just friends in a friendly way, playing catch up."

Maya groaned. "Please, Dani. Not the ketchup gag."

Dani green eyes widened. "Would I do that?"

"You absolutely would." She turned to James. "I've been the victim of that one myself. Don't let her draw you in with that innocent face or she'll pull it on you, too." To Dani, she said, "Give me a minute and I'll ride with you as far as the cabin."

"Yes, Maetyrm." Dani bowed slightly, then pivoted on her heel and left.

James watched her go, amused in spite of himself. "She's something, isn't she?"

"She absolutely is," Maya agreed. She stood and caught Olaf's eye. "We'll be here for a few days if you have any questions about my proposal."

"I appreciate that. Thanks for considering me."

"Oh, you're very welcome. We could use someone at the IECS with your particular skill set. I hope you'll decide to join us."

"It would be hard to turn you down," he admitted.

"That's the idea. See you on-site tomorrow?"

James nodded, shook her hand, and for the umpteenth time, cursed the attraction flowing between them. It was distracting and would be a damn nuisance if he accepted her offer.

She picked her way through the crowd, said farewell to the Lindbergs, then waved at other members of the group who called out goodbyes as she left. Without meaning to, he imagined working with her on a daily basis, feeling the nascent attraction bloom into something stronger, and maybe even acting on it.

He cut the thought off abruptly. Too much, too soon. He wasn't ready for that kind of entanglement. Still, it had been a good long while since he'd thought about a woman that way. He just didn't know if doing so was such a good idea, particularly when the woman in question was as attractive and mysterious as Maya Bellegarde.

THE SHRILL RING of her phone woke Maya from a deep sleep. She groped her way to the nightstand, picked it up, and glanced at the small bedside clock. 2:47 a.m. Alarm shot through her. "Hello."

"It's Dani. Come to the site now. There's been a break-in."

Maya scrambled out of bed and grabbed clothes, dressing one-handed. "Are you and Indigo ok?"

"I'm fine." Dani sucked in a breath. When she spoke again, her voice was tight and thin. "Indi, not so much, but she'll live."

"Does Dr. Lindberg know?"

"Yeah. Indi called him and Dr. Terhune."

"Any damage?"

"Yeah." Bitterness crept into the younger Daughter's tone. "Everything's a mess, but at least a couple of the documents were taken."

Maya closed her eyes, a deep dread creeping through her. "I'll be there as soon as I can."

As she finished dressing, her mind flashed rapidly through the situation. Dani still had the rented Volvo out at the borg, leaving Maya temporarily stranded. There was no way around it. She'd have to run the five-odd miles from the cabin to the borg. She yanked the laces of her boots tight, grabbed a flashlight out of her suitcase, and exited the cabin, locking it behind her.

"Maya!"

She swung around, searching for the speaker. James was standing half in and half out of his rental car, waving her over.

"C'mon," he said. "Indigo said you needed a ride."

The next few minutes were tense. The streets were empty and James took advantage, whipping the car along the roads winding through open farmland at a breakneck speed. Maya gripped the car's door with one hand and the edge of her seat with the other, questions jostling around in her mind. Who was behind the theft? What exactly had been taken? And why had the dig been targeted right after she and Dani had arrived, or was that a coincidence? As much as Maya would like to believe that, she couldn't quite bring herself to, not given the potential importance of the anomalous burial to the People.

They arrived at the site within minutes and tumbled out of the car as soon as it was safely parked. A cluster of flashlights huddled near the trailer. From the number of voices, Maya guessed most of the students had already arrived. She clicked her flashlight on and hurried toward them, James close behind her.

Her steps slowed as she neared the trailer. Indigo sat on the steps leading into it, an ice pack pressed to the back of her head, a bruise spreading across her jaw. Helene leaned over the other Daughter, gently patting her back. Dr. Lindberg and two of the students were standing close by, in deep conversation. They turned toward her and James as they approached, Olaf shaking his head.

Maya knelt on the lowest step in front of Indigo and gently grasped her chin, turning her bruised face into what little light there was. "Are you all right?"

"Maetyrm." Indigo winced and touched her fingers to the bruise along her jaw. "Whoever it was got the jump on me. Knocked me out cold. I didn't even hear them coming."

Apprehension tightened the skin on the back of Maya's neck. Not many people could move quietly enough to elude a

Daughter's keen hearing.

"I've failed." Indigo dropped her head into one hand. "Failed Dr. Lindberg, failed the People. I'm so sorry."

"Oh, bosh," Helene said in her thickly accented English. "These hoodlums, they did this to you. Steal the artifacts, loot the dig, and then hit this poor girl on the head as she tried to do her work."

"Can you tell me what happened?" Maya asked.

Indigo nodded, then winced and held her head still. "Dani was still here. We lost track of time talking and were a little late making our last round. I stopped to wash my hands. Popcorn. Hate having dirty hands." Her shoulders rose and fell on a deep sigh. "Anyway, Dani said she wanted to stretch her legs, so she went out ahead of me. She hadn't been gone two minutes when the lights went out. I came out of the bathroom and took a blow to the jaw, then one to the head. It must've knocked me out for a minute. When I woke up, Dani was hovering over me assessing my wounds."

"Where is she?"

Indigo hesitated and cut her eyes toward Helene. "I think she's trying to restore power to the trailer."

Dani jogged around the end of the trailer, flashlight in hand. Her gaze zeroed in on Maya. "Around back," she said, then pivoted and disappeared into the dark behind the trailer.

Maya stood and studied Indigo's wan features. "I'll be right back. Try not to move too much until we can have a doctor look you over."

"Yes, Maetyrm."

James appeared at Maya's elbow. "I'm coming with you."

She looked him square in the face, saw the suspicion blooming there, and nodded. "Yes, that would be best."

Dani was standing under the power lines, her flashlight playing over the spot where they intersected with the trailer. She flicked her flashlight at Maya and James, then fixed it back on a spot on the trailer's exterior. "Power was cut here, probably with bolt cutters. Stupid."

Maya nodded. Cutting a live power line like that was bound to cause sparks, maybe even a fire, if it didn't electrocute the person cutting it first.

"From the roof or the ground?" James asked.

"Definitely the ground." Dani stepped back and played her flashlight over a block and the ground around it. "Somebody used this as a boost. There's a footprint here."

Maya knelt beside the print. "Any thoughts?"

"Yeah, lots, and none of them good." She crouched beside Maya and pointed at the print, her finger well above the ground. "By the size and shape of the print and the use of a block, I'd say it was somebody small and lightweight. Probably a woman. Possibly a man with really narrow feet, but I'm thinking a woman, maybe five seven, a hundred and thirty pounds. Small but strong."

Maya stood and brushed dirt off the knees of her pants. "Any other damage?"

"Lots. The bolt's broken on the storage shed."

"Hence the use of bolt cutters here," James said.

Dani pushed herself into a stand. "Looks like. I only took a quick peek in there, but it's pretty messy. Same with the storage containers under the tent. I'd say the looter started there..."

"Looter?" Maya asked sharply.

"Oh, yeah," Dani said, nodding. "Just the one. She, or he, started with the easy stuff under the tents, then hit the storage shed, and finally the trailer. I can't be sure because I don't know what's supposed to be here, but it doesn't look like a lot was taken. I mean, a lot of the boxes in storage were dumped out. Stuff is everywhere, but there's an awful lot of it, so I'd guess not much was taken."

"So the looter, singular, was looking for something in particular and kept looking until he found it," James said.

Maya glanced at him. "When Dani called, she told me some of the items taken were linked to the gravesite."

"That's a big coincidence, you showing up the day before a looter breaks in and takes the very thing you're here to see."

Dani stiffened. Maya laid a hand on her arm and shook her head slightly. "Yes, it is, but we aren't responsible, not directly at any rate."

"You have to admit it looks bad."

Dani's eyes turned frigid. "If you think we're responsible, just say so."

Maya tightened her grip around Dani's arm. "Stay calm, Dani. Anyone else would think the same thing. It's best to clear those suspicions up now before they take root and distract everyone from finding the real culprit."

"Yes, Maetyrm." Dani relaxed slightly, though her gaze remained cold. "If you don't mind, I'd like to check on Indigo."

"Of course."

As soon as Dani was out of earshot, James said, "She's got a short fuse."

"Not usually. I'd suggest not provoking her further, though."

He shot her a startled look.

Maya tucked her hands into the pockets of her cargo pants and shrugged. "People look at Dani and see only the surface, a bright, energetic young woman who charms and flirts her way through life, much to the detriment of anyone who crosses her. I assure you, Daniella makes a formidable enemy."

James crossed his arms over his chest and scowled. "Is that a threat?"

"Merely a friendly warning. Stay on her good side." Maya smiled, mischief getting the better of her. "Chocolate usually helps."

"I'll remember that."

"If it helps, keep in mind that it takes a lot to anger her. The looting and Indigo's injury have upset her. This dig is as important to Dani as it is to anyone else here. Once she's able to take a positive action to resolve the situation, she'll find her calm."

34

"Right."

James' voice betrayed his doubt, but Maya let it go. Better for him to be at least a little wary of the young warrior.

They walked around the trailer and joined the main group. The students were chattering quietly among themselves. Olaf, Helene, and Dani hovered over Indigo, who was still holding an ice pack to the back of her head.

While Maya was checking on Indigo, a lone police officer arrived and cordoned off the areas with the worst damage. Very little of the site had remained untouched, with the exception of the pits themselves. Helene finally convinced Indigo to go to the hospital to check for a concussion. Dani insisted on driving, and Helene tagged along as the navigator.

Maya spoke briefly with Dr. Lindberg and offered her assistance in sorting through the artifacts. Restoring order to the dig would give her a chance to assess what had been taken, but it would also give her a chance to covertly monitor the police's investigation and begin her own. The students gave statements to the officer and, with Olaf's encouragement, wandered back to their lodgings for a few hours' rest, leaving Olaf, James, and Maya to guard the site.

As daylight broke in the eastern sky, Maya found herself drawn to the undisturbed anomalous grave. The skeleton still wore the ancient copper armband, the symbol of Marnan just visible through the patina. Maya was certain the burial was of a Daughter, but questions circled endlessly in her head. Had the Daughter really been buried around the time of the massacre? If so, why had she been buried when all the other victims had been left where they'd fallen, at a time when it was more common to consecrate the dead with fire? Would the fragments contain an as yet unknown part of the Daughters' history? Or would the writings the Daughter carried contain a dire warning for their future?

Most of all, Maya considered the who. Who was this Daughter and how had she ended up in Scandinavia? And who was behind the looting? Was it simply local artifact hunters looking for a quick money-making scheme, or was it someone, or something, more deadly?

Dread settled low in Maya's gut. Their ancient enemy had been silent for decades. She fervently hoped they'd stay that way, but if her suspicions were correct, *they* were behind the looting. Her mind buzzed with the consequences of their reappearance, to the Daughters and the IECS, to herself and her own daughters, and to the people they loved.

Maya checked her watch and calculated the time difference for the third time since her arrival in Sweden less than twenty-four hours before. She called Director Upton and caught her just after the other Daughter had gone to bed. In spite of the late hour, the director's voice was crisp, calm, and cool. Maya outlined the situation with the artifacts, including Indigo's injury, and assured the director that she'd remain on site as long as she needed to.

She'd just hung up when a scuffed footfall alerted her to someone else's presence. She glanced over her shoulder. James was ambling slowly toward her. In the distance, Dr. Lindberg sat in a chair, head in hands, talking to the police officer.

Maya tilted her head toward Olaf. "How's he holding up?"

James halted beside her, his gaze drawn to the partially uncovered skeleton at the bottom of the pit. "He's fine. Tired, worried. The usual."

She nodded. Looting at an active dig was heartbreaking, especially when you were in charge.

"Listen." He exhaled sharply and stuffed his hands into the pockets of his jeans. "About earlier. I don't really suspect you or Dani or the IECS of being behind this, and I apologize for implying that."

Maya slashed a hand through the air. "Don't worry about it. It's natural to suspect us. If I were in your shoes, I'd do the same."

"Yeah, maybe." He jerked his chin toward the skeleton.

"What was she carrying that was so important?"

"I was just asking myself the same thing."

"And if those artifacts were the target, how did the looter know what to take? Is there a spy here at the dig? Has somebody been feeding information to an outsider?"

"That's unlikely. All of the students are loyal to Dr. Lindberg, which leaves only me, Dani, and you." Maya slid a sly glance toward him. "I can vouch for me and Dani. What about you?"

He laughed softly. "Touché."

"On the other hand, if data were being transmitted electronically, it would be easy to spy on the dig without being on site, simply by listening in on phone calls or tracking e-mails. How did Dr. Lindberg convince you to visit?"

James grimaced. "By e-mail and in great detail."

"It's not that difficult, if you know what to do."

"Yeah, but it's illegal."

"Only if you get caught."

"Good point."

They stood for a few moments more, until the sun had fully risen and the police officer finished his conversation with Dr. Lindberg. Another officer arrived and, by mutual consent, Maya and James walked across the site to meet her.

THREE

THE FIRST FULL DAY after the looting was long and tedious. Maya convinced James to scrounge breakfast for them from a nearby restaurant while Dr. Lindberg dealt with the police. The students drifted back on site, though the police refused to allow anyone inside the taped off areas.

James returned with breakfast for Maya and Dr. Lindberg. Behind him came the County Police Commissioner and the head of the County Administrative Board, the local authority charged with protecting and overseeing cultural heritage sites like Sandby borg. James retreated to the less onerous task of overseeing the students, leaving Maya to help Dr. Lindberg handle the politicians. More officers arrived to process the scene and created as much of a mess as the looter had. A crew from a Stockholm television station arrived and made a polite nuisance of themselves.

Helene, Dani, and Indigo returned not long after, joining the growing crowd mingling around the site. At midmorning, James drove Maya to her cabin and dropped her off there to shower and change clothes while he did the same in his own cabin. They grabbed food for the students and, by the time they returned to Sandby borg, the police had finished their work and cleared the students to begin clean-up. A single officer stayed behind to serve as a guard and a liaison. He promptly chased the television crew away.

Maya and James cleared one of the tables and set out a variety of sandwich fixings and sides. Everyone except the Lindbergs ate standing up, huddled into a group. Once lunch was done and cleaned up, duties were assigned and the real work began.

The students were divided between the tents and the storage shed. Paper inventories were printed out so that item tags could be compared against box labels and artifacts checked off as they were sorted and repacked.

Maya and James volunteered to sort out the trailer. Dani's assessment of the looter's path through the site had been spot-on, surprising Maya not at all. The younger Daughter had told Maya in an odd moment that she'd been away from the trailer less than five minutes total while the looter was on site. She'd started on the normal rounds around the perimeter, familiar after the previous two rounds she'd made with Indigo, and hadn't gone far when the power was cut. She'd immediately returned to the trailer and found the door wide open and Indigo bleeding on the floor, and had started after the looter only after making sure Indigo was conscious.

The looter had escaped into the shadows, leaving very little of himself behind. The police had dusted for prints, but Maya suspected they'd find none that shouldn't be there.

After straightening up and cleaning away fingerprint dust as best they could, James began sorting the photographs while Maya searched for any fragments or photos that might've slid under furniture. Indigo entered the trailer just as they finished sorting everything out. She sat down on a cushy, worn-out upholstered chair and nodded to both of them.

"How are you feeling?" Maya asked.

"Better." Indigo's gaze slid from Maya to James and back again. "A few days resting should do the trick."

"See that you actually rest," James said.

Indigo smiled wanly. "I'll be fine. I promised Dr. Lindberg I'd help you sort through this mess. Dani and I removed some of the document fragments from storage last night so we could take more photographs and study the writing."

"Thank God you did," James said, "or the looter might've gotten the whole lot."

"As it is, the darkness that confounded me also confounded the looter, at least in here. He must've rushed after taking me out. Maybe he knew Dani was on the grounds and his time was limited." She shrugged and her mouth twisted into a thoughtful frown. "He grabbed mostly print copies of some of the photographs taken when the items were catalogued. A few original textual fragments, yes, but mostly photos, and he completely missed the storage boxes under the coffee table."

"Hmm. I saw these." Maya knelt and pulled one of the boxes out. "What's in them?"

"Documents that are too fragile to handle. We only brought them in to use as a comparison. See?" Indigo opened one of the boxes. Inside were three small pieces of parchment, each rolled up and tied with thin twine. The parchment had been burned, but some text was still visible. Indigo pointed to a symbol on one. "I remembered seeing this symbol on several of the fragments, but couldn't find it on the photographs."

"So you decided to pull the boxes out of storage and photograph them again," James said.

"Sort of. We were going to compare the photos against the parchment tonight and have one of the other students photograph them again tomorrow morning when the light's better."

"Have any other items been discovered missing?" Maya asked.

"No, not yet. There's just so much to go through. Part of the artifacts have already been sent to the University, including the metal box we found the documents in. Anything with writing of any kind was left here in anticipation of Dr. Terhune's arrival."

James scrubbed a hand over his hair. "So if it weren't for me, the entire contents of the grave might already have been put into more secure storage."

"We don't know that." Maya laid her hand on his arm. His skin was warm through his shirt and a little too tempting for her peace of mind. She allowed her hand to slide away and faced Indigo. "Has Dr. Lindberg called the University to check on the status of items sent ahead for storage?"

"Not yet, but he will."

Indigo and Maya shared a long look. What he might find was anybody's guess. A looter here, maybe another there, and no one the wiser as to the whys, not yet anyway. As soon as they knew exactly what had been taken, Maya would set Dani on the looter's trail. If anyone could hunt down the thief, she could.

The three began cross-checking the few fragments Indigo had brought to the trailer against a copy of the inventory, storing each item as soon as it was accounted for. Indigo remembered only two items she'd removed from storage that were missing from the lot, a small piece of papyrus no bigger than her hand and a larger piece of parchment.

Once they'd gone through the inventory, they sorted the photographs and placed them back into their respective folders, one for each object. Several appeared to be missing, but Indigo waved that problem away. "These are print copies of digital images. Even if the looter knew which computer they were stored on, it wouldn't matter. They're also on an external hard drive and in cloud storage."

James stacked the folders into a carefully constructed pile. "Dr. Lindberg sent some of the images to me so I could begin working on deciphering and translation."

"So there are digital copies everywhere," Maya confirmed. "But the looter still has some of the photographs. He can begin deciphering and translating the way you have, depending on which photos were taken."

"Is that important?" James asked.

Maya glanced at Indigo, the other Daughter's frown a twin to her own. "It could be."

"Let's hope not," Indigo said, and Maya silently agreed. Everyday looters wouldn't care what information those documents contained. They'd simply be looking for a payout. But plenty of people might be interested in the contents, and it was those individuals Maya suspected might've stolen them. It wasn't something she liked to consider, but it wasn't something she could rightly ignore, not for the sake of a thorough investigation.

THAT POSSIBILITY stayed in the back of Maya's mind throughout the afternoon as the site was reorganized. While she, James, and Indigo cleaned the trailer and sorted out its contents, Dr. Lindberg called in an electrician to restore power.

He'd also called Lund University and been met with bad news. The artifacts in storage there had been pilfered. Any artifact found with the anomalous burial had been stolen, including the metal box that had once housed the Daughter's cache of documents. It hadn't been scheduled for study yet, but the drawings and photographs of it were still available. Those would come in handy, if she could persuade Dr. Lindberg to share copies.

Maya's resolution hardened into grim purpose as the sun crept westward on its daily voyage. Supper was eaten on site amid hushed whispers and quiet speculation. After, the group gathered together under one of the tents to hear the final count. All of the artifacts stored in the shed related to the Daughter's burial had been taken. An external hard drive was also missing and two computers had been sabotaged, but beyond that, the only other items not accounted for was a sign-out sheet for items stored in the shed and three cylinder seals.

"Whoops," James said. "I signed those seals out last night so I could begin working with them. When we went out for lunch today, I boxed them back up and put them in the trunk of the car. I forgot about them in all the fuss."

Dani held out her hand, her expression flat. "Keys."

James dug them out of his pocket and handed them over, his shoulders hunched, and Maya bit back a laugh. The poor man had a lot of work ahead of him where Dani was concerned.

Dani grabbed one of the students, a strapping young archaeology major named Lars with shaggy blond hair and a friendly smile. Maya shook her head. Trust Dani to pick out the handsome one.

The two returned shortly and compared the contents of the storage box James had signed out against the inventory. A collective sigh of relief filtered through the group when all the items were accounted for.

"Some good news, then, thanks to my friend." Dr. Lindberg set the end of his cane against the earth and pushed himself into a stand. "And so, we have lost some items, but have found some, too. Now, I think it's time we all get some rest. Tomorrow, we must continue our work."

The students drifted off, heading toward the parking lot. The University and the Kalmer Läns Museum had each chipped in money towards private security until the dig's season ended. None of the students would have to stay overnight while the looter remained at large.

As the students were leaving, Maya caught Dani's eye and nodded toward the trailer. The two slipped quietly away, leaving Indigo to distract James and Dr. Lindberg.

When she and Dani were out of earshot, Maya asked, "Did you find any other signs of the looter today?"

Dani rubbed a narrow hand over the nape of her neck. "None."

"You know what to do, then."

"Yes, Maetyrm."

"Get some rest before you start."

Dani glanced at the trio still gathered near the array of tents sheltering the dig's equipment. "I'd like to say goodbye to Dr. Lindberg first."

"Of course." Maya cupped Dani's shoulders and squeezed lightly. Dani had been a beautiful child, as bright as the sun, full of laughter and warmth. It was the child looking at her now out of the young Daughter's eyes, and so it was the child Maya addressed. "This wasn't your fault, Daniella."

Dani's head bowed. "I feel responsible."

"You did what you could and that's all that can be asked of you. Don't take on the burdens of the world, eknon."

Dani's mouth tipped into a slight smile. "I haven't been called a student in a long time."

"Yet you continue to call me teacher."

"I still have a lot to learn from you."

Maya slid her hands down Dani's arms and gripped her elbows. "No, Dani," Maya corrected gently. "We have many things yet to learn from one another."

Dani touched her forehead to Maya's. "I won't fail you, kaetyrm."

"Nor I you."

Dani bounced off with some of her normal vigor. Maya gave her a few moments to say her farewells, then trailed behind her and said her own goodbyes for the night.

FOUR

J AMES LEFT TWO DAYS after the looting. He would've liked to stay longer, but duty called him back to the States. As it was, he'd made not even a small dent in identifying all of the scripts used in the fragments Dr. Lindberg had been so anxious for him to see, but he had digital copies of the photographs to work with and a few prints. Indigo's keen eye for detail had not only saved some of the texts from the looter. It had also made the photographic evidence more complete.

He'd fully intended to work from the physical prints during the flight home. His thoughts were caught instead by the three women so tightly bound to one another. What were the real relationships between Maya, Dani, and Indigo? They seemed too close, too respectful even, to be teacher and students. The fact that the three women appeared nearly identical in age was also a puzzler, yet there was no question that Maya was older than Dani and Indigo. The deference both paid her was obvious, and Maya's poise was well beyond that of a woman in her early to mid-twenties, as he'd assumed her to be.

Maya commanded respect with little effort, regardless of the people she interacted with. Even the Lindbergs had deferred to her judgment. James had no doubt that right at that moment, she was sweet-talking Olaf into handing all of the remaining burial-related artifacts over to the IECS. The permits needed to get them out of the country would be a piece of cake by comparison.

On the other hand, the IECS was undoubtedly the best place for the artifacts to be. Their facilities were, by reputation, some of the best in the world, and their campus was rumored to be one of the most secure. Somebody had targeted those artifacts. Even if the IECS wasn't the best facility for conservation or restoration, the level of security they had would at least deter further attempts at theft.

He hoped so, anyway.

With the artifacts almost certainly on their way to the IECS in the next few weeks, the only question remaining was whether or not he'd join them. He could easily continue working on identifying the scripts and possibly translating the texts from photographs during his free time back home, but would he be satisfied with that, knowing the documents could literally be in his grasp if he'd only accept Maya's offer?

He shifted in his seat, stirring the forgotten photographs resting on his lap, and stared blankly at the seat in front of him. Thinking of Maya led him to a completely different set of problems. She was an attractive woman. He closed his eyes and an image popped into his head, of her at the bar the night they'd met. The dim lighting had turned her hair into a dark halo of wild curls and her eyes had glowed with the mysterious secrets only women knew.

He wanted to get to know her better, maybe spend time with her and see if the attraction was mutual. The thought surprised him. Had another woman ever tempted him this much? Of course, he could never act on that temptation. His life was in Connecticut with Amelia and his job, hers was in Georgia at the IECS, and ne'er the twain shall meet.

Unless he took Maya up on her offer.

James blew out a sigh. His mind was going around in unproductive circles, like a puppy chasing its tail. That's about what he felt like right then, a puppy with an intriguing new toy dangling just out of its reach.

The realization that he might want the toy didn't really help bring it into his grasp.

He shook his head clear and focused on the photographs in his lap. This, at least, he understood. Women? Never. Dead languages in forgotten scripts were far easier to deal with.

MAYA SPENT nearly three frustrating weeks gaining permission to take the artifacts out of Sweden. The attempted theft of all, and the actual theft of some, had set the entire heritage bureaucracy on its collective ear. It seemed every bureaucrat and politician in the country wanted a say in how the remaining artifacts would be handled. She certainly felt as if she'd spoken to all of them, personally or by phone, or if not them, then a myriad array of receptionists, secretaries, assistants, and junior bureaucrats.

With Dr. Lindberg's backing and the sterling reputation of the IECS behind her, it was difficult for resistance to her request to linger, even among those insisting the artifacts should remain in Sweden. With permission gained at last, she personally oversaw packaging and ensured that the whole was shipped directly to the IECS via a trusted private courier. No chances would be taken with those precious items.

The Lindbergs were sorry to see her go, they assured her, and made her promise to visit again, with "that lovely girl, Dani." Maya had grown fond of them as well and made a note in her calendar to plan a future trip with Dierdre. Her daughter would love the countryside, and maybe they could spend time exploring and just hanging out.

Maya's plane touched down in Atlanta on what felt like the most sweltering day of the year. She pushed her way through security, avoided the groping hands of a lothario disguised as a TSA agent, and climbed gratefully into her garaged car for the trip home.

It wasn't a bad drive in spite of the heavy traffic, all of which seemed to be going northeast with her. Halfway home, the sky opened up and a thunderstorm burst out. The rain slowed the traffic down only slightly. Cars continued to whiz by her at upwards of eighty miles per hour, weaving in and out of traffic without the use of turn signals or apparently any concern for the proximity to other vehicles.

Driving in the Greater Atlanta area wasn't for sissies.

The IECS compound was located more than two hours from the airport by car. The Daughters had settled in the area during the French and Indian War, living among the native tribes in relative harmony and even fighting alongside them on occasion. No one loved a good fight like the Daughters.

The natives had eventually been driven out. Most of the Daughters had remained on the land, gaining legal title to it under new governments as they rose, and adopting an outward face that was compatible with the social mores of each passing era. Underneath, though, they were still the proud, fierce warrior women the Cherokees had befriended.

The compound itself had been built over time. What had begun as a pre-Revolutionary War village had developed into a small town serving as a gateway to the IECS campus. The inhabitants were largely Daughters and Sons, with exceptions granted rarely. Property was never sold or bequeathed to anyone outside of family. Outsiders posed too big of a security risk, for one, and too many immortal Daughters lived and worked in or around the compound. Mortal humans tended to notice when someone didn't age as she should. The Daughters had learned how to deal with that long ago, but it was nice to have a place where it wasn't such a worry.

The thunderstorm petered out during the drive and ended completely by the time Maya rolled past the city limit sign for Tellowee and parked in the still-damp driveway of her two-and-a-half story American Queen Anne style home. The previous owners had maintained it in close to its original condition, expanding and modernizing it over time, sticking to the original style whenever possible. She'd fallen in love with the intricate design, with the two round towers, the sweeping staircase leading to a rounded side porch, and the crenellated eaves, and with the interior rooms that were by turns spacious or cramped, depending on the function and exterior design. The house had an almost haphazard feel to it that most people never associated with her reserved personality, but it suited her family's needs well. When she'd bought it a few months prior to Dierdre's birth, it had seemed like the perfect home. She still felt that way, even after a grueling month overseas dealing with red tape.

Maya spotted a section of loose shingling and cursed inwardly. Well, it was *mostly* perfect.

Dierdre ran out of the house, all gangly arms and legs. Maya opened the car door and stepped into a full-bodied hug, holding her youngest daughter close for a long moment.

At last Dierdre stepped back. Maya caught her hands and held them out so she could look her fill. "You've grown. Again! Look at you." She smoothed a hand over her daughter's curls, far tamer than her own kinky brown mass.

"Well, geez, Mom. You were gone forever."

"Hardly, sweet girl." Maya squeezed Dierdre's hands and turned toward the trunk of her car. "It feels like it, though, doesn't it?"

"Yeah." Dierdre heaved the kind of heartfelt sigh only a fourteen-year-old girl could make. "I hate it when you have to leave."

"Me, too, Squiggles."

They emptied Maya's baggage out of the trunk and walked slowly into the house and up the stairs to Maya's bedroom where they dropped the entire load. Dierdre chattered on about all the latest happenings, who was dating whom, which teachers were on the outs with the students, the A+ she'd received on her end-of-year history essay.

The fact that Johnny Linton had tried to sneak a kiss from her after their mixed martial arts class.

Maya made a mental note to speak to Johnny's parents. Her eyes narrowed to slits. No, she'd speak to Johnny himself.

Nothing like a centuries-old warrior to dampen a young man's hormones.

Her daughter had plopped onto the bed and was still chatting away. Maya realized she'd lost part of the conversation with her motherly thoughts. "I'm sorry, what?"

Dierdre rolled her eyes skyward. "I said, then I put him on his hiney 'cause he didn't ask."

"Johnny?"

"Yes, Johnny," Dierdre repeated patiently. "Honestly."

Maya leveled a steady look on her daughter. "Be respectful of the old woman."

Dierdre hid her grin behind one hand. "Yes, ma'am."

"So you took him down for kissing you. Then what?"

Dierdre casually buffed her nails against her shirt, then flicked her fingers outward. "I hauled him back up and laid a big one on him."

Maya scowled. "Whatever for?"

"'Cause I wanted to. Why else do you kiss a boy? Geez, Mom, are you feeling ok? Like, maybe you left part of your brain in Sweden or something?"

"Very funny, young lady."

Dierdre grinned, bounced off the bed, and threw her arms around Maya. "I just love you, Mom."

"I love you, too." Maya drew back and slid her hands over her daughter's shoulders. "Movie night later or do you have homework?"

"Just a little. Should I start supper?"

"Homework first."

Dierdre nodded, not questioning the priority. Self-discipline was taught at an early age to the children of Daughters, usually by necessity. It rarely failed to blossom.

"I have to talk with Director Upton first, but that shouldn't take long," Maya said. "Will you stay the night here or at the dorm?"

Dierdre grimaced. "At the dorm. We've got a hike first

thing in the morning and I don't want to miss it, not with the exhibition coming up."

Maya stifled her disappointment. A month-long absence wasn't enough to justify skipping planned activities no matter how much she'd missed her daughter. "An early night, then. Maybe we can make up for it with a little extra family time this weekend."

Dierdre lightly hit the side of her head and cupped a hand behind one ear. "I'm sorry. Maybe I didn't hear you right. What was that you said about taking me to the mall on Sunday?"

Maya laughed and shooed the giggling teenager into her bedroom and the homework awaiting her daughter's attention.

HALF AN HOUR LATER, Maya knocked on the door leading into Director Upton's office.

"Come in," a muffled voice called.

Maya entered and closed the door behind herself. Rebecca was seated behind her desk talking on the phone. Maya looked politely away, giving the director at least the appearance of privacy.

The room was spacious and richly appointed, a testament to the wealth and power the Daughters had accumulated over time. An antique settee and two matching chairs were artfully arranged on top of an antique rug to one side. Rumor had it the rug had been gifted to a previous director by an infatuated foreign dignitary, and that the man had pursued the Daughter over the ends of the Earth.

The truth was probably far less romantic, but even the most pragmatic Daughter sighed over the tale, true or not. Maya preferred the romance, even as she chastised her soft heart.

Late afternoon sunlight filtered through the curtained windows, showcasing the sitting area. She'd be out in the sunshine tomorrow, maybe on a nice winding trip through the forest surrounding the IECS along one of the dedicated bike trails. The chain on her bicycle had probably rusted from disuse. She could do a thorough check on it that night after the movie, unless Dierdre changed her mind about staying home.

Maya rolled her shoulders, easing her disappointment, and shifted her gaze. The opposite side of the room held glass cases filled with Director Upton's personal collection of antique weapons and memorabilia, including her first sword, Silverthorn, earned during the Battle of Hastings when the director was very young. Many Daughters had similar collections, though most put theirs to the uses they'd been created for. Rebecca had retired her weaponry when she'd fallen in love with her husband nearly thirty years before, but she still kept her hand in. To do otherwise would be suicide. Even if *they* hadn't made an appearance in a long while, it was never wise to allow one's defensive skills to wither. No Daughter worth her salt would be so unwise.

The phone clicked into its cradle, and the director rose and crossed the room. "Maya. It's so good to see you."

"And you, Director." Maya bowed as Rebecca stepped lightly across the wooden floor, dressed in one of her signature power suits, this one carnelian red paired with matching heels. Maya preferred the freedom of her loose cargo pants and camp shirt, but had to admit the director looked lovely in her tailored outfit.

Rebecca perched elegantly on the settee. "How was your flight?"

Maya dropped into one of the chairs and crossed an ankle over one knee. "As expected."

"And Dierdre?"

Maya smiled. "Also as expected."

"I saw her a few days ago. I couldn't quite resist checking up on her during your absence."

"I appreciate that."

"She's getting so tall now." A wistful note entered the director's voice. "They do grow up quickly, don't they?"

"Much too quickly," Maya agreed, and bit back her own nostalgia. Dierdre *had* grown an inch or so over the past month, and Maya had missed seeing it.

"Down to business then, so you can get back to your reunion with her. The artifacts' delivery is on schedule, I take it."

"Yes, Director. I spoke with our courier just before leaving Sweden. They should be here tomorrow afternoon."

"Good. I'll rest better once they're here."

"We all will."

"And the pictures?"

Maya pulled a flash drive and a photograph out of a side pocket of her pants and handed both to the director. "Digital images of all the artifacts are on the thumb drive, but I thought you'd like a hard copy of this particular one."

Rebecca laid the flash drive aside, her eyes riveted to the photograph. "The Eye," she breathed. She traced a finger lightly over the glyph captured within the photo. "Surely the Daughter buried at Sandby borg was of the line of Marnan."

"We might be able to know that for certain."

Rebecca glanced up. "Oh?"

"The students finished excavating the skeleton before I left. Her skull was bashed in, by the way, but her head was turned during the burial so the damage was hidden. It was probably the blow that killed her."

"So she might've died in the massacre?"

"It's possible. We'll know more once the artifacts are dated. In the meantime, Dr. Lindberg hopes we'll be able to extract DNA from the bones."

"Will we be allowed to examine them?"

A spurt of triumph shot through Maya. "Dr. Lindberg agreed to release the skeleton to us. I slid it in under the same permit as the artifacts. It'll arrive by courier next week."

Rebecca laughed and grasped Maya's hand. "Well done, kaetyrm."

"I can't take all of the credit. Dani's charm softened the

Lindbergs to our cause and Dr. Terhune spoke on our behalf. The IECS does have a certain reputation."

"Yes, it does, with many thanks to people like you. Will Dr. Terhune be joining us?"

Maya shifted in the chair. She'd managed to put the attractive-but-not-quite-handsome language expert out of her mind for a few days. "He was undecided when he left Sweden, but I believe his hesitation will give way once he fully considers the situation."

"I'm sure you sweetened the pot."

"Of course. He could be a valuable asset."

"Agreed. Let me know what I can do to help."

Maya nodded. "A letter from you might go a long way toward convincing him. He knows how difficult it is to gain access to our archives, though he doesn't know why."

Rebecca tapped the edge of the photograph against her palm. "He wants access? How badly?"

"I don't know. He has a pet project he implied would depend on accessing our holdings, but he never elaborated on it. There simply wasn't time. But, I believe his wish to fulfill this personal project is quite strong."

"Reminding him of that desire could tip the cards in our favor. I'll compose a letter to him as soon as I can, reiterating your offer."

"Thank you." Maya pursed her lips, containing her relief. "I thought it would be harder to convince you."

"Am I that difficult to manipulate?"

Maya's eyes widened as a breath wheezed out of her. "I'd never do that, Director."

Rebecca threw her head back and laughed. "Oh, Maya. You mustn't let me tease you so. After all that time with Dani, and you're still so literal." She placed a light hand on Maya's arm. "You must promise me you'll work on that."

Maya inhaled deeply, willing her heart to calm. Imagine, the director teasing. What had the world come to? "I will."

"I imagine you'd like to spend some time with your lovely daughter, now that you're home." Rebecca rose gracefully. "I've arranged a meeting with the Council of Seven for next week. They'll want your full report. I'd like to have a copy ahead of time, if possible."

Maya stood. "Of course, Director. I'll have it on your desk first thing Monday morning."

"Make it Tuesday, and take the weekend for yourself. You've earned some rest."

"Thank you, Director."

Rebecca shook her head. "Always so formal."

"It sets a good example," Maya said with a small smile.

"Go on then. I'll see you Tuesday morning and not a moment earlier.

Maya bowed and left the room, her heart still skittering over the director's little joke. She must be mellowing, Maya thought as she made her way out of the building. A hundred years ago, the slightest hint of someone manipulating her would've had the director reaching for a weapon. Maya shook her head and bounded down the outside steps. Must be the husband's influence.

She fell into a jog and tucked the incident away for another day's worry. Right then, she wanted to spend some q.t. with her daughter and catch up on the exact nature of Dierdre's relationship with young Johnny Linton.

AFTER MAYA LEFT, Rebecca resumed her seat behind her desk and lost herself in thought. Shadows lengthened across the room as the sun slipped behind the surrounding hills, cloaking the office in a deepening darkness.

She'd propped the photograph of the armband up against a framed picture of her family. It was one of her favorite portraits, taken weeks after her son turned five years old and a mere eight years after she'd surrendered her immortality by trusting Robert.

No, that wasn't quite right. She'd loved him enough to trust him, and that had been the key she'd needed to finally break the curse of immortality.

Her gaze lingered on the portrait. In it, she sat facing her husband with their son between them and her youngest natural daughter standing behind them. It had been a happy day, though she'd forgotten exactly why, and they were all smiling, even Jerusha. Four of her daughters yet lived with the curse, including her youngest. Rebecca leaned forward and picked up the photograph of the armband. Would the texts found with this innocuous adornment lead them to a way to break the curse for all of the Daughters?

There were rumors that there was a way, always rumors. The Daughters had been chasing them for millennia. For nearly thirty years, the task of heading that search had fallen to her. Was there hope at last or were they following yet another dead end?

"You have found her."

The voice startled Rebecca out of her reverie. She hadn't heard anyone enter her office. A figure stepped from the shadows into the light cast by her desk lamp and Rebecca's heart skittered and sank. The woman in front of her wore a hooded, knee-length leather jacket over a plain cotton tank top tucked into jeans, with lineman's boots laced up to her knees. Her face was fully hidden behind a mask, save for eyes as black and cold as midnight. A thin, white scar circled her neck, the only skin showing on the woman's entire body.

To the People, she was the Woman with No Face, an almost mythical figure of doom and death. Most people, mortals included, believed she was an assassin. Very few saw her and lived to tell the tale, but she was known widely by the mark she carved into her victims, a triangle set on one point with a half circle hanging from the top line. No one knew her true identity. None was brave enough to pursue such information, though whispered tales found their way into plenty of ears.

Rebecca had met her once before, in 1939. Fear had etched

the incident into her memory with a clarity few other emotions had the power to convey.

She had never wished to see the Woman again.

The fear rose, clogging her throat, stultifying her breath. Rebecca gathered her will and shoved the emotion aside. "Who have I found?"

The Woman raised one gloved hand and pointed at the photo of the armband. "Her."

"Who is she?"

The hand dropped and the figure stared at Rebecca, eyes unblinking behind the mask.

Silence stretched between them. After a moment, Rebecca cleared her throat and tried again. "Is she important?"

"You will see."

The mask muffled the Woman's voice, unnerving Rebecca. She stifled a shudder and trained her gaze carefully on the assassin. "Why have you come?"

"I bring a warning, Rebecca of the Blade. Your enemy approaches and is aided from within. Strengthen your gates and arm the People, for the time draws near."

"The time for what?"

The Woman pointed again to the photo. Rebecca placed it carefully onto her desk and spread her trembling hands flat against its surface.

The Woman stepped forward, one step, then two, until she was barely an arm's length away. Cold chills broke out along Rebecca's skin.

"Is the child well?"

Rebecca searched her mind frantically for a moment before memory caught. "She's doing very well."

"You named her for her father."

A breathy laugh sputtered out of Rebecca. "I could hardly name her for her mother."

The Woman nodded. "You have done well by her. For this, you have my gratitude."

The sentiment was so unexpected, it caught Rebecca by surprise. Not knowing what else to say, she settled for, "Thank you."

"Her task approaches. She must complete it without hesitation. The fate of the People depends upon it."

"I'll warn her."

"No." The word snapped through the air between them, hard and flat and terse. "She must do this on her own. I have foreseen it."

"As you wish."

"As the Lady Goddess wishes," the Woman corrected.

"Of course."

The Woman's expressionless eyes bore into hers. Rebecca found herself drawn into them. She leaned forward and, as quickly as a striking cobra, the Woman snatched Rebecca's hand into a painful grip, squeezing hard enough to draw an involuntary gasp from Rebecca. Blackness swam in front of her eyes. Gradually, a scene appeared, of seven women sitting around a campfire, laughing. They were replaced by the chaos of battle, the screams of the dying. A woman holding another who'd been mortally wounded, then pain and more death before the campfire scene returned. One by one, the women faded into shadow. The Woman let go and Rebecca collapsed against her desk, her breaths panting audibly out of her lungs, her vision swimming.

"The One who Sleeps. Is she well?"

Rebecca drew herself up by sheer dint of will. "I'm sorry. What?"

"I believe you call her the Oracle."

"Oh, yes. Of course." Rebecca inhaled a deep, stuttering breath. "She still sleeps."

"Protect her, Rebecca of the Blade. She may yet be your salvation, or perhaps your doom. This I have yet to foresee."

Rebecca nodded and swallowed the questions crowding into the back of her mouth. She closed her eyes and rubbed them, trying to clear her vision.

Find the traitor, child, a voice whispered in her mind.

Rebecca glanced up, certain she'd imagined the soft words. The Woman with No Face was gone. A breeze stirred through an open window, wafting the summer night into Rebecca's office.

She looked down, expecting to find the photo of the armband, but it was gone. In its place was a small, thin piece of homemade paper containing a rough charcoal drawing of an upside down triangle with a half circle dropping from the top line.

FIVE

THE ROOF'S GRAVELED SURFACE bit into Dani's skin through the tough leather pants she'd chosen for that night's recon. She shifted and wished for the dozenth time that she'd chosen a better surveillance position.

Of course, then she wouldn't have been able to observe the muscled spectacle in front of her. Correction, the *shirtless* muscled spectacle. Definitely a two hubba sight, maybe even three. She pondered it for a minute and decided to split the difference, placing Shirtless Wonder at a solid two point five on the Hubba Meter.

She'd seen a three point fiver once, but she didn't like to think about him. He'd gotten her all hot and bothered, and then, bad boy that he was, she'd had to give him the smack down, totally ruining it for her. A grown man pleading for mercy was not a turn on, especially when she hadn't even shown him her A game.

"Oh, yeah, baby," she murmured. "Lift that box. Mmm. Make 'em ripple for me."

She set the binoculars down and reviewed her notes as Shirtless Wonder hefted a box to Muscled Nitwit, who, yup, dropped the box. Again.

Geez. Didn't Nitwit know he was handling precious cargo?

Tonight was her first night staking out this warehouse. It showed real promise as one of the last resting places of the artifacts she was tracking. After saying goodbye to Dr. Lindberg, she'd scouted the area around the dig, checking rooms for rent, restaurants, shops, anywhere a visitor to the island would've been.

When it became clear that the looter had zeroed in on artifacts from the Daughter's burial site, Dani had known they were dealing with a stranger and not a local. She wasn't sure why or how, she just *knew*. Knowing that had tailored her plan of action. The island of Öland had been relatively easy to case. She'd done a thorough job there, even though her gut screamed that the looter had already left the island.

She'd hit Stockholm next, visiting dives that would've given anybody the heebies, she assured herself. Then London, and ditto, because where else would a gal find out what was going on in an area except in the lowest of the low? And finally here, back in the States in a warehouse near the docks in New York City. The looter was long gone. Dani hadn't been able to turn up a single, solid description, but at least she'd been able to figure out that the artifacts were in the Big Apple. She intended to find them before they went any farther.

Dani picked the binoculars back up, fitted them to her eyes, and blew out a soft whistle. "Well, hello there, big boy."

A new player had arrived. Six two, maybe six three, two hundred twenty-five pounds of solid muscle encased in a plain black t-shirt and faded jeans. His face was obscured by a battered Chicago Cubs baseball cap.

"Ouch," she murmured. "No taste, dude."

New Guy was obviously a member of this team. Shirtless and Nitwit both stopped unloading boxes from the truck trailer they'd been emptying to talk to him. Body language said it was a serious convo. New Guy pulled his cap off, ran a hand over his hair. She got the impression of strong features before he yanked the cap back on. He turned and stalked off, and as he did, Dani's stomach jumped and urgency grabbed hold of her. *This one*, her gut said. She stuffed her gear into her backpack and did exactly what instinct demanded.

A WEEK PASSED QUICKLY as Maya settled back into her normal routine. As promised, she'd had her report on the director's desk the Tuesday after she'd arrived, then presented the report in person to the Council of Seven. She'd tried to convey the amazing promise the artifacts presented, particularly the texts, without giving undue hope. As it usually did, meeting with the Council had drained her.

The next day, bad news arrived from Dr. Lindberg via Lars. Someone had hacked into their computer system and systematically destroyed the digital images taken of the stolen artifacts. E-mails that had pictures attached were gone on both ends and the cloud storage where the pictures were being held had also come under attack. Some of the images had previously been printed, but not all. Between the missing inventories, the damage to the on-site computer and hard drive, and the electronic attacks, Dr. Lindberg feared that some artifacts from the Daughter's burial were bound to be overlooked and would thus never be found. A computer expert had been called in to try to beef up their electronic security, but it was probably too little too late. Indigo had called separately and told Maya that they were compiling a handwritten list of the artifacts based on everyone's memories of the burial, and Maya promised to contribute as well.

She talked to James only once, and that not long after her talk with Indigo. He didn't mention whether or not he'd made a decision on working at the IECS, and she didn't push him. She did make sure Director Upton had mailed a personal letter to him.

Maya tried very hard not to linger on thoughts of Dr. James Terhune. Her lab needed a good cleaning before the artifacts arrived, so she settled her mind there instead of on him. Sometimes it was easy, others not so much. If anything, the avoidance made her uncomfortable. It felt like a lie, hiding from her interest in him. That was what she was doing, she admitted to herself, hiding like a child who'd broken a rule and couldn't face the punishment.

She was knee deep in boxes and packing materials when she realized that. The courier had come with the first shipment of artifacts, a delivery she'd personally overseen, and now she'd taken on the task of making sure that everything shipped had also arrived.

Sitting in the middle of near chaos, with the possibility of finding answers, of uncovering enough of the People's past to make a difference to their future, and she was avoiding thinking about the possibility of a relationship holding that same potential, simply on an individual scale. Maya threw down the pen she'd been using to check off artifacts against inventories and pushed her hands through her hair. Honesty. It was something she'd always promised herself, so now she'd be brutally honest.

She blew out a breath and leaned back in her chair. The bright lights of her lab illuminated every corner, from the gleaming countertops to the high-backed barstools she preferred to all of her equipment. This was as much home as her house was. She felt comfortable there surrounded by history, in a way she'd never been comfortable inside her own head, particularly in matters of the heart.

But history was also the problem here. She'd lost her parents so young, then more recently Dierdre's father, and in between was a long line of people who'd hurt or betrayed her, whether intentionally or not. Trust was always an issue for Daughters. It was part of their nature. For her, the inability to trust had been built over a long, long time. She rubbed grubby fingers over tired eyes. Yes, she'd lost the ability to trust, so gradually she seldom thought about it anymore.

She had people she trusted, at least to an extent. Her daughters, the director, a handful of other Daughters she called friends, but trusting a man and particularly with her heart? Her mind immediately recoiled from the idea, so swiftly she realized another emotion must be at play here. It took her a moment to recognize fear, something she so seldom acknowledged. The thought of actually opening herself up to a man as something other than a friend or colleague shriveled her insides, and that made her a little angry. Fear was the first thing a Daughter learned how to conquer, yet it had been driving her for weeks now. That couldn't be allowed, not for any reason.

No, she *wouldn't* allow it. She was a Daughter, a proud warrior of the People, respected in her own right for the gifts and abilities she'd cultivated through years of hard work and sacrifice. She'd be damned if a mere man caused her to act like a child cowering from the dark. Maybe she'd never be able to trust a man again, but she certainly *could* control her fear.

JUNE TURNED TO JULY without James making a decision. The pictures of the documents found in the Sandby borg grave languished on his desk, neglected while he vacillated between going to the IECS or not.

It wasn't work holding him back. He'd already spoken with his department chair and knew he'd be able to take an indefinite leave, given where he'd be going. Though he tried to quell the rumors, word spread rapidly through the department that he'd be taking an assignment at the IECS. The number of requests he'd already received from colleagues to pull records in the IECS Archives was astounding. He'd promised nothing, but that hadn't stopped anybody from slipping notes under his door containing scrawled pleas for access.

No, the problem here wasn't work. It was Amelia. As much as he wanted to seize the opportunity, he simply couldn't abandon his daughter to her mother's loving but occasionally neglectful care. For only the second time in his life, he was torn between what he wanted to do and what he needed to do. Both times had involved his beautiful child.

The window of opportunity for accepting Maya's offer was closing, and quickly. He'd received a letter from Director Rebecca Upton just two days before, restating the job offer and personally extending an invitation to him to access the IECS Archives. While Director Upton hadn't said so outright, he'd inferred that access was contingent upon his acceptance of that offer.

He sat in his car outside his former residence, the house he and Linda had tried and failed to turn into a home. Since the divorce, they'd continued to have family night once a month, more often if their schedules allowed. At first, it had hurt being there not as a husband and father, but as a guest. Now, he relied on these evenings with his daughter in a normal setting where they could be a family without the bickering and hatefulness he'd witnessed after some of his friends had divorced.

Director Upton's letter burned a hole in his pants pocket where he'd stuck it on his way out of his office. Tonight he'd have to make a decision, but first, he had to tell Amelia and Linda.

He got out and slammed the car door shut. Almost immediately, the front door burst open and his daughter ran out, her elven face wreathed in smiles, her mahogany hair glimmering in the late evening sun. James held out his arms and grabbed her as she bounded down the sidewalk and into a hug. He held her close, breathing in the perfume he'd gotten her for her thirteenth birthday. His heart expanded with the joy of holding her, and ached, too. Soon, she wouldn't be his little girl anymore, and he dreaded the day she finally grew up on him.

Amelia drew away and beamed at him. "You're late. We've been waiting forever."

James made a show of checking his watch and nodded solemnly. "Yes, I see I'm all of three minutes late. I'll have to do better next time."

"See that you do," Amelia replied, her chin tilted at a pert angle. She abandoned her reprimand and tugged on his hand. "C'mon. Mom let me make supper."

They walked hand in hand to the door, Amelia chattering about school, James teasing her into blushes. He followed her into the kitchen, where Linda was peering into a large pot, slowly stirring the contents.

Linda looked up when he and Amelia walked in and smiled, then offered her cheek for a perfunctory kiss. Except for a strand or two of silver in her strawberry blonde hair, the years had been very kind to his ex-wife. Maybe a laugh line or two had been added since they'd met eighteen years before as freshmen at the University of Connecticut, but otherwise she looked very much like the young woman he'd fallen in love with.

Amelia sidled up to Linda and the two bent their heads together, one dark, the other light, identical smiles on their faces. They looked more like sisters than mother and daughter. Every time he looked at Amelia, Linda's gray-green eyes stared back, and maybe that was a good thing. His heart lightened. Yeah, maybe it was better Amelia resembled her beautiful mother instead of her scruffy old dad.

He leaned a hip against the counter. "Smells good."

"Oh, well, we've been having a little fun," Linda said, her voice light. "No promises on edibility."

James grinned. "Isn't that usually the case?"

Linda smacked his arm and Amelia laughed.

"Go on then, you two," Linda said. "For that you can set the table."

Not long after, they ate at the small, square kitchen table. The meal was more than edible, a simple red sauce over pasta accompanied by salad and bread. James listened as Linda and Amelia chatted about school and work and everything in between, and he settled in, comfortable and happy for the first time in days.

After they'd cleaned the table and sat down again for healthy slices of his favorite cake from a local bakery, James cleared his throat. "I have some news."

Linda's brow furrowed. "Nothing bad, I hope."

"No, nothing bad. I've been offered a temporary job at the Institute for Early Cultural Studies in Georgia. They want me to work with some of the documents found at the Sandby borg site."

"Oh," Linda said. "I heard you might be going there."

James stifled a grin. God bless the college rumor mill.

Amelia set her fork on her plate. "What'll you be doing?"

"I'll be translating some documents found in that dig, maybe help conserve them, and while I'm there, I can work on some personal projects."

Linda leaned forward, her eyes bright, and peppered him with questions. Amelia tilted her head. A small frown pulled her lips into a downward curve. The more questions he answered, the deeper her frown got.

When Linda wound down, Amelia said, "How long will you be gone?"

James sighed and leaned back in his chair. "I don't know, honey. Anywhere from a few weeks to several months or maybe longer."

"Will you come back home at all?"

"Sure." He gripped her smaller hand, squeezing lightly. "If I go, I'll come back as often as I can, and you can visit, if your mom says it's ok. I've heard the IECS campus has all kinds of biking and hiking trails we can explore."

Amelia nodded, her brow furrowed. "I'll miss you is all."

"I haven't made a decision yet. It may be that I can't go."

Linda rose and stacked their plates into a pile. "This is a good opportunity for you, James. You should take advantage of it while you can."

He glanced toward Amelia. "There are still some things I have to take into consideration."

Linda set the plates down in the sink, then turned and rested her back against the counter with her arms crossed over her chest. "Amelia, darling, why don't you go get your fall school schedule so your father can look it over?"

Amelia rolled her eyes. "Geez, Mom. That wasn't obvious at all. If you want to talk to Dad in private, why don't you just say so?"

"Ok, then," Linda said evenly. "I want to talk to your father in private, but I'm sure he'll want to see your schedule, too."

"Yes, ma'am." Amelia rose and left the room, her stride just short of flouncing.

"When did she grow up on us?"

Linda sighed and faced the dirty dishes piled in the sink. "When we weren't looking, I promise."

James rose and joined her. He rummaged for a dish towel and slung it over his shoulder. "What did you want to talk about?"

Linda waited until the sink was full of sudsy water to reply. "I know you're worried about leaving Amelia here with me. I'm not the irresponsible parent you make me out to be, James."

"I never said you were irresponsible."

"Right." She laughed, the sound rough and bitter. "I forget to pick her up from school one time and suddenly I'm a monster."

James gripped the edge of the sink, tamping down the slow burn of anger rising in him. "It's more than forgetting to pick her up from school, Linda, and you know it. You get so wrapped up in work you forget she's there."

"I do not."

"Yes, you do," he insisted. "You used to do the same thing to me. You'd shut me out while your mind was filled with some project you were working on and it drove me crazy. It's one thing to do that to your husband and something else to do it to your kid."

"I never shut you out," Linda said flatly. "You stopped listening to me. You stopped caring, James."

James reared back. "No. I always cared."

"If you did, you didn't show it." Linda slumped against the counter. "I thought you were having an affair."

"I never cheated on you. Never."

"But you didn't come home, either."

"God, Linda. I was working."

She nodded. "I know. You took on extra classes, extra projects, more students, anything to keep you away from home."

"I was giving you the space I thought you needed."

"I needed my husband."

"Jesus." He barked out a short, humorless laugh. "Why didn't you tell me that before we got divorced?"

The tension drained out of Linda's shoulders and a half smile curved her beautiful mouth. "Stubbornness?"

"Hunh. Maybe some on my part, too." God, wasn't that the truth. Both of them were too stubborn for their own good, and it was well past time they got over it. James shook his head. That wasn't a wound he wanted to prod again. "I don't want to leave you and Amelia alone."

"You won't be." She slid her arms around his waist and rested her head on his shoulder. "If we need help, you'll be just a phone call away."

He wrapped his arms around her and rested his chin on top of her head. "Sure. It's just..."

"No." Linda pulled away and met his gaze evenly. "No buts. You're going, and while you're gone, you'll call every night or two, and you'll come up or Amelia will come down. It'll all work out."

"I can have Jena drop in to help out."

She shuddered. "No, thank you. Your sister hates me, and I can't see her willingly stooping to helping me out, not even for Amelia."

James acknowledged that with a shrug. Linda and Jena had never gotten along, though he'd always put it down to differences in personality. That and his sister didn't like anyone, not even herself.

Amelia flounced in, schedule in hand, and James let the conversation slide. He settled in and watched a movie with them, and was pleasantly surprised by how smoothly the rest of the evening went. Linda had set some of his fears to rest, enough that by the time he left to go home, he'd made the decision to take

Maya up on her offer to work at the IECS. He'd make the arrangements the next day and by the end of the week, he'd be on his way.

Seeing Maya Bellegarde again had nothing to do with the excitement pinging through him, nothing at all.

SIX

REBECCA STUDIED the final draft of the notes she'd made detailing her encounter with the Woman with No Face. It had taken days to finish the report, first to calm down, and then to tease all the nuances of the meeting from her memory.

She'd started locking her office windows at night, though she suspected it would do nothing to keep the Woman *out* should she wish to be *in*.

Rebecca read the report a final time, then placed the typed notes into a file folder along with the piece of paper the Woman had left on her desk. The morning after the encounter, she'd called down to the Archives and had them gather every scrap of information on file about the Woman, several linear feet of material dating back at least three millennia, as far as Naomi Spillfeite, the archivist, could tell.

So much information, yet no one knew the Woman's true identity.

Surely she was a Daughter. Her skills and age attested to that, assuming the mask hadn't been taken up by several successive individuals. Rebecca was certain, at least, that the one who'd brought the infant to her in 1939 was the same woman who'd visited her office just days ago. Beyond that, who knew?

A quick phone call to the Archives ensured that an intern was on the way to drop off the first box of material and simultaneously pick up Rebecca's notes to add to the collection. She'd waited until her report was finished to begin reviewing the files they maintained on the Woman, quite deliberately. It wouldn't do to taint her memory with the recollections of others.

Still, she was anxious to begin and was grateful, not for the first time, that the People had gone to the trouble to collect and maintain such an extensive database on themselves, their allies, and their enemies. Or, in the case of the Woman with No Face, a person of an indeterminate relationship.

A hard knock rapped on the office door and Rebecca smiled. The second phone call she'd made after the Woman's visit had been to someone she trusted nearly as much as she trusted herself. As the door opened, she rose and studied her youngest natural daughter.

Jerusha had grown from a laughing child into a solemn adult, but that was to be expected. The lives the People led were somewhat easier now than they had been when Rebecca was a child, but it was still difficult, particularly for the youngest daughters. Those were the ones who witnessed their mother's happiness, if such was fated, and the birth of the long-awaited first son. Some daughters grew jealous of their younger male sibling. Thankfully, not her own.

"Jerusha, love," Rebecca gestured for her daughter and the two met in a hug. In spite of her heels, the top of Rebecca's head was inches shorter than her daughter's. Thank the Goddess Jerusha had gained her father's height instead of her own. "It's been too long. How's London?"

"Decadent," Jerusha replied, a hint of sarcasm tingeing her voice. Her crystalline blue eyes sparkled, adding a mischievous hint to her expression. "Digging in the dirt, reconstructing skeletons, guarding the loot. I'm constantly overwhelmed by the excitement."

Rebecca smiled and led her daughter to the sitting area. "I'm sorry to have to pull you away from your work, especially now."

Jerusha shrugged and dropped into an overstuffed chair. "It'll be there when I go back."

"Hopefully." Rebecca settled onto the settee. "Have you heard about the Öland Island dig?"

"Yeah. I ran into Dani in London while she was tracking the artifacts. We had a high time on the town searching for clues."

"The two of you must be mellowing. The last time you and Dani painted a town red, I had to send in the cavalry."

Jerusha snorted. "We've aged a little since then."

"Yes, you have. I'm quite proud of the both of you. A mother couldn't ask for finer daughters."

"Nor could we have asked for a finer mother."

Tears welling up in Rebecca's eyes at the standard, formal exchange, said so often between Mother and Daughter. She quickly sniffed them back, appalled at both the overflow of emotion and the lack of control. Truly, being mortal had its drawbacks. "Well. I'm sure you're wondering why I asked you to drop everything and come home."

Jerusha arched a black eyebrow and leaned back in the chair. "I did wonder a time or two what was so important."

"I have a job that needs doing and I need someone I can trust to help me. You mustn't tell anyone, not a single soul," Rebecca cautioned. "This mission depends upon your utmost discretion. Will you help me?"

"Of course. What do you need?"

Rebecca took a deep breath. She'd thought long and hard about telling Jerusha of her meeting with the Woman with No Face and had decided against it. Only a handful of individuals needed to know of that incident, and knowing might hinder Jerusha's work. "I've received intelligence that our enemy grows strong. I need you to confirm this."

"They've been quiet for decades now. Do you have any specifics?"

"Unfortunately, no, but it shouldn't be hard to assess their strength."

Jerusha pushed herself off the chair. "I'll get on it right away."

"There's more." Rebecca hesitated as Jerusha sat back down on the edge of the chair. "My intelligence says we've been betrayed."

"By who?" Jerusha asked, a hard edge to her voice.

"By a Daughter."

"You're certain?"

"As certain as I can be without hard evidence."

They shared a moment of silence. Some Daughters opposed the majority's goal to overcome the curse for them all. A few clung to their immortality, using it as a shield against love, against trust. Others simply had no wish to ever become mortal. Still, all were more or less open about their feelings on the subject, or pretended to be. Very few would ever stoop to such an insidious act as betraying the larger cause, but determining who would've done so might be difficult depending on a number of factors Rebecca refused to consider. She was no longer in the loop where efforts to contain the Eternal Order were concerned, but they were rumored to have been forcibly disbanded long ago. Surely this wasn't their handiwork.

"I'll get that proof for you."

A weight lifted off of Rebecca's chest. "Good. Now, Robert and Bobby will want to see you while you're in town."

"I'll stop by tonight after I've visited the Archives."

"I put in a request a few days ago for the files you'll need. They should be waiting for you, but please don't hesitate to request additional information."

"I won't." Jerusha smiled and the mischief returned to her expression. "My mother, the director. Always so on top of things."

Rebecca laughed and settled in for a little girl talk with her daughter.

NIGHT HAD FALLEN by the time James reached the IECS compound. Once he'd gotten the ball rolling with a call to Maya, it hadn't taken long to make arrangements for an extended leave from work and find somebody to take over his classes.

Saying goodbye to Amelia had been the hardest part. Even the promise of frequent calls and her visit during the Labor Day holiday before school started hadn't been enough to dampen her tears. When he'd stopped by to see her the night before he'd left, she'd clung to him, and the guilt of leaving her had nearly overwhelmed him. Linda had reassured him they'd be ok a dozen times, but it hadn't assuaged his worry.

Because his time at the IECS was likely to be long, he'd opted to drive down over two days. The long journey had left too much room for second thoughts. Several times, he caught himself searching for exits so he could turn around and head back home. Each time, he forced himself to remember that Amelia would be fine, his work was important. He'd see her soon.

He called Maya when he crossed the South Carolina-Georgia line and let her know he was near. An hour later, he entered Tellowee, the small town bordering the IECS. He pulled over twice and checked the directions Maya had e-mailed him, and finally found the main gate.

James stared at it, glanced around and glimpsed the IECS sign, then stared again. From where he sat, a ten-foot high brick wall extended to either side, bright lights scattered evenly along it. Two guard shacks flanked the main entrance on the outside. A sturdy iron gate blocked the road into the compound. In the distance, he could just make out guard towers, adorned with what he could've sworn were machine guns pointed toward the peaceful town.

Surely not. He blinked, shook his head, and put the vision down to two days of hard driving.

Maya stepped into the beams of his headlights, startling him. She waved, then came around to the passenger's side and slid inside. "Hey. The guards need to do a vehicle check, and then we're good to go. Pop the trunk and the hood, would you?"

What followed was surely the most bizarre security check James had ever been through. Four guards stepped out of the guard shacks, two from each one. A fifth approached from the side holding the leash of a German Shepherd. All were dressed completely in black, with Kevlar vests visibly thickening their torsos and handguns strapped onto their waists. Each carried a machine gun slung over a shoulder. The dog handler was the only male. The rest were tall, well-built Amazons, their expressions so neutral and flat, their faces might as well have been made out of stone.

One guard stepped to the back of James' car and rummaged through the trunk. Another walked around the car holding a long-handled mirror to the ground. A third inspected the engine.

James glanced helplessly at Maya.

Her mouth twitched into a slight smile. "Sorry. I forgot to warn you about security."

"What are they doing?"

"Checking for bombs."

He did a double take, eyes wide, and clamped his teeth shut over his astonishment.

"It's routine," she said. "No one expects you to actually have a bomb."

"Well, that's a relief."

"Roll down the window and I'll introduce you."

"I don't know. I think that one's got it in for me." He nodded toward one guard, a pretty blue-eyed brunette. She'd stood to the side the entire time his vehicle was being inspected, staring intently at him, her rifle held crosswise over her body. James was pretty sure she was itching to use it on him.

Maya shot him an exasperated look. He obligingly rolled the window down.

"Y'all knock it off," she said. "You're scaring our guest."

The pretty brunette slumped and slung her gun back over her shoulder. "We were just having a little fun."

"I know. That's why I let you go so long." Maya winked at her. "I remember what guard duty's like."

James closed his eyes, unsure whether to laugh or bang his head against the steering wheel.

The guards dropped all pretense of searching his car and crowded around his open window, neutral expressions replaced by sheepish grins. Maya introduced them one by one, and James shook their hands, trying to keep names with faces. After a few minutes of chatting, during which each one called him "Dr. T.," the brunette (Andrea, maybe?) jogged into one of the guard shacks and triggered the gate open.

He drove slowly through it and followed Maya's directions around the IECS campus. To the left, a standard-sized oval track with bleachers on both sides dominated the open field. The landscape rose behind it, dotted with other buildings whose functions he couldn't quite figure out.

The other side of the road seemed more familiar. Maya pointed out each feature in calm, even tones. The first building they passed held classrooms, offices, the library, and a small museum. The road branched and Maya gestured to the right. He turned off and drove past the main administrative building, a small cafeteria, a building devoted to labs, and finally, the building containing quarters for guests and interns. The entire compound was lit by security lights and was bright enough that he could clearly make out people exercising or walking around the grounds.

After he parked, Maya led him up two flights of stairs to rooms used, she explained, specifically for visitors to the Archives. "Elevator's out. Should be fixed in a few days."

She opened the door into a great room with a small kitchen on the left and a sitting area to the middle. Two doors on the right led from the main room into what looked like bedrooms. What captured his gaze, though, were the windows framing a view across a good portion of the compound. Maya caught his stare, crossed to one window, and pulled down a shade. "Sorry about the light. It can get annoying, but if you pull the shades down and close the curtains, it should be dark enough to get some sleep at night."

James nodded, a little dazed from the long drive or the lack of sleep, or maybe reality was setting in and it was just different enough from the way he'd envisioned it to throw him off. "Is all that security really necessary?"

"It's not just the IECS we're protecting." She tugged on the shade. It slid upward, revealing the view. "We have a school on the other side of campus, plus the Archives."

"Ah," James said, though he certainly didn't understand. He'd never seen a campus with such high security. The White House, maybe, but not an institute devoted to studying the past, and though he'd heard rumors of the IECS' high security, the reality was a long way from what he'd imagined.

Maya crossed to a round table situated near the kitchen and picked up a folder. She wiggled it at him before setting it back down. "Your welcome packet. There's a map to campus, keys and directions to your office and lab, and so on. You'll likely need it for a few days. Just stick to the IECS side of the campus and you'll be fine." She walked toward the door and put her hand on the knob. "Oh, and the running trails and such. There's a town business directory in the packet, but if you have questions, just call. Do you need help getting your bags in?"

"I'll get them, thanks."

Maya smiled. "All right, then. I'll come by in the morning and give you the tour."

James nodded and showed her out, then flopped into one of the chairs in the sitting area. It was surprisingly comfortable and after a while, he nodded off. In his dreams, Maya chased him, German Shepherd in tow, the Guard Pack hot on her heels gleefully waving paintball guns at each other.

SEVEN

MAYA KNOCKED on the door of James' suite early the next morning. He'd looked tired the night before, security's prank on him notwithstanding. Hopefully, he'd gotten a good night's rest.

For her sake, she'd hoped the attraction she felt for him would've dimmed by the time he arrived in Tellowee. No such luck. He'd been so cute the previous evening, gawking at the guards as if he'd never been through a security check point before. They'd been a little rough on him, all in the name of good-natured fun. Poor kids.

And he'd been so *cute*, though he probably wouldn't appreciate that particular description.

A grin still lingered on her features when James opened the door, alert and apparently well-rested. He was sharply dressed in a sky blue button-down shirt and khaki slacks and he'd even taken the time to shave.

She eyed his clean-shaven jaw, a steady sinking sensation filling her gut. How could she possibly prefer his lean face covered in stubble? She didn't even like men with facial hair.

"Hey." He stepped aside and gestured her in. "Just a minute more. Briefcase? Ah, there it is."

"No rush."

He nodded absent-mindedly, shoved his welcome packet in the briefcase, and slammed it shut. "All set then. So, what's on the agenda today?"

Maya waited until he closed and locked the suite's door. "Not much. I thought you'd appreciate a day to settle in before we get to work on the artifacts. Breakfast first at the cafeteria, then I'll show you around."

Sunlight bathed the campus in early morning heat as Maya led James from his suite to the cafeteria. There, they joined a growing line of teachers, professors, interns, students, and other campus residents. Maya helped him juggle his briefcase and a tray of food as they worked their way through the line and to a table.

As they sat down to eat, James leaned forward and quietly asked, "Is it just me or is everybody staring?"

"It's not just you. We don't have many visitors here. The word's already out on who you are and why you're here. Office hours." She waggled her spoon at him. "Trust me."

Dierdre bounced up to them, tray in hand, a huge smile on her face. She set her tray on the table and plopped into a chair. "So, this is the famous Dr. T., huh, Mom?"

James swung his head toward Maya and mouthed, *Mom?*

Maya introduced James to her daughter, adding, "Dierdre attends school here."

"Pleased to meet you," James said, nodding.

Dierdre nodded back solemnly, then turned in her chair and held up two fingers. A group of girls at a nearby table broke into giggles and gave her two thumbs up all around.

Maya bit the inside of her cheek and glanced at James. He appeared to be completely engrossed in his bacon except for a faint tinge of red creeping up his cheeks.

"What brings you by, Squiggles?" Maya asked.

Dierdre feigned an innocent look. "Gee, Mom. Can't a daughter have breakfast with her only mother without it being a big deal?"

Maya stared steadily at her daughter.

"Ok, all right. Geez. Everybody wanted to know what Dr. T.

was like, so I volunteered to come check him out." She waggled her eyebrows. "And I have to say, he is *hawt.*"

James dropped his head into a hand and muttered something under his breath that sounded suspiciously like, *God save me from teenage girls.* Maya stifled a laugh.

"But the mother-daughter thing was totally true, too," Dierdre said, her brown eyes wide.

Maya had pity on James and changed the subject. "How are plans for the Labor Day camping trip coming along?"

Dierdre perked up. "It's gonna be totally awesome. Except, you know, not many of us are going. But Maetyrm Holly said some of the interns might go, too, which would be *sweet* 'cause they know all the good ghost stories and stuff."

"How long will you be gone?" James asked.

Dierdre lifted one shoulder in an off-hand shrug. "Just two nights so we can be back for the Labor Day stuff in town."

"There'll be a parade, then fireworks," Maya said. "Most people bring a supper picnic and sit out in their yards or on the athletic field here on campus for the light show."

"Sounds like fun. My daughter Amelia's coming down the week before Labor Day, so maybe we'll go." In an aside to Dierdre, he said, "School doesn't start back home until mid-September."

"Oh, well, Fall Term hasn't started here yet either."

"Many of the students choose to attend a summer session where they can work on particular skills," Maya explained. "Dierdre is taking classes in martial arts and horseback riding."

"And outdoor survival skills," Dierdre added.

"Hence the camping trip," James guessed.

"You bet." Dierdre beamed at him, then screwed her face into a thoughtful frown. "Your daughter can go camping with us, if she wants to."

"That's a generous offer. I'll ask her, but she'll probably want to spend most of her time here with me, since we won't see each other again until Thanksgiving."

"Aw." Dierdre wrinkled her nose. "She's not a girly girl, is she?"

James laughed. "Only when she wants to be. She used to be more of a tomboy, and then she discovered the magical land of shopping."

"Woot!" Dierdre shot a triumphant look at Maya. "Mall of Georgia, here we come!"

Maya sighed. "Don't encourage her, please."

He crossed a finger over his chest and held up a hand, palm out. "No more. You have my word as the Payer of Shopping Bills."

Maya laughed as Dierdre giggled and clutched her stomach.

"Whew! You're a riot, Dr. T." The table of girls Dierdre had signed to earlier rose and gathered their breakfast trays. One of them called Dierdre's name, and she looked around. "Time to go." She rose hastily, dropped a smacking kiss on her mother's upturned cheek, and said, "Laters!" She held up two fingers to Maya and grinned, then bounded off, joining her friends as they emptied their trays and pushed their way outside. The cafeteria was noticeably quieter after the girls left.

Maya picked up her spoon and stirred her oatmeal. "Sorry about that. If I'd known she was stopping by, I would've warned you ahead of time."

"No problem. Just two questions, though. First, Mom?"

"She's my youngest daughter."

James' eyebrows shot up. "What were you, twelve when she was born?"

"Hardly. I told you, I'm older than I look."

He eyed her critically. "Are you sure she's not adopted?"

Warmth pooled low in Maya's abdomen, curling through her in insidious tendrils. She reined it in and cleared her throat. "Positive. Your other question?"

"What's with the peace sign?"

"Dierdre's been hanging around Dani too much. Two fingers means you're a two hubba guy."

"Hubba?"

"You know, *hubba, hubba.*" Maya sipped her coffee and peered at him over the cup's rim. "She's got good taste. You're definitely at least two hubbas."

James leaned closer. His eyes bored into hers and the warmth in Maya's middle morphed into breathlessness need.

"So, does that mean you think I'm *hawt*, too?" he asked.

Maya laughed and the spell was broken. "I'm so sorry. She's not normally that bad."

"It's ok. Amelia's about the same age, and she and her friends do the same thing. You'd think I'd be used to it by now."

"I don't think anybody can ever get used to teenagers," Maya said wryly.

After breakfast, Maya took him by the office he'd use during his time at the IECS, then by a small room in the lab building where he could work with the artifacts. She showed him where her office and lab were, then took him to meet Director Upton, who graciously welcomed him to the IECS.

In between, she filled him in on the history of the area, the town, and the IECS in particular. Some of the buildings dated back to the Civil War era, including the main administrative building where Director Upton's office was located.

"This structure," she explained as they left the director's office, "was built just after the war to replace an earlier one destroyed by fire."

"Sherman?"

Maya shook her head. "That's what everyone thinks. The truth is much less glamorous. At that time, the building was used primarily as a school for girls. The local Sheriff heard rumors of a large Federal force nearby and took it upon himself to come by and check on the students, and one teacher in particular who, rumor has it, he was sweet on. Unfortunately, he was a bit tipsy at the time and not quite steady on his feet."

"I can see where that might be a problem."

"Oh, yes," Maya agreed. "He tripped over a chair, knocked

over a lantern, and managed to spill his flask full of corn liquor into the fire. The building went up in flames too fast for it to be saved. Fortunately, everyone was evacuated before it was fully engulfed, including the Sheriff."

"Lucky save, then, but what about the budding romance?"

"Those seeds never bore fruition," Maya said, mildly and with a straight face. The poor man had chased after her for months. After the fire, he'd been too embarrassed to approach her again and had eventually married a local girl and raised a large family.

She and James chatted comfortably as she guided him back to their offices. Had she imagined the heat she'd felt earlier when he'd teased her over breakfast? He was so at ease, so laid back, she simply couldn't tell if he felt anything in return.

And she wasn't a teenaged girl, so why was she obsessing about it? Yes, he was *hawt* from his lean, athletic build to the keen intelligence hidden behind his rich, gray eyes. She itched to explore him, to learn every curve of muscle and the exact feel of his skin under her fingers, but he was just a man. Nothing to be afraid of, nothing to fret over.

He held the door open for her, and she entered the air conditioned interior of the building that held their offices, the library, and several classrooms. Her arm brushed his as she passed and a spark jumped over her skin.

She sucked in a breath. Maybe there was something to fret over after all.

Their footsteps echoed in the hallway as they walked to his office. When they arrived, James groaned. Half a dozen notes were tacked to the corkboard affixed to a wall beside his door. "This is like being back home. I've not even been here a full day, and look at this." He pulled down two separate requests for consultations on doctoral dissertations and shook his head, then took down a third note and held it out to her. "Is Dr. Upton who I think he is?"

"That's the director's husband. He's our resident

genealogist."

He glanced at the note. "Hmm. Wonder what he wants."

"I'd guess he wants help translating something written in an obscure archaic language."

"Har." James pinned the notes back onto the board. "Tomorrow."

"Post office hours," Maya reminded him. "You're the only language expert in residence right now, so do yourself a favor and set limits while you still can."

"I'll do that." He turned his back on the corkboard and leaned casually against the wall, his mouth tilted in a grin, his gaze warm. "So, what does a beautiful woman like you do for supper around here?"

Maya eyed that grin and cursed the answering heat rising within her. "Are you asking me for a date or trying to weasel the names of the best local restaurants out of me?"

"Both," he admitted. "I can't take you out for a thank you meal if I don't know where you like to eat."

"You don't have to take me out."

"Oh, I insist."

He brushed his hand over her shoulder. The fleeting touch heated Maya's skin through the barrier of her cotton shirt and she shivered. One touch from him, one charming offer for a meal, and she was ready to yank him close and discover how his mouth would fit against hers.

"After all, you protected me from the vicious security guards and a gaggle of teenaged girls. A meal's the least I can do to thank you." His voice dropped a notch as he leaned closer. "Is it so awful, spending time with a man who thinks you're attractive?"

Maya narrowed her eyes. "Are you flirting with me?"

He straightened away from the wall and lifted both hands in a shrug. "I must be rustier than I thought if you have to ask."

"Not that rusty."

Two female students walked by, chatting quietly with each other, both surreptitiously studying James. One held up two fingers to Maya and winked broadly, and Maya heaved a sigh. Dierdre had been busy that morning.

"Does everybody know about the two hubba thing?" James asked.

"Probably."

"But it'll blow over, right?"

"Eventually, if you're lucky." Maya bit back a grin and tapped the notes tacked to the corkboard, then turned toward her own office. "You have bigger problems right now and I'm late for my own office hours. We can set a schedule for lab work tomorrow, if you like."

"Sure. How's Thursday sound?"

She turned back to him, puzzled. "For what?"

"Supper."

Maya paused and really looked at him. "You're serious."

"Is that so hard to believe?"

She shook her head. "I'll think about it."

His smile was slow and sexy, as if he knew thoughts of him had already kept her up at night.

Damn him.

She turned on her heel and left, ignoring the skip in her heartbeat and the charming man watching her walk away.

JAMES CALLED AMELIA the next night. He'd spent his first afternoon at the IECS setting his office up and familiarizing himself with the campus. True to her word, Maya had stopped by earlier that morning and scheduled lab time with him. Apparently, Linear A was a hobby of hers. She'd been trying to crack it for years.

James snorted. So had every other language geek in the world, including himself.

The phone rang three times before Amelia picked up. She squealed when she heard his voice, then chatted with him about shopping, boys, Linda, boys, summer camp, and boys, in that order.

For some reason, Dierdre's face popped into his head.

After the fourth time she mentioned a boy named Mark, James interrupted, purely for her own good and not because he already wanted to strangle the young man his precious baby apparently had a crush on. "Has your mom bought your plane ticket yet?"

"Geez, Dad, no. I did that with the credit card you gave me."

"Ah." He made a mental note to have somebody pick up his mail and forward it to him, now that he had an address, so he could pay the credit card off when the bill came in. Because he knew he'd forget, he searched through his briefcase for a scrap piece of paper and a pen. "You're going to love it here. I've got a suite with a spare bedroom and there's a school on campus with lots of kids your age."

He hesitated for a moment, unsure whether or not to mention Maya, and decided *why not*. Amelia had to know that he and Linda would eventually begin dating again. "The woman I'm working with. Maya? She has a daughter around your age. You're invited to go camping with her when you come down."

"Oh?" Amelia's voice was as carefully casual as his own. He could picture her winding a strand of hair around one finger, a habit she'd developed as a child. "What's she like?"

"Dierdre?"

"No, Maya."

"Ah, well." He searched for something innocuous to say, sure his thirteen-year-old daughter wouldn't want to hear how compelling and sexy he found Maya, and that he spent entirely too much time daydreaming about kissing her. "She's pretty and smart."

Amelia's sigh distorted the phone's signal. "So's Mom."

James winced. "Er, yes, she is."

Please don't ask why we divorced if I still think she's pretty and smart, he thought.

87

The phone gods had mercy on him, or maybe Amelia didn't want to talk about that either. "What about Dierdre? Is she, like, cool or what?"

James exhaled a relieved sigh and sent a silent thank you to the god of phone conversations. "I've only met her once, but she seems nice. She's in summer school here taking martial arts and horseback riding. She mentioned taking you to the mall."

"The Mall of Georgia? That's, like, the biggest mall in the South."

Imaginary credit card bills danced through his mind. He grimaced and rubbed a hand over his eyes. "I don't know if we'll be able to go yet. There's a picnic on Labor Day and fireworks and an awful lot of interesting things to do around here."

"Dad, the Mall of Georgia is a historical landmark or something. Just think of what an enriching experience it would be to go there."

"Har."

"Please?"

"We'll see," he promised.

A knock came at the door and he rolled his eyes, hoping it wasn't another student dropping by to meet him or a teacher needing advice on curriculum planning. After the third interruption the day before, he'd finally done as Maya suggested and posted office hours on the corkboard outside his office door. The knocks petered off, but when he left for lunch, his corkboard had been covered with notes.

He opened the suite's door. Three men of various ages and builds stood in the hallway, all strangers. He held up a finger, then pushed the door nearly shut.

"Amelia, I have to go now. Somebody's at the door."

"Sure, Dad. You're just trying to avoid the mall talk."

"No, I promise. We'll talk about that later, ok?"

"Ok. Call soon!"

"I will. Love you."

"Love you, too, Dad."

He hung up and opened the door. The men were looking at each other, their expressions puzzled. One gestured to the phone. "Wife?"

"Ah, no," James said. "Daughter. Why?"

The men grinned and high-fived each other. One, a burly young man in his mid-twenties with wide shoulders and sandy blond hair, said, "Tom's got a hypothesis. Long story. I'm Phil Walters, this is Tom Fairfax." Phil pointed to a tall, lanky man with a touch of gray in his dark hair. "And that's George Howe." George was a stocky young man with a slight pooch and stylishly cut golden hair. "We're the other three visiting professors."

He shook each man's hand in turn. He'd known there were other visitors, just not who. "James Terhune."

"We know," said George. "You're the talk of the campus."

"Two hubbas." Tom shook his head. "Dani only gave me a one point seven five."

James leaned a shoulder on the doorframe. "You know Dani?"

Phil crossed his arms and rocked back on his heels. "Who doesn't? It's a small community. You'll find that out soon enough."

Tom hitched a thumb over his shoulder. "We're going out to The Omega, a local sports bar. Thought you might like to tag along."

"Sure." James patted his pockets. Crap. He still had on his office clothes. He motioned for the men to enter and shut the door behind them. "Sorry about the mess. I'm still getting settled in. I, ah, need to change. Be just a minute."

The men wandered around the suite, chatting amiably. James changed into jeans and a t-shirt emblazoned with a UConn basketball logo, then followed the men outside to Phil's car.

THE OMEGA was located a short ten minute drive away in Tellowee's tiny downtown business district. It was crowded for a

Wednesday night and seemed to be less of a sports bar than a local watering hole, judging by the large age range of the people wandering around the interior. The staring guard from his first night was in one corner, playing darts with an older man James didn't recognize. A group crowded around the bar, fixated on the baseball game showing on a large flat screen TV mounted to the wall. Several bar-height tables with high-backed stools took up the middle space, while a small stage with a dance floor in front of it occupied a large space in another corner.

Through a large, arched doorway, James spied pool tables. Several women clustered around one, watching silently as a young woman with a very fine rear bent over to make a shot. She stood and turned, and recognition hit. Maya. He rocked onto the balls of his feet and stuffed his hands in his pockets. Suddenly, the evening looked a lot more promising.

James followed George to an empty table away from most of the crowd while Phil and Tom made the rounds, greeting people they knew, just about everybody as far as James could tell. He took a seat where he had a clear view of Maya's game. As if she could feel her eyes on him, she glanced around and raised an eyebrow, and he grinned. Yup, very promising.

When all four of the men were settled at the table, a waitress came by and took their drink orders, smiling flirtatiously with the other three men.

As soon as she whirled away, James said, "Is it just me or did the waitress give me the cold shoulder?"

Phil barked out a laugh. "Word is, you're as good as taken, my friend. The women here don't poach, if you know what I mean."

"No, I really don't."

"Oh, come on," George said, his expression as skeptical as the tone of his voice. "Don't tell me you're not in a relationship with Dr. Bellegarde."

The waitress came back and set their drinks on the table in front of them. She was friendly to James, but no more than that.

He took in the men's knowing glances and a light went off in his head. Dierdre and her two hubbas.

The waitress whirled away again, her tray held high. James focused on the three men staring at him with thinly disguised curiosity. "I barely know her."

Tom waggled his eyebrows. "But you'd like to, right?"

"She's a beautiful woman."

"Understatement," Tom said.

Phil tilted his bottle of beer toward the crowd. "Here's to the beautiful women of Tellowee, Georgia."

George raised his glass of coke. "I'll second that."

James clinked his beer against the other men's drinks. "Speaking of, what's with all the women? Everywhere I turn, there's another young, athletic female. It's kinda weird."

"Ah." Tom leaned back and scratched his lean torso. "You've noticed the low male-to-female ratio."

"Here it comes," George muttered into his glass.

Tom ignored him. "But you've not been here long enough to notice that most of the younger men seem to be relatives."

"Can't say that I have," James confirmed.

"And most of the older men are married," Phil added.

George's pudgy face sagged. He glanced toward one corner of the bar. "Regrettably."

James followed George's gaze toward where the staring guard and the older man were playing darts. He really needed to learn her name. "She doesn't look old enough to be married."

"She's not," Phil said. "That's her step-father."

George's round shoulders slumped. "He's got a shotgun and he's not afraid to use it."

Tom leaned close to James and muttered, "George found that out the hard way."

"No shots were fired," George said, "but I got the picture."

James reassessed the couple playing darts. "I don't know. She looks like she can take care of herself."

Phil snickered. "George found that out the hard way, too."

91

"If one of 'em offers to teach you a little hand to hand, don't do it," Tom offered. "Fight like wildcats."

"Skilled wildcats," Phil said. "But man, oh, man, what a sight."

"Gotcha." James filed the advice away in the corner of his mind. Truth be told, he wouldn't mind Maya putting her hands all over him, hand to hand combat or not. He glanced casually at the pool table and caught her watching him. He saluted her with his beer and she nodded back.

Phil glanced around, saw Maya, and turned back to the table with a low whistle. "You sure you're not seeing her? 'Cause the look she just gave you was *scorchin'*."

"There was a definite heat factor," George said.

Tom's thin lips twitched. "Or a *hawt* factor."

James sank lower in his chair.

Phil's mouth stretched into a knowing grin. "Yeah, we heard about that, too."

"Jesus. Does anybody here do anything but gossip?"

"Sure." Tom pointed to George, then Phil. "Shorty there is a genius with genetics, Phil's doing his doctoral dissertation. Don't ask or you'll never hear the end of it."

"Hey, now," Phil said.

Tom waved away the protest. "And I'm working with the Archives to upgrade their procedures for storage and conservation. We all work hard."

George raised his glass. "That we do."

"But at the end of the day, we're visitors to a very small, tight-knit community. Everybody here's curious, so we've gotten to know a lot of the permanent staff, the locals, hell, even the school kids."

"And a lot of that community consists of good-looking, eligible women," Phil added.

Tom leaned back in his chair. "Which brings me back to my hypothesis. It's a definite possibility that with the shortage of eligible men around here..."

Phil interrupted. "Who aren't relatives."

"Right, who aren't relatives," Tom said, "that we were deliberately brought here to widen the gene pool."

"Though some of the relatives date, just not their own family," George said.

Phil gave George a *well, duh* look. "Tom's been here the longest. He's had time to study on this."

"How long have you been here?" James asked.

Tom ruffled his hands over his dark hair. "A year and a half, and in all that time, only a handful of women have been invited to study at the IECS."

"Far as we can tell, most of those were relatives of people who live or work here," Phil pointed out.

"True," Tom acknowledged, "which makes my case even stronger. The men invited here are, without a doubt, some of the top minds in the world in their field. So, they're strongly intellectual and, more importantly, they're all single."

James stared at Tom across the width of the table. "Are you serious?"

"Absolutely." Phil slapped his hand against a muscled thigh. "And the women, the eligible ones, are very straightforward. Not many game players here, if you know what I mean."

Tom nodded. "If they want you, they say so, though I wouldn't call any of the ones I've gone out with promiscuous."

"Nope," Phil agreed. "But there's no hesitation. It's like a meat market and we're prime rib, baby. Even George managed to snag a date or two before he got caught by Lady Love."

"It's not like that, guys," George said softly.

"But you." Tom tilted the neck of his beer bottle toward James. "You're already spoken for, so rumor mill has it. The ladies might look, but they'll never touch, not while you and Maya are an item."

"We're not an item," James said evenly. He was beginning to wish they were, but that was a far cry from actually being in a relationship with her.

"Poor, delusional sap." Phil slapped his back in sympathy, or maybe pity. James couldn't tell which, and maybe that was a good thing. Wasn't it bad enough everybody thought he and Maya had a thing going? Any more protests would only add fuel to the fire.

A slow song came on the jukebox, drowning out the baseball game. A few couples drifted onto the dance floor. The staring guard appeared at George's shoulder and tugged him out of his seat. Two women James didn't recognize claimed Phil and Tom, leaving him sitting alone.

He glanced up, searching for Maya. She was watching him, her expression impassive. She was surrounded by women, and even as long as he'd been out of the game, he knew a lone man didn't approach a crowd of women in a bar. That was a sure path to an ego's quick and untimely demise.

Their gazes caught and held, and the rest of the room faded away. Without a word, she handed her pool cue off and glided across the room toward him.

EIGHT

MAYA WENDED her way across the bar toward James and called herself all kinds of fool for doing so. She wanted him, yes, more and more each time they met, but actually entering into a relationship with him seemed too much like tempting fate. Hadn't she learned her lesson already, more than once?

He sat calmly at the table, watching her walk, and stood when she reached his chair. Maya took his hand and led him to the small dance floor, hesitating on the edge as a shaft of fear pierced her heart. She took a deep breath and willed herself to overcome it.

I'm not afraid of this. I refuse to give in to fear.

James' hand slid to the small of her back. He guided her gently the rest of the way onto the floor, as if he knew she needed an encouraging push. Maya steeled herself, then slipped into his embrace. He took her right hand and held it against his chest over his heartbeat, steady and strong. It filled her with courage, enough to run her other hand down his shoulder and grasp his triceps. She admired the firm muscle under her fingers, then slid her hand to the back of his shoulder and stepped fractionally closer.

He was warm against her, steady, and in his arms, she felt safe and comfortable and a hundred other things she'd never expected to experience again with a man. Need swirled inside her, hot and strong. She tried to tamp it down, to rein it in and regain her reason, and failed miserably.

Other couples moved by, talking softly or swaying to the music. James leaned down. His lips brushed her ear and she shuddered as desire stabbed at her. She closed her eyes and leaned into him a little more. Their legs brushed as they moved slowly in time to the singer's lyrical voice.

"So, what's a pretty girl like you doing in a gin joint like this?"

A startled laugh erupted from her. "Girls' night out. You?"

"Boys' night out. Phil, Tom, and George showed up on my doorstep an hour ago and shanghaied me."

"Mmm."

He brushed his chin against her cheek. His late day stubble scratched along her skin and liquid heat swirled through her. Oh, yes. She preferred him a little scruffy.

"I have a confession to make," he said.

"Oh?"

"I've wanted to hold you like this since that night at the bar in Borgholm."

She drew away and pinned a narrow-eyed stare on him. "Really?"

"Absolutely. James, I said to myself, there's a beautiful woman. You should make it a priority to dance with her."

"Do you always have conversations with yourself?"

"Often, particularly where beautiful women are concerned."

"I'm flattered."

"Funny." James relaxed his hold and met her gaze, an odd expression on his face. "You don't sound flattered."

Maya drifted to a halt. What had she been thinking? It really had been wrong of her to dance with him, so horribly wrong to lead him on that way. "I'm sorry. I don't think it's a good idea for us to get involved."

"Who said we had to get involved?" James pulled her back into the dance, cradling her body against his at a distance that wasn't quite decent. "We're just two colleagues with a lot in common who happen to be attracted to one another and are expressing that attraction with a dance. That's not involved. That's exploring an opportunity."

Maya breathed out a laugh and relaxed against him. "And how far would you like to explore that opportunity, Dr. Terhune?"

"Oh, as far as you'll let me, Dr. Bellegarde." His grin was wicked and sharp, and held the heat of a man enjoying his view. "I am a man."

One song melded into another. Couples left the dance floor, others entered it. It was so easy to lose herself in his kindness, his calm. As they swayed to the music, she felt as if she'd stepped out of the storm and into the deceptive safety of its eye. "So this counts as a date, then?"

"A date is where I pick you up and take you out to a nice restaurant, maybe a movie afterward. We sit and talk and get to know each other, and then I take you back home and try to sneak a kiss when I walk you to your door."

She hid a smile against his shoulder. "So that was your plan when you asked me out."

"Yup. Dinner, a movie, and a kiss. Sounds like a perfect night in my book." He pulled her closer and maneuvered them into a less crowded spot on the dance floor. "Unless you're into sports. We could have hotdogs and a game, and then a kiss. Hey, whatever makes you happy."

Maya snickered, couldn't help it. "What if I like opera?"

"That might be pushing it. We manly men can't be seen at such places."

She shook her head, amused by the banter. He seemed so shy, even reserved at times. It was easy to overlook his sly sense of humor, easy to overlook how attractive that humor was.

And she was attracted, more so every day. In spite of that, Maya didn't want to rush into anything with him. She could *feel* that they were headed into something, something she couldn't quite make out. It was leading her, maybe leading them both. She wanted desperately to not be afraid of that pull, but that didn't mean she had to give in to it completely.

They swayed through several more songs, all slow and romantic, and they talked quietly about nothing in particular, their bodies syncing to the music's rhythm.

At nine o'clock, Maya reluctantly pulled away, feeling for all the world like a young lover facing the dawn and her parents' stern disapproval. In this case, a fourteen-year-old had set the curfew, not in disapproval, but so they could have their ritual mother-daughter chat before bedtime. It wasn't something Maya easily surrendered, not when her job forced her away from Dierdre so often.

"Tomorrow's Thursday," James said. "Any chance you're going to take me up on my offer?"

Maya slid her hand down the back of his arm. "I need to think about it, just a little more."

"All right." He hesitated, then bent down and pressed his lips lightly to her cheek. "I'll see you tomorrow, then."

Maya nodded and left. Her thoughts lingered on him through the rest of the evening. She fell asleep and dreamed of holding him under a moonless sky, their bodies entwined in passion, their hearts beating to the rhythm of the music they'd danced to.

NEW YORK CITY might be a Yankee town, but its summers were just as sweltering as any Southern town Dani had ever visited. Night had fallen an hour ago and still the humidity lingered. She eyed the low, thick clouds hanging overhead and hoped for rain, even if it would ruin the outfit she'd chosen for that night's work, black leather pants, a matching lace-up tank top, and thick-heeled motorcycle boots, also black and adorned with crisscrossing straps and shineless buckles.

A woman could never have too many buckles.

And there was her target, the man she'd followed a few nights earlier. He jogged toward her, his long, muscled build a well-oiled machine, his attention on the path ahead of him as if he had no idea she was waiting for him.

Well, how could the dear man expect somebody to follow him, spend a week figuring out who and what he was, and show up on one of his carefully randomized running routes, waiting to ambush him with his secret?

And it was a very big secret. Naughty boy.

He slowed to a stop and bent over, his breaths panting out in regular huffs. Even in ragged running clothes dampened with sweat, he caught her interest, though she couldn't pinpoint exactly why. His clean-shaven features were attractive in an ordinary way, his dishwater blond hair cut close, his clothes chosen for their plainness. He blended, deliberately so, just your average underworld stooge working his way up the ladder of criminal success.

Not.

Dani stepped out of the shadows. He glanced at her, his expression blandly curious, no more, no less. Did he practice that look in a mirror or what?

"Hello, G-Man."

He stood, hands on hips, and inspected her from head to toe. "Do I know you?"

She shrugged. "How could you? We've never met."

"Ok." He appeared completely unruffled, as if he had conversations with strangers in the middle of the night in a deserted park all the time. "Can I help you?"

"Oh, yes," Dani purred. She stepped closer, pleased when wariness flickering through his expression. "So glad you asked. I need an inside man, Davy boy. You've got a lot of practice at being an inside man, don't you?"

His expression went flat. "I have no idea what you're talking about."

"Don't be coy." She took another step and another, and

planted herself inches away from him. She caught the collar of his t-shirt between two fingers and twisted it playfully as she leaned against him. "I need information and you're gonna give it to me."

His hands came up, grasping her elbows lightly. "Or what?"

She stood on tip-toe and whispered, "Or I'm gonna spill your little secret into the wrong ear and blow your cover."

His fingers tightened on her elbows and he hustled her into the shadows of the tree she'd been using for cover. As soon as they were out of sight of the path, she twisted her arm, loosening his hold. She brought her other arm across his body and slammed it into his chest in a blow that would've knocked a less sturdy man off his feet.

He grunted, dodged a blow she aimed at his jaw, then swung her around and shoved her against the tree, holding her there with the full weight and length of his body. Her short staff dug into her spine where she'd anchored it earlier and she wiggled, trying to ease the ache. He shot her a droll look and leaned harder into her, bracing his forearms against the trunk above her head.

His head bent toward hers. "What do you know?" he demanded in a low voice.

In the low light from a distance, they'd look like lovers, if anybody was watching, which they weren't. She and her handy-dandy short staff had taken care of the little problem of Feebi tails and criminal watch dogs alike.

Some days, she loved her job, usually on the days when she got to crack skulls.

But she had to wonder why Davy boy was being watched so heavily. That was something she hadn't dug up. Yet.

"I know who you are." She breathed deeply, inhaling the masculine scent of sweat and soap. Too bad the dark masked the color of his eyes. Were they as deliberately bland as the rest of him, or would they give her a different picture of him all together? She shook her curiosity off and focused on the reason they were there. "I know what you're doing and I know why."

"I doubt that."

"Oh, Davy. Don't be naïve. An informant here, a computer hack there, and I know everything about you from where you were born to the size of your shoe."

"Jesus," he breathed.

"Hardly," Dani said drily. "Just money applied to the right person at the right time."

"I want names." His voice was hard, uncompromising, and his body firm against hers.

Naturally, she obliged, though probably not in the way he intended. Why make it easy for him? "David Allen Winstead, twenty-nine years old. A Taurus, born and raised in a little town outside Kansas City to a farmer and his wife. Graduated from Notre Dame with honors and a degree in criminal justice, a minor in psychology." She hesitated, giving him time to understand that she really *had* found out everything about him. "Were you deliberately aiming for a government law enforcement job or were you just tired of growing wheat?"

"Oh, my God." He closed his eyes and beat his forehead twice against the tree's trunk. "I've been working on this case for two years and a castoff from a Goth vampire porn novel blows my cover on a damn whim."

Dani gaped, torn between outrage and amusement, then remembered her outfit. Her lips curled into a snarky smile.

Dave's eyebrows veed over an angry glare.

"Your cover is perfectly intact, Davy. You'd be no good to me if it weren't."

He hissed out a breath and pushed away from her, stepping back into a wide-legged stance with his arms crossed over his chest. "Ok, you've got my attention."

Dani allowed a hint of triumph to creep into her smile. "I knew you'd come around," she said, and then she explained exactly what she needed him for.

THE FIRST FULL DAY in his lab, James devoted his time to deciphering the half dozen cylinder seals unearthed in the anomalous burial at Sandby borg. Each one was between one and one and a half inches in height, though they were made of different materials. They were meant to be rolled over clay as a signatory, so that's exactly what he did.

The flat impressions were much easier to work with than the seals. After taking additional pictures of the tiny cylinders, he packed them away and sent them to the Archives for storage. He snapped more images of the flat impressions, then set them out of the way where they could dry and harden for later use.

The previous day, before his adventure with Phil, George, and Tom at the bar, James had taken the time to sort through the pictures taken at Sandby borg and pin them up onto the corkboard taking up an entire wall in his lab. As a decorating scheme, it left a lot to be desired, but it was handy for his purposes and probably why he'd been assigned that particular room.

Now, the photographs were arranged chronologically, with earlier writing systems on the left and later ones on the right. There was a pattern there, he was sure. It just hadn't jumped out at him yet.

He'd started working with the cylinder seals first since their inscriptions, rendered as images partnered with a smattering of cuneiform, represented some of the oldest inscriptions found in the Sandby borg grave. The language was Sumerian or maybe Akkadian, but he wasn't quite sure. In spite of his reputation as an archaic language expert, the ancient Near Eastern languages weren't his specialty and he was a little rusty there. He'd often wondered if he'd spent too much time on the Classical languages, their origins, and derivatives, and now he was absolutely sure of it.

But he had a book that might help. He peered around at the lab's fixtures and ran a frustrated hand through his hair. The book was in his office in a box he hadn't unpacked yet. He uttered a mild oath and set out, bringing copies of the photographed impressions with him. Now that he had those, he could just as easily work in his office.

Maya had been right about the weather in Tellowee, he reflected during the short walk between buildings. It was miserably humid during the day. The frequent afternoon squalls rarely helped. The days would grow warmer as summer progressed and the humidity with it, and he was confined to a business casual dress code. What he wouldn't give to be able to work in shorts and a t-shirt. On the other hand, walking around in only his running shorts might not be such a good idea, given the number of women on campus.

The previous evening popped into his mind, bringing with it an image of Maya swaying with him to some slow jazzy number, her eyes half-closed, her body relaxed against his. He'd taken liberties there that he wouldn't normally, but had figured at the time that, given her standoffish attitude, the opportunity to dance with her might not come again for a long time, if ever. So he'd held her a little closer than propriety deemed correct and for a little longer, too.

It had felt good, holding her, and somehow right.

Now, if he could just convince her to go out on a date with him.

He laughed quietly as he opened the door to the building housing his temporary office. He'd never been the hound dog some of his friends were. He didn't date a lot, but in the past, when he'd been interested in a woman, nobody had turned him down. Of course, the last time he'd dated seriously, he'd ended up married to her, and hadn't dated since their divorce. Maybe he was a little rusty there, too.

The building was cool and dim compared to the bright summer heat. His footsteps echoed in the empty hallway, eliciting an odd nostalgia. That sound always reminded him of his father, a professor at UConn when James was young. His father had often taken him to work on the weekends at his office on campus. It had been a happy time for both of them. Those childhood memories had spurred James into academia as an adult, a place he'd grown comfortable with long before he decided on a career.

He rounded the corner and pulled up short. Dierdre dawdled casually outside his office. She wore a black tank top and calf-length Yoga tights, each embroidered with the high school's logo. Her dark hair was braided into thin plaits that were pulled back into a loose pony tail. The outfit emphasized her lean, toned figure. James stifled the urge to find a shirt for her to wear over the revealing clothing.

She pushed away from the wall, her shoulders stiff. "Hey, Dr. T."

"Hello, Dierdre." He unlocked the door and opened it. "What brings you by?"

"Oh, you know, just checking to see how you're doing."

James studied her carefully. Her words didn't sound like a lie, but they didn't quite ring true either. He tilted his head toward the door. "Come on in."

She followed him into his office and plopped into one of the chairs placed in front of his desk. The room had come furnished, as had his lab and the suite he was using. Maya had told him to take what he needed from basement storage, but he'd been satisfied with the simple furniture already gracing this room. The walnut desk was a little dinged, but it was sturdy and functional. The bookcases lining the walls were mostly bare. He'd only had room to bring four boxes of books on the trip down and already missed the rest of his home library.

A loveseat was shoved into a corner across from his desk. It was covered in a hideous floral print, but it was comfortable. A small desk lamp sat near the edge of his desktop. The only other furnishings were three chairs, one behind the desk and two for visitors. It wasn't much, but it would serve him well during his time at the IECS.

James dropped into the chair behind his desk and set the

pictures aside. Dierdre pulled the ends of her hair over her shoulder and twirled one thin braid around a finger. Her wide-eyed stare was fixed on him. She opened her mouth, closed it again, and frowned.

"Yes?" he prompted.

"I know you're interested in my mom," she blurted out in a rush.

Her words caught him off guard. He searched for a polite way of agreeing and came up blank. How did a man even begin to discuss his interest in a woman with her daughter?

"I'm ok with that," she continued, her voice a little firmer.

"I'm glad?" he ventured cautiously.

Dierdre nodded, as if he'd said exactly the right thing. She dropped the ends of her hair and drummed her fingers on the chair's arms. "You should be, 'cause I could make your life real difficult if I weren't."

"I'm sure you could," he said with as much sincerity as he could muster.

"I know what you're thinking." Her gaze was steady and calm, reminding him eerily of her mother. "You think I don't know what's going on, but I do."

"Er," he said, confused. "What's going on?"

"Duh, Dr. T." She crossed her arms over her chest. "I know about the birds and the bees. I know you want to have sex with Mom."

Heat flooded his cheeks. "Jesus, Dierdre. We haven't even been on a date, yet."

"Yeah, but that's what comes after. I'm not stupid, you know."

James stifled a curse and rubbed a hand over his eyes. "If we did do...that, it wouldn't be anything you'd need to know about."

"Yeah, ok, whatever." Dierdre rolled her eyes. "The important thing is that you want to snag Mom. You're not gonna get her if you play all shy and stuff. I mean, it's sexy and cute and all, but it ain't gonna work, you know?"

He groaned and buried his head in his hands. "Dierdre, stop. Please."

"I'm sorry, Dr. T."

James looked up and caught an unguarded yearning cross the teenager's features, so fleeting he thought he'd imagined it.

"It's just, I want my mom to be happy and stuff, and she likes you, she really does." Dierdre leaned forward, her voice earnest. "But she's got this hang up about dating and I think she's scared to try again, and if you don't do something, she'll never go out with you and then we'll be all alone again, like after Dad died, and I don't want that."

Her lips trembled and tears welled up in her eyes, and his heart ripped just a little.

"Hey," he said softly. He stood and walked around the desk, intending to pat her arm and maybe reassure her, and never got the chance. Dierdre launched herself at him, wrapping her arms around his waist, clinging to him with a muffled sob.

He froze. God, a crying female. He'd never been good at dealing with them, never been good at comforting women, and this one baffled him completely, poised as she was between the maturity of womanhood and the longing of a child for her father. Another sob hit his chest, so he did the only thing he could. He wrapped his arms around her and patted her hair and hoped for the best.

"When did your Dad die?" he asked.

Dierdre sniffled and pulled away, her cheeks flushed pink, her eyes wet. She ran a careless hand over her face, dashing away her tears. "I was, I don't know, four maybe? I remember him, though, and I miss him, so much."

His heart nosedived. Is this what Amelia had gone through since the divorce? He hadn't died, but still. Living apart from him might've felt like it to her. Familiar guilt stabbed at him and he shoved it down. There was nothing he could do about the situation with Amelia that he wasn't already doing.

"He must've loved you a lot."

"That's what Mom says. I think she misses him, too, but probably not the same way."

"Probably not," he said softly.

"It's been a long time since he left. Like, forever, you know? And she hasn't dated or been interested in a guy or anything, not 'til you."

He perked up, interested in spite of himself. "Oh, really?"

Dierdre tilted her head and peeked at him from the corners of her eyes. "And she really likes you."

"Hmm."

She huffed out a sigh. "Any other guy would be pumping me for information right now."

"Been through this before, have you?"

"Dude, guys, like, fall all over the women here. It's embarrassing."

He lifted one eyebrow. "Is it, now?"

"Yeah, but Mom's not interested, no matter how many guys throw themselves at her."

"Maybe they're going about it the wrong way." When she narrowed her eyes at him, he shrugged and added, "Just a thought."

"Maybe," she conceded. "But I know for sure she'll put you off forever if you don't make a move on her or something. Like last night at the bar. I heard you had some smooth moves, Dr. T."

He didn't even wonder how she knew about that. Small town rumor mill. He was getting used to it.

"So, I came up with a plan."

"Er, I've got my own plans, Dierdre."

"Yeah, but too slow, dude. I'm in a hurry here." She sat back down in her chair and crossed her legs, her demeanor that of a general strategizing a war. "Now, I know you asked her out and she wouldn't go, so here's what I'm thinking. There's an exhibition coming up next week. Lots of us are competing. You know, demonstrating our skills with weapons and hand to hand

and stuff. You'll come, right?"

He nodded slowly. "Sure."

"'Cause I'm competing and I want you to be there, ok?"

"Ok."

"Also, Mom will be, too, and..."

He sat bolt upright. "Wait. Maya's competing?"

"Um, yeah, 'cause she was a teacher here, like, ages ago, and since she's in town, she'll be put on the roster."

"She won't by any chance be wearing that outfit, will she?"

Dierdre looked at her own outfit, then grinned broadly. "Oh, yeah, Dr. T. She will be."

"Hmm." Visions of Maya in tight exercise clothes flitted through his head and heat throbbed through him. He casually turned and sat down behind his desk. Some things a daughter didn't need to see, no matter how worldly she thought she was.

"Anyhow, after the exhibition, you'll say how you were impressed and all, and then you'll, like, ask her to teach you how to fight."

"What?" James snapped abruptly out of his daydream. "Oh, no. No, no, no. I've been warned about that already. No fighting, absolutely not."

"Aw, c'mon," Dierdre wheedled. "She won't hurt you."

She said that as if it were a given that Maya was the better fighter, which she probably was. What did he know about fighting?

"But I've heard the older girls talk about how, you know." She gestured helplessly. "Fighting leads to other stuff."

"Stuff?"

"Don't be dense, Dr. T. *Stuff.*"

A light dawned. "Right. *Stuff.*"

"But you'll tell Mom you won't do that *stuff* with her unless she'll go out with you first." She brushed her hands together and relaxed confidently into the chair. "Easy, peasy."

He somehow thought it wouldn't be all that easy. "How about if I reserve the fighting lesson as a backup in case my plan falls through?"

Her expression turned doubtful. "I dunno, Dr. T. Guys never come up with good plans."

"Thanks a lot, kiddo."

"Ok, fine. So, here's another one. After the exhibition, I'll invite you over for movie night. We'll grab a pizza for supper and have popcorn and stuff. It'll be fun."

"And you think Maya won't see through that."

"Oh, she'll see right through it," she assured him. "But once you get there and snuggle with her on the couch, you can wear her down and talk her into a date."

Not for one second did he believe Maya would allow any of that to happen. "We'll see."

"Trust me, Dr. T. It'll work." Dierdre glanced at her watch. "Whoops! Gotta run. Class starts in ten. Don't wanna be late." She jumped up and rushed over, hugged him hard, and hustled toward the door. "Don't forget the plan, Dr. T. I'm counting on you."

She shut the door behind herself. James slouched into his chair, torn between amusement and exasperation. How sad was it that a fourteen-year-old girl thought he needed her help getting a date with her mother?

Pretty damn sad and probably true. Maya hadn't caved after The Dance, and while he wasn't in a hurry to start a relationship with her, he'd at least like to see where this attraction would lead. To do that, he had to talk her into a date or at least find a way to spend time with her outside of work.

The fighting lesson Dierdre had suggested was out of the question and having Maya's daughter invite him over was just pathetic. Surely no man could ever be that desperate. Nope, he'd stick to his own plan and hope for the best.

God help him.

NINE

MAYA SPENT A WEEK avoiding James outside of work. No more girls' nights out, no more running on the track on campus, just in case. Meals were a little trickier, since they saw each other every day as the translations steadily progressed, but she'd managed to avoid him there as often as not.

He hadn't asked her out again.

She threw her pen down in a huff. What was wrong with the man? One minute he was giving her the shy man's version of a full court press, and the next, he barely gave her the time of day. Fickle man.

Grimly, she shoved him out of her mind and stared at the photographs in front of her, trying to concentrate on the text she had to translate into English. The urgency to decipher the texts found in the unknown Daughter's grave pushed at her each day. While James had started on the older scripts, she was tackling the easiest, a scroll written in Latin dating possibly from the third century C.E.

She'd chosen this particular document not to horn in on James' territory, but because it was one language she was very familiar with. Unlike most schools in the U.S., schools for Daughters and Sons still taught Latin and ancient Greek, for the same reason their children learned to read and write cursive handwriting, to preserve their history. The IECS Archives and its counterparts around the world held documents written in a variety of languages, including the Classical languages. It would be foolish to let them die out and thus lose the ability to read their own history.

Five more minutes of futile effort, then ten, and Maya realized her concentration was shot. With a discouraged sigh, she rubbed her hands over her face, tugging her fingers through her hair in frustration.

Maybe she needed more sleep. Her nights over the past week had been restless. Pushing her body to the breaking point night after night hadn't kept her from reliving that evening at the bar in her sleep, or, as she usually thought of it, The Foolishness. What had she been thinking?

It was useless to dwell on it. She knew this. There was no changing the past and no point wasting time with regrets.

Except, a small, secret part of her didn't regret the evening spent in James' arms. She'd tried very hard to quell that part of herself, without success.

Would it be so bad to go out with him? She folded her arms on her work table and rested her head on them, eyes closed as she imagined a date with James. She'd wear the dress Dierdre had talked her into buying on their last shopping trip, a filmy little black number with a fluid skirt that swirled to a stop just above her knees. He'd be in slacks and that shirt she liked, the sky blue one that was slightly fitted, with a tie and jacket. They could go to Mama G's, have something fabulously decadent, and listen to a good live band. And at the end of the evening, after they'd laughed and talked and danced until the wee hours of the morning, he'd bring her home and pull her into his arms and press his lips against hers...

A knock rapped against the door, startling Maya awake. She scrubbed her hands over her face and bit back a curse. How sad was it that she'd fallen asleep daydreaming about James?

Dierdre popped her head around the door. "Come on, Mom. We're gonna be late."

Right. The exhibition. She'd almost forgotten. Maya

checked her watch. If she hurried, she had just enough time to change. "Sorry, Squiggles. I dozed off for a minute."

"I knew it! You've not been getting enough sleep."

"No biggie," Maya said, smiling softly. "Just a lot on my mind."

Dierdre cocked her head, her own smile sly. "Like a certain Dr. T.?"

"Knock it off, shorty, or I'll rearrange the roster so I can spank your little bottom tonight."

"Bring it, Big Mama."

Maya grabbed her gym bag and slung it over her shoulder. "Speaking of, who did I pull in the draw?"

Dierdre grimaced. "India Furia."

"Great." To be matched against that particular Daughter on top of everything else. Maya pursed her lips, quelling a sigh, and shared a commiserating glance with her daughter as they locked up Maya's on-campus lab.

The walk across campus relaxed Maya, enough for her to shunt aside her unease over fighting India. She and Dierdre joined the steady stream of Daughters, mortal and immortal alike, making their way into the gym's dressing rooms.

The youngest students were marching onto the gym floor by the time Maya finished dressing. She hurried through the final touches so she could watch them. It was always her favorite part of these events, seeing the happiness on their cherubic faces, before time and reality had a chance to dull it.

Dierdre spotted her training coach and jogged off to join her group, shouting goodbyes over her shoulder as she went. Maya tugged a jacket on over her athletic clothes and hurried into the gym, settling herself into the bleachers on the opposite side of the crowd.

Just as all Daughters and Sons learned certain academic subjects, they also all spent a lot of time on physical development and training. Gymnastics and martial arts were started at young ages, training the mind and body to be flexible and disciplined.

As the children began their routines on the mats scattered across the gym's floor, a tiny tingle shivered up Maya's spine. She glanced up and spotted James on the opposite side of the gym. He was leaning against the railing at the top of the bleachers chatting with Robert Upton, but his eyes were fixed on her.

The strangest feeling shuddered through her. Her muscles clenched and butterflies fluttered in her stomach. It took Maya a moment to figure out that those butterflies were her nerves setting up a ruckus. She closed her eyes and groaned. How could a nearly three hundred-year-old woman skilled in the warrior arts possibly be nervous about a simple exhibition fight?

James was still watching her, and it hit her then that she was nervous because *he* was there.

When he looked away, she slipped into the dressing room to warm up and unwind. She'd need all of her focus tonight and simply couldn't afford to have anything distracting her, not even the increasingly attractive James Terhune.

THE GYM WAS NEARLY FULL by the time James arrived. He pushed through the crowded foyer into an empty spot against the railing overlooking the gym floor, painted in standard lines for basketball and volleyball. The bleachers were jam packed, so he leaned against the railing instead, his eyes scanning the crowd. An older man in a wheelchair rolled up beside him. James scooted over, making room.

"Good crowd," the man said, his lined face set in a friendly smile.

James nodded. The number of people in attendance had surprised him until a group of four and five year old children had walked onto the floor. The exhibition must feature a large variety of age groups. Looked like the whole neighboring town might be in attendance. "Do you have a child competing?"

"Oh, no. My children are too old for this." The man stuck his hand out. "Robert Upton."

James shook Robert's hand. "Director Upton's husband."

"Right on the first try. You must be our new language expert. I've been meaning to catch up with you."

"You and everybody else," James said, his smile wry.

"New kid on the block. It'll wear off in a couple of months, once everyone's had a chance to pick your brains."

"Don't think I'll have anything left once this crowd gets through with me."

Robert laughed, a hearty, infectious boom.

Across the gym, people trickled in and out of dressing rooms. Dierdre came out with a group of people her age, giggling and cutting up. A few minutes later, Maya entered the gym floor and found a seat in the bleachers across from him. Disappointment twisted through him. She wore a coat over athletic wear similar to the outfit Dierdre had worn to his office the week before. He'd been waiting a whole week to see Maya dressed that way and had hoped reality came close to his imagination. Heat spilled into his gut, strong and steady, and he shifted against the railing. Maybe not too close to reality, not in public anyway.

The youngest group of children finished their set of gymnastics and martial arts forms to enthusiastic applause, their young faces beaming. After, two successively older groups performed ever more complex maneuvers. A break was called and the mats were rearranged across the hardwood floor, leaving four behind.

James chatted off and on with Robert, surprised to discover the other man had known James' father during their early days as professors at UConn.

"I was teaching history at the time to large groups of students who were more interested in dating than studying," Robert said. "Then I came here to do some research, fell in love with Rebecca, and that was that."

A group of middle-school students ran out and divided into four groups of nearly equal size. Two students from each of the groups stepped onto one of the four mats and faced each other, bowed, and assumed fighting stances. The other students sat down out of the way as referees stepped up to the mats. A bell sounded and the students on the mats sprang into action, attacking each other with fierce punches and kicks.

The crowd went wild, cheering the students on. Robert managed a shouted explanation over the noise. Each pair was given five minutes to score three points or knock their opponent completely off the mat. Two of the fighting couples were composed of a male and a female each instead of the students being paired by sex. James made a mental note to ask Maya about that later, then patted his pockets absent-mindedly for a piece of paper to write the reminder on.

Another bell dinged and the competitions immediately stopped. The spectators broke into applause. The students bowed to one another and, without fail, walked off the mats grinning, their arms slung around each other's shoulders. Two more students settled themselves onto each mat and the competitions began again, cycling through all the students waiting on the sidelines.

Dierdre's group came out next carrying wooden sticks.

James nodded toward the floor. "Should I be worried?"

"Ah, yes. I heard you were stepping out with Maya."

James didn't bother denying it. What was one voice against the community grape vine?

Robert threaded his fingers together at his waist. "As far as worrying, there's no need. These young people can take of themselves. You'll see."

And James did. Dierdre stepped onto one of the mats, her body relaxed, her face a picture of intense focus. A young man stepped onto the mat facing her. The two bowed and assumed ready positions.

"Who's her opponent?" James asked.

"Johnny Linton. I hear he has a crush on her."

James frowned as the bell dinged and the students began

sparring. He soon saw that Robert was right. Dierdre could certainly take care of herself. She scored her first point by coming in under Johnny's swing, sweeping him off his feet with her staff, and tapping him lightly on the chest with the staff's end. Johnny took the next point on the rebound, catching Dierdre off guard as she stepped away and gave him room to regain his footing. Her face hardened and she went into a controlled attack that would've been brutally vicious if not for the fact that when it came time to score points, the hits were lightly made.

The bell dinged a moment after she scored her third point. She and Johnny bowed to one another, slung casual arms around each other's shoulders, and walked off grinning. As she sat down, Dierdre shared her grin with James and waved at him.

He waved back, ignoring the curious stares and whispers directed his way.

After Dierdre's group finished, another break was called and the floor was rearranged again. This time, a single mat slightly larger than the others was pulled out into the center of the floor.

"Ah." Robert leaned back in his wheelchair and rubbed his hands together, a huge smile wrinkling his face. "Now the real sport begins."

Two women entered the mat, each carrying a sturdy, yard-long stick similar to the ones Dierdre and her crew had used. One of the women was older and looked vaguely familiar, though James couldn't quite pin down why. Like most of the people he'd seen in his time at the IECS, she was trim and fit. Her light blonde hair was pulled into a ponytail high on the back of her head. He searched his memory, trying to put a name with her face, and came up blank.

The women fell into ready stances, the bell dinged, and they circled one another. The younger woman said something, the older woman smile, and then the attacks began. They used the sticks as if they were swords, slashing and stabbing at one another, blocking and dodging when needed. The younger woman swung her staff in a waist high, back-handed arc. The older woman jumped back and blocked the cut with her own staff. The younger woman did a three sixty and swung her staff around her body into a back-handed upper cut at the torso of the older woman. She calmly blocked again, then twisted her staff around the other woman's, disarming her.

"Atta girl!" Robert shouted.

"Eh," James said. "You know her?"

"My wife, Rebecca. You've already met her, I believe."

"Briefly."

James turned his attention back to the competition. Rebecca had stepped back, allowing the younger woman time to pick up her staff. James tried to reconcile the two images he had of the director, on the one hand, the powerful middle-aged woman who ran the IECS with a velvet-gloved iron fist, and on the other, the woman who expertly wielded a weapon as if it were an extension of herself.

Robert leaned toward James. "Rebecca the Blade, they called her."

"Excuse me?"

"Before we were married. They called her Rebecca the Blade because of her skill with the sword. She stopped teaching and fighting when our son was born, but she still keeps sharp. Practices every day."

The bell dinged, ending the round, and the women bowed and hustled off the mat. Two more women assumed stances on the mat, each carrying a staff, and the round began. When they finished, a third pair of women with no weapons stepped onto the mat. After their bout, a fourth pair entered the mat holding two short sticks each, one per hand, and wielded them with dizzying speed.

James watched the competitions, fascinated by the women's grace, strength, and obvious skill. The matches often ended with only one point being scored, sometimes none.

His parents had never allowed or condoned fighting, not

even for competition. In spite of James' strong desire to learn a martial art or maybe boxing, his parents were firm pacifists and had discouraged his interest. He and his sister hadn't even been allowed to watch fighting as a sport, a restriction James had broken as an adult. He'd long since realized that violence didn't beget violence, as his parents feared, and that there was a large difference between healthy competition and war.

Still, when Amelia had wanted to enroll in a Kung Fu class, he'd automatically dismissed her wish out of hand. It was one of the few things he and Linda had fought about. She'd insisted that a woman should be able to defend herself, but he had, in a rare burst of shortsightedness, never envisioned his daughter growing up enough to leave the house. He seldom acknowledged the fact that she *would* grow up. Deep down, he wanted her to stay his little girl forever, but now, here she was a teenager within a few years of dating, and he was beginning to worry about how she'd handle herself when she was, God help him, alone with a boy. After watching Dierdre take down a young man a full head taller and at least thirty pounds heavier, maybe he should reconsider his opposition.

The crowd's furtive whispers drew James' attention back to the exhibition. Maya walked onto the mat carrying a short staff in her left hand, swinging it around in slow, testing circles. James took a closer look at the other woman and frowned. "I thought Indigo was still in Sweden."

"She is." Robert's mouth thinned. "That's her twin, India. They're nearly identical in looks, but their personalities couldn't be more different."

The crowd hushed. Even the younger children grew still and quiet.

The bell dinged and India attacked. Maya calmly countered, quelling the onslaught of India's fury with steady, even strokes of her staff.

And it was fury, unlike in the other matches where even the youngest participant exhibited an amazing degree of control.

India wore her anger like a shield, attacking in short bursts of speed that would've left another opponent winded and likely seriously injured. Horror crept slowly over him as Maya broke into a light sweat, her body moving continually into a defensive position, never an offensive one. What was she waiting for?

India attacked again and again, her fury seeming to mount at Maya's steadfast refusal to attack and at her inability to break through Maya's defense. She screamed. The sound echoed eerily through the tense silence. The bell dinged, signaling the end of the round, and the fight continued, Maya circling away, India pursuing in short, brutal attacks. James glanced around. Why was nobody stepping in to stop the fight?

Several minutes after the bell rang, Maya shifted the stick to her right hand and went on the offensive. India's fury never dimmed, her strength never waned. Maya, on the other hand, looked as if her second wind had hit. She swung her stick up under India's guard and bashed the other woman's ribcage twice in short succession, *thud, thud*, each blow hard enough to crack a rib. India skittered away and rebounded, popping her staff around one-handed. Maya ducked under the swing and thrust the end of her staff into India's abdomen. India gasped and staggered back, nearly losing her balance. Maya waited, her body loose and ready. India's shoulders heaved as she sucked in breath after breath, her beautiful features pulled into a furious glare. Maya murmured something too low to carry and India laughed, harsh and bitter. She leapt forward and lashed out, apparently unfazed, and Maya countered, graceful and calm.

Just when James was ready to go down there and break up the round himself, injury be damned, Maya crouched and swept a leg around, hitting the back of India's legs above her ankles. India crashed back first into the mat. Maya popped up and calmly tapped the end of her staff lightly against India's cheek.

"Yield," Maya said, her clear voice ringing through the gymnasium.

"Never," India declared. She snaked one hand toward

Maya's bare ankle. Maya twirled her staff down, cracking it against India's forearm, sweeping the limb aside, then dropped to one knee and punched India's jaw with a balled up fist. India's face jerked to the side and her body went slack.

Maya rose and stood over the limp figure of her opponent, her expression oddly dispassionate. Director Upton walked over and spoke quietly to Maya, then directed two of the women standing on the sidelines to remove India from the floor. They weren't gentle about it, either, dragging the unconscious woman out in by her ankles, leaving her head to bounce against the floor and anything else in their path.

The crowd began murmuring, softly at first, the noise building into a normal volume as Maya and Director Upton left the gym floor and another pair of women approached the mat.

James pushed himself away from the railing, torn between his need to check on her and the urge to respect her privacy.

Robert's hand shot out and latched around James' forearm. "Give her some time. Trust me, she needs it."

James sighed. If anybody knew how to handle a woman like Maya, it would be Robert. After all, the older man had a woman like that for his own. "Sure," James said, but he couldn't bring himself to relax against the railing again. He watched the final few matches while worry niggled at him, and counted down the minutes until he could break away from the crowd and find Maya and Dierdre.

ONCE THE MATCHES ENDED, the crowd spilled onto the gym's floor. Maya pushed her way through the crush of people, searching for Dierdre, greeting friends and acquaintances as she went.

No one mentioned her bout with India.

The match had drained her, not physically, no, but emotionally. India had once been a shining star of potential, destined to be one of the greats, but her spirit had been corrupted by envy and a twisted hatred fueled by a crushing need to conquer, to grind her enemies into the dust.

That was not the way of the People.

India was tolerated because the People were so few. Their numbers needed to be preserved. And India rarely allowed her anger to burn in such a reckless display. Maya feared the younger Daughter might've gone too far this time.

Guilt swamped her, bringing anger in its wake. India had once been her student. Maya had had the chance then to help her find redemption, and had failed. For a Daughter, such failure was intolerable. It had taken a long time for Maya to understand that the failure was not her own and never had been. India simply didn't recognize the difference between friend and foe. Still, the guilt chased Maya and, inevitably, the anger.

James was still standing at the railing talking to Director Upton and her husband. Maya had caught the exchange between him and her daughter and had puzzled over it. Now, she wondered why he hadn't made his way down to the floor to find them, to find her.

Had he even noticed her outfit?

Maya bit back a groan, embarrassed at her own thoughts. Of course, he had. She was wearing skin tight Lycra that left little to the imagination. Any man with half a brain and a working penis would notice. By the Goddess, what was wrong with her? Here she was covered in sweat, not a stitch of make-up on, her hair frizzed into a rat's nest, and she was worried that a man might not have noticed her. As if any woman in her right mind would want to be noticed in such a state.

Which just proved she wasn't in her right mind.

He peered down, his eyes homing in on her as if he'd known where she was all along, yet he made no move to join her.

Was he playing hard to get? No, that wasn't right. *He* was chasing *her*. She just hadn't decided yet whether or not she wanted to be caught.

She was leaning more toward getting caught every day, but

only if he pursued her.

With a frustrated *hmph*, she turned her back on him and finally spotted Dierdre plowing her way across the crowded floor, Johnny Linton in tow. When they reached her, Dierdre asked, "Where's Dr. T.? I thought he'd be down here by now."

Maya shrugged and affected an innocent look, as if she didn't know exactly where he was right at that very minute.

Dierdre narrowed her eyes. "Did you chase him away? Geez, Mom. What is that, like, a record?"

"I did no such thing."

"Uh-huh. Well, let's go find him. I want him to meet Johnny."

"Why don't I meet the two of you outside? I could use a little fresh air."

That last was the truth, at least. The gym had grown stifling over the evening. After the confrontation with India, all Maya really wanted was the cool breeze on her face and an hour of silence.

Dierdre snagged Maya's arm in an iron grip. "Oh, no, you don't. I know you're interested in Dr. T., and he's interested in you, and we're gonna go up and meet him and invite him over for pizza and a movie, and you're gonna like it and that's that, young lady."

Maya pursed her lips, trying and failing to suppress a smile. "Oh, really?"

"Really." Dierdre's sternness melted away. She slung her arm around Maya's shoulders and squeezed. "Come on, Mom. It'll be fun."

And it was.

There was no awkwardness as Maya extended the invitation to James, nor at the pizza parlor where many of the Daughters gathered after the exhibition, nor during the movie when she, James, Dierdre, and Johnny all slumped into on the overlarge sofa Maya had purchased when it became evident that her daughter enjoyed having people around her.

They sat shoulder to shoulder during the movie with Maya and Dierdre in the middle and "their fellers," as Dierdre insisted on calling James and Johnny, sitting on the outside. Dierdre had picked an old favorite, an adventurous, fantastical romp with a pirate, a giant, and a Spaniard facing the forces of the evil prince to gain the heart of the princess.

After the scene where the pirate and the Spaniard fought a duel on the cliffs, James tilted his head toward Maya and whispered, "You're not left-handed either, are you?"

She shook her head, her heart melting a little. He'd noticed her switch during the fight. The move had been intended to incite India into rash behavior. Any Daughter would've understand that Maya was insulting her by using her weaker hand to defend, but India, with her hair-trigger temper and wavering control, would take it doubly so, and it had worked. India had burned through her energy and lost focus, allowing Maya to control the fight from start to finish.

Later, James reached behind her to tease Dierdre by pulling at one of her braids and left his arm across Maya's shoulder.

And she didn't mind.

He didn't ask about India or the oddness of their match. He didn't push her to go out with him or try to take advantage of the situation. He just waited, his presence firm and strong and reassuring.

It was exactly the right tactic to take.

Maya allowed her head to fall against his shoulder during the final scenes, when the Spaniard was searching for his father's murderer and the pirate overcame the dastardly prince. She sighed as his arm tightened around her, engulfing her in the safety and warmth she'd reveled in the night they'd danced.

She'd have to go out with him. He was wearing her down just by being himself, an intelligent, reserved man with deep wells of compassion and humor. If she didn't act soon, the attraction between them would spiral out of control, and then where would she be?

As the credits rolled across the TV screen, she leaned her head back and whispered, "Ok."

"Ok, what?"

"I'll go out with you."

He smiled down at her, the corners of his eyes crinkling. "Next Friday?"

"Sure."

He laid his cheek against the top of her head, and she closed her eyes, hoping she'd made the right decision.

TEN

THE TRANSLATIONS progressed nicely. The cylinder seals, the first items James had tackled, had presented less of a problem once he'd remembered that the symbols engraved on them could be symbolic representations other than language. Scenes of worship, maybe, or historically significant events.

If he hadn't been so distracted by his growing attraction for Maya and his worry over Amelia, he would've realized that a lot sooner, a fact that nagged at him. To effectively do the job he'd been hired to do, he'd have to find his focus sooner rather than later.

He checked his watch. Maya would be at the lab any minute now to go with him to present their findings to Director Upton. He finished packing the small impressions of the seals and stuffed the reports he'd prepared in his briefcase, eager to get through the meeting.

Tonight was the Big Night, his date with Maya. He'd taken the entire week to plan this one evening. He scrubbed his hands down his thighs and exhaled a shaky breath. Had he ever been this anxious over a date before or so worried about its outcome?

Maya was still a tantalizing mystery to him. She'd been more open since the exhibition. God knows why, but that night seemed to have been some kind of turning point for her. Curiosity over the match she'd fought with Indigo's sister ate at him, but he refused to bring it up. It had obviously been a difficult night for her, and if she wanted to talk about it, she would. His nagging would only push her away. Still, the whole incident tugged at him. Maybe she'd open up once she felt more comfortable around him.

On the other hand, maybe she'd never trust him enough to open up. He had no end game in mind with her except to, as he'd told her during The Dance, explore the possibilities. What was wrong with two intelligent, unattached adults who were attracted to each other trying to find common ground?

When he'd presented that question to the Three Professorteers, Phil had leveled a pitying look on James and said, "You're overthinking it, man. Just go with the flow."

Maybe Phil was right.

A hard rap on the door startled him back to the present. He jerked his gaze around. Maya leaned against the doorframe, her mouth curled into a smile. "You looked like you were a million miles away."

"Yeah. Sorry. Just, ah, thinking."

Not in a million years would he tell her what he'd been thinking about.

The walk to Director Upton's office went quickly. She was waiting for them in a small sitting area set up on one side of her office. "Punctual as usual, Maya. Dr. Terhune, would you like something to drink before we begin?"

James settled onto the overstuffed chair to Rebecca's left. "Thanks, no."

"I'll start, then." Maya perched on the loveseat next to the director and launched into an explanation of her progress translating one of the texts from the burial. "One of the problems I've had is that the text seems to be written in a strange dialect of Latin, possibly one that was in the early stages of becoming its own language. If so, it's not a dialect I've encountered before."

James nodded. "It's possible the account was rendered in Latin as a translation of another, quite different language.

Normally, that wouldn't make a difference, but if the text's author wasn't a native Latin speaker, it could account for some of the oddities Maya's encountered."

"How far along are you?" Rebecca asked.

"About halfway through." Maya pursed her lips and shrugged. "It seems to be an account of an event that must've had some importance to the woman in the grave, though it's not an event I'm personally familiar with. There were a few names and places mentioned that I'd like to research in the Archives, once I'm finished translating the whole. "

"A sound approach," Rebecca said. "I'd like to read the account myself. I wouldn't mind helping with additional research, if you need a hand."

"Of course, Director."

Rebecca turned her pale gaze on James. "How is your work coming, Dr. Terhune?"

"Steadily. I've been working with the cylinder seals. They seem to be the oldest textual artifacts." James opened his briefcase and pulled out the reports he'd printed. He handed one to each of the women and kept one for himself, then placed the box of impressions on the table, opening the top so that they were displayed against the foam holding them in place. "The seal in the first picture of the report corresponds to this impression."

One by one, James took the director through an explanation of the cylinder seals, describing the materials they were made of, the time period they might've been created during, and linking each to a possible place of origin.

Rebecca scanned through the report, lingering over the images embedded into it. "The carvings on these are incredibly intricate. What was their function?"

"Anything from a scene of worship to the equivalent of a notary's seal or a signature. I haven't yet determined that for most of these." He flipped to an image of a limestone cylinder seal and pointed out the corresponding impression. "This one for example. The image begins here on the left with seven figures, two groups of three stacked on top of each other with the seventh rendered twice as large as the others. Next is what could be a grove of trees, and finally a four-legged creature of some sort. That section is too worn to really lend itself to a solid identification."

Rebecca leaned forward, studying the impression. "What does it mean?"

"I'm not sure," James admitted, "but there are a couple of observations I've made that might be important to determining the meaning. These figures are clearly female. It's difficult to make out in the smaller figures, but the larger one has definite breasts. Usually, cylinder seals depict men or possibly goddesses, but ordinary women aren't often portrayed."

"Are these goddesses, then?"

"I don't think so. They're carrying weapons, specifically quivers for arrows, not unheard of for a goddess. But, normally when gods are portrayed on these seals, it's during an act of worship or the god-figure is accompanied by a name or symbol. That isn't the case here."

Rebecca and Maya exchanged a look James couldn't decipher. He glanced between them. "What?"

"Seven women, a grove of trees, and a four-legged creature," Maya murmured. "Sounds familiar, doesn't it."

"Indeed," Rebecca said.

James raised his hand. "Mind cluing me in?"

Maya ignored him. "I thought so, too, when I first saw the seal, but..."

"You didn't want to get your hopes up." Rebecca ran one finger lightly over the impression of the scene. "It may be time, Maya."

Maya's gaze pierced through him as if he were paper thin. "Not yet, Director."

"Soon, then," Rebecca said firmly.

James huffed out a breath. "What are the two of you talking about?"

Rebecca set her copy of the report on the table. "We have some documents here that might have bearing on your work with these seals. I'd like the two of you to finish the translations or as much of them as you can before you have a look at those."

"Context is everything when interpreting images like these." James exhaled sharply and rubbed his hands down his thighs. "Part of the reason I can't tell you what these mean is because they're isolated from their time period and the locality where they were created."

"The fact that they're part of a collection is just as important and probably an overriding factor to other possible contexts," Maya pointed out.

"Yes, of course," James agreed. "But if you have relevant information that could shed light on the original context..."

"All in good time, Dr. Terhune," Rebecca said. "You have my word."

James slumped into his chair. They were holding back something important, that much was clear. On the other hand, he wasn't willing to risk his removal from the project. If they wanted him to wait, he would, but it rankled. "As you wish."

Maya shot him an exasperated glare.

Rebecca flipped to images of two seals James had deliberately included on the same page. "These look as if they were made of the same material."

"They're lapis lazuli." James pointed out the appropriate impressions. "These appear to represent two different individuals. Notice the mixture of symbols and similar cuneiform. It's possible they were made at the same time or in the same locality."

James continued his explanation of the possible meanings and origins of each seal. He concluded by pointing out the holes drilled into the top back side of each one. "It was fairly common for cylinder seals to be strung and worn as a necklace or in some other fashion."

"Is there any possibility the woman from the grave wore all

129

of these on the same necklace?" Rebecca asked.

James mulled the idea over. "It's possible. Of course, it's equally possible they were carried in a pouch. At this point, it'd be unwise to rule out any possibility. We simply don't know enough yet."

"Mmm." Director Upton studied the impressions, her fingers brushing over each one. "Well, I've kept you long enough. The two of you have made excellent progress. I hope you'll have more news for me soon."

After packing the impressions away and saying goodbye, Maya and James left the director's office. When they were outside under the hot Southern sun, he said, "I can do a better job if you share whatever it is you're holding back."

"I'm not holding anything back."

He snagged Maya's elbow and pulled her onto the grass, earning a startled look from a passing student. "Except whatever documents the IECS has that might be related to the seven figures seal."

Maya shook his hold off. "It's not important, not yet, anyway."

He scrubbed his hands over his hair and glared at her. "How do I know that if you won't show it to me, whatever it is?"

"Because I'm telling you it's not important right now."

"So you want me to trust you, is that it?"

"Yes, I do."

He glanced away. "But you don't trust me."

Maya edged closer and laid a gentle hand on his arm. "Where these artifacts are concerned, yes, of course I do."

"But not enough to share important information with me."

Maya exhaled a heavy sigh. "It's not really my decision."

"Director Upton didn't seem to think so."

"Ok, it's partly my decision, but you have to understand that there's a lot at stake here. I'm not the only one..." Her voice trailed off. "There are things here you don't understand."

"Because you won't tell me," he gritted out.

Maya leaned her head back, closing her eyes against the sun's brightness. "People could be hurt."

"It's just a cylinder seal, Maya."

"No, it's not." Something close to sadness flitted across her normally tranquil features. "It's potentially something much greater."

"Then let me help. Tell me what's going on."

"I can't, not yet." She squeezed his arm lightly and warmth spread through him, rippling away from her simple touch. "Have a little patience and trust me, ok?"

She seemed so anxious and a little tired, as if a heavy weight had settled on her and she was the only person available to carry the load.

He clenched his hands into fists, relaxed them. "You have to show it to me eventually."

"Soon, I promise."

He walked her back to her office and left her there with a reminder that he'd pick her up that evening at six thirty sharp. As he returned to his own office, the conversation whirled through his head. How deep did Maya's secrets run? And what was so sacred she couldn't share it with him?

MAYA STUDIED her reflection in the mirror, examining her appearance. She'd deliberately chosen the apricot sheath because it was *not* a dress she'd dreamed of wearing on a date with James. It was simple and sleeveless, cut high at the neck, and dipped to a few inches above her waist in the back. The fabric clung to her figure, accentuating her flat stomach and the curve of her breasts and hips, and stopped just below mid-thigh. She'd paired it with a simple two-stranded, gold necklace and a matching bracelet, and a shawl, heels, and purse all in black.

She twisted to and fro, examining her three-inch heels in the mirror. They'd put her nearly eye to eye with James. A thread of uncertainty worried at her. She straightened her shoulders and pushed it away. He didn't seem the type to care about a woman's height, and if he was, better to find out now so she could usher him right back out of her life.

Dierdre whistled softly and flopped crosswise onto Maya's bed. "You're totally rockin' that outfit, Mom."

Maya smoothed a hand down her stomach, eyeing her reflection critically. "You're just saying that because I'm your mother."

"No, I'm totally serious. Dr. T. is gonna, like, go wild over that dress."

"You think?"

"Oh, yeah." Dierdre's eyes widened and she nodded emphatically. "He totally digs your bod."

"Dierdre, honestly." Maya paused and glanced at her daughter. "Really?"

"Yup. He got all hot and bothered when I told him what you were gonna wear to the exhibition."

"And you talked to him about that when, young lady?"

"Oh, er, you know." Dierdre flipped over and stared at the ceiling. "When I went to his office and invited him to come."

Maya shook her head. Curls bounced around her face and she whirled toward the mirror in a panic. She and Dierdre had spent half an hour taming her hair into a chignon, leaving some curls pulled out in strategic places to achieve a *sexy mama* look.

Dierdre certainly had a way with words.

Maya brushed her fingers over the stray curls and exhaled. Everything was in place, right where it was supposed to be, but if she didn't get ahold of herself, she'd never make it through the evening in one piece.

"Besides," Dierdre said. "He doesn't mind. I stop by all the time to chat with him."

"Define all the time."

"Well, not, like, every day or anything."

"Dierdre, honey, James is here to work."

"I know." Dierdre rolled onto her stomach and rested her

chin on her folded hands. "It's just, he's nice and everything, and he likes to talk to me."

The words were soft spoken, her daughter's voice small and thin. Dierdre was so independent, so self-assured, it was easy to forget she was still young. Maya joined her daughter on the bed and stroked a hand over the teenager's braids. "Just don't make a nuisance of yourself. Now, what time are you going to the movies?"

They discussed Dierdre's plans for a night out with friends, and Maya reiterated the rules. Home by ten or as soon as the movie let out if they went to a late show, no friends inside the house, and cell phone set to vibrate or ring at all times. Dierdre was a Daughter, true, but she was a *teenaged* Daughter. Not setting firm limits tempted fate.

The doorbell rang. Dierdre bounced off the bed and loped down the stairs. Maya followed at a more leisurely pace, taking her time navigating the wooden steps. It had been a while since she'd worn heels. She pressed a hand to the nerves dancing in her stomach. It had a while since she'd been on a date, too.

 She was a few steps away from the foyer when James glanced up and saw her. His gaze drifted slowly down her body and up again, scorching a trail of heat along her skin. His eyes met hers, his so hot, a thrill shot through her. Dierdre had been right. James *was* attracted to her, more than a little. How could Maya have missed that?

He glanced away and cleared his throat, and a hint of pink tinged his cheeks. He turned to Dierdre and handed her a small, elaborately wrapped box. "For you."

Dierdre's eyes widened. "Wow. Really?" She tore the wrapping off, revealing a box of expensive chocolates. "Thanks, Dr. T."

"You're welcome, kiddo." James took Maya's hand and helped her down the last few steps, then handed her a bouquet of wildflowers. "These reminded me of you."

Maya buried her nose in the flowers, hiding a pleased smile.

"Maybe I wanted the chocolates."

He grinned and tucked his hands into his pants pockets. "You're teasing."

"I am."

"You do it so rarely, sometimes it's hard to tell."

"I'll have to do it more often, then. Let me put these in water."

"Take your time."

Maya walked into the kitchen, one ear on Dierdre and James' conversation. They seemed so familiar with one another, casual even. She scrounged for a vase and filled it with water. She'd have to ask him about that later, make sure Dierdre really wasn't bothering him. Her youngest could be a bit too persistent sometimes, especially when she really wanted something. Maya set the flowers on the kitchen table where the blooms would greet her each morning at breakfast and worried on her lower lip. What could Dierdre possibly want from James?

BEFORE SHE AND JAMES LEFT, Maya restated the rules for Dierdre's night out one last time.

Dierdre rolled her eyes. "Yeah, yeah, I got it, Mom. Just give me a hug already."

Maya tsked and kissed her daughter's cheek. "We won't be late."

"Geez, Mom. Be late." Dierdre hopped onto tiptoes and kissed James' cheek. "But, you know, let me know if you can't make it home before bedtime."

James grinned and tugged one of Dierdre's braids. "Ok, Mom."

Dierdre shooed them out, grinning madly as she shut the front door behind Maya and James.

He was dressed exactly as she'd pictured him, in the sky blue shirt she liked with khaki slacks and a navy blue sports jacket, the epitome of a college professor out for a night on the town. He was clean shaven, his hair slightly damp from the shower. As they settled into his car, she caught a whiff of woodsy cologne and smiled. *Mmm.* A scent to get closer to.

He started the car and pulled out onto the street. His radio was on, the volume low as the DJ wound up a commercial and played a classic rock ballad. Maya crossed her legs and folded her hands in her lap. "Where are we going?"

His eyes were fixed on the road as they cruised through Tellowee, but the corner of his lips turned upward into a grin. "It's a surprise."

"No hints?"

"Not a one," he said cheerfully. "I love your house."

"I'll give you the grand tour later."

"I'd love that. How did you find it?"

"When I was pregnant with Dierdre," she explained. "I wanted to put down roots, at least while she was young. Director Upton heard I was looking to settle and offered me a job at the IECS. This house came up for sale right after that. It seemed like serendipity."

"I love it when a plan comes together. When was it built?"

"About 1893. It had been in the same family since then, and they took wonderful care of it."

They chatted off and on during the half hour drive, though Maya had trouble keeping her full attention on the conversation. Once she discovered that James' eyes followed her legs each time she shifted, she couldn't help wiggling a little more than was strictly necessary.

The desire to tease him into a physical reaction surprised her. She'd played plenty of games before with men, becoming shy and coy or bold and reckless to fit the situation, but she'd never been a tease. It had always struck her as somehow dishonest. Too many women enticed men into lust without following through and it was wrong.

James brought out the temptress in her, with his shy sidelong glances and hesitant touch. The look he'd given her earlier, as if he were imagining exactly what she looked like underneath her dress, had been so unlike him. Even after Dierdre had told her that James wanted her, Maya hadn't quite believed it, in spite of their dance at the bar, in spite of Dierdre's insistence. That look had convinced her, and now, she wanted to see it again, even if it meant teasing him.

The restaurant he'd chosen was in a neighboring town, a good half hour's drive from Maya's home. It was also one of her favorites, especially during summer weekends when local bands played in the outside eating area. How had he known?

Dierdre, she guessed. The rat.

James placed his hand on the small of her back as they waited. It should've been polite, would've been if he'd placed his hand a little lower. His fingers brushed over the bare skin of her back, warming her, and inched upward along her spine. He leaned close and whispered, "Are you wearing a bra?"

She arched an eyebrow. "What do you think?"

He groaned softly. "I was trying to be good, Maya."

She grinned. "Yes, but I wasn't."

The restaurant's service was slow, the food excellent. Over salads, homemade rolls, and fresh pasta, their conversation roved from movies and books to parenting, and even to the forbidden first-date topics of politics and religion. Surprisingly, they agreed more than they disagreed, given his reserved Yankee upbringing and the gypsy-like lifestyle of the People.

The sun slipped behind the mountains, bringing a slight chill to the air. A singer-songwriter stepped onto the raised platform serving as a stage, guitar in hand. Maya and James fell into a companionable silence as the performer sang one bluesy original after another. His hand crept to the back of her chair, to the ends of her hair, to her bare shoulder, and she shivered.

Wherever he touched her, heat rose, delicious and sweet, and a fine tension spooled between them. It tugged at her, distracting her from the songwriter's performance and the hefty slice of white chocolate cheesecake their server brought them.

Anticipation. How long had it been since she'd anticipated the end of an evening and the kiss that was sure to follow? Everything else, the dinner, the music, the conversation, was merely leading to that one moment when he'd draw her close and lower his lips to her own.

She sucked in a breath and pressed her hand over the desire pooling within her. She wanted that kiss, needed to feel his mouth on hers. Did he want that, too, or had he only mentioned it as a matter of course?

After the performer's second set, James paid the bill and they left. He helped her with her shawl, his hands lingering on her nearly bare shoulders, and rested his hand on her waist as they left the restaurant. His heat seared her through the thin fabric of her dress. Blessed Ki, why did he have to be such a gentleman?

The drive home seemed twice as long as the drive into town. Maya crossed her legs, tapped one foot nervously to the rhythm of the radio, then stilled. What was she doing? Daughters never got nervous. It wasn't in their nature, yet here she was, fidgeting, her mind tangled in knots over the possibility of a kiss, her fingers twisted together at her waist. What must he think of her?

She glanced at James. He stared straight ahead, his attention seemingly focused solely on the road, and her heart sank. Why didn't he say something, anything to break the silence?

Maybe he was waiting for her to speak.

She bit her lower lip and searched for an appropriate topic. The only thing that came to mind was the kiss, his mouth on hers, his hands gripping her waist and skimming over her back. She swallowed and leaned her head against the cool glass of the passenger's side window.

Maybe he was nervous, too.

At last, they arrived, and Maya bit back a relieved sigh. James helped her politely out of the car and walked with her to the front door, holding her hand lightly in his.

At the top of the steps, she said, "Thank you. I had a lovely time."

His eyes crinkled at the corners in a gentle smile. "Me, too."

Still, he made no move to leave.

She grasped her purse with both hands and gnawed on the inside of her cheek. "Would you like some coffee?"

"Thanks, no." He stuffed his hands into the pockets of his slacks. "I should probably head home now."

"Ok. Well." At a loss, Maya turned and walked to the door, hesitating with her hand on the doorknob. His hands cupped her shoulders, strong and warm, and she turned and met his gaze with her own, that sweet gaze, so intense and hot. Her heart flipped over and her breath shallowed, and she stepped back, bumping into the solid wood of the door.

"You're so beautiful," he said. His hands slipped to her waist and he leaned into her, his face inches from her own. He brushed his lips over hers, once, twice, lightly as if giving her a chance to say no.

The feathering touches set butterflies loose in her stomach. She dropped her purse and gripped his shoulders, urging him into a deeper response. His lips pressed firmly against her own, and she shuddered. It felt so good, his kiss. Her skin tightened and heat pooled within her as he explored her mouth, slowly and thoroughly, his hands tightening against her waist, drawing her firmly against him. The solid length of his body aligned perfectly with her own. He leaned into her, pressing her into the door, and his hardening need pushed into the juncture of her thighs, inches from the center of her own desire.

She twined her fingers into his hair, clutching the cool, silky strands. He groaned and rocked against her, and his mouth left hers and trailed hot kisses down her neck. He bit her gently, and she gasped as fire raced through her.

"James," she whispered. "Please."

He soothed the sting with another kiss and murmured, "Please what? Please more, please stop, please don't ever let you go?"

The porch light flickered violently off and on, and Maya sagged against the door. Dierdre. What perfectly awful timing.

James' soft moan whispered against her ear, sending shivers over her skin. "Saved by a teenager."

"Soon to be a grounded teenager," Maya muttered.

He laughed softly and kissed her, slow and easy, and slid his hands up her arms to her neck. "I've mussed your hair."

Maya bit her lip, hiding a smile. "You're the only man I know who'd put it that way."

"It's the truth." He wound one of her curls around his finger, tugging gently. "When can I see you again?"

"When do you want to see me again?"

Heat reignited in his eyes. He nuzzled her neck, licked her pulse. "I don't think you want to know the answer to that question."

"Fair enough." Though, secretly, she already did, and was glad that he, at least, had enough restraint to pull away. Five more minutes, ten tops, and she would've yanked him inside the house and had him in the foyer.

Thank the Goddess for Dierdre.

"Tomorrow?"

"Movie night with Dierdre." She hesitated, weighing one need against the other. "Would you like to come?"

"It won't be an intrusion?"

"No," she said firmly. "As long as you don't mind the movie. It's Dierdre's turn to pick."

"Ok. Just one more," he murmured, and kissed her again, claiming her with a need equal to her own.

One turned to two before James left, and Maya couldn't blame him, not for the kisses, not for the reluctance to leave. She had just enough control left to keep herself from staggering inside. She locked the door, against temptation as much as anything. *Mmm.* Who would've thought James' reserve hid such passion? And boy, did he know how to use it. Hidden depths were the best finds, always.

Dierdre had retreated to the couch and was watching a movie. Maya stuck her head in the living room and said goodnight, then climbed the steps to her room, her gait not quite steady. She undressed slowly, her mind caught on the night she'd shared with James, and his kiss. She fell into bed smiling and slept soundly through the night.

ELEVEN

THE EARLY MORNING LIGHT illuminated the practice room in Rebecca's home. Every morning, she rose early and went through her routine, stretching, exercising, and training. Achieving mortality hadn't been enough to overcome centuries of habits.

This morning, she eschewed weapons practice in favor of yogic stretches. Her body was aging and needed more work to stay limber and flexible, something she hadn't had to worry about as an immortal, or not as much. She emptied her mind and flowed through several forms, holding each pose before easing into the next, breathing through the stretches.

Here in her home, she felt safe enough to relax, but not so much that she lost awareness of her surroundings. The door to her home gym opened, disrupting the meditative rhythm of her exercise. Jerusha entered, murmuring a hello and an apology in one breath.

Rebecca rose from her final pose and greeted her daughter, examining her from head to toe. Dark circles marred the skin under Jerusha's eyes and her shoulders were slumped. "When did you get in?"

Jerusha rubbed a hand over her nape and yawned. "Just now. I have some info. Thought you'd want it as soon as I could get it to you."

Rebecca exhaled slowly. Whatever news Jerusha carried,

whatever she'd dug up, it must be bad. "Why don't you take some time to freshen up? I'll make you some breakfast and then we can talk."

Jerusha nodded and headed upstairs, her steps slow and even. Rebecca threw a track suit on over her workout clothes and bustled into the kitchen, her thoughts buzzing over Jerusha's news. Good or bad, and it must be truly gut-wrenching, it would be easier for Jerusha to deliver it on a full stomach, and easier for Rebecca to absorb and act on it. Breakfast, then, a hearty one. She pulled bacon and fixings out of the fridge and tucked her worry away as she prepared a meal.

Half an hour later, Jerusha bounced down the stairs wearing clean clothes, her expression alert. Robert followed her into the kitchen and maneuvered his wheelchair over to Rebecca. "Look who I found wandering around upstairs."

"The prodigal daughter has returned." Rebecca bent down and planted a firm kiss on his mouth. Three decades had failed to dim the sweetness of his touch. "We'll kill the fatted calf tonight and have a feast fit for the Seven."

Robert waggled his bushy eyebrows and grinned. "That we will. Nothing's too good for my girls."

Bobby stomped down the stairs whistling and ducked into the kitchen. His handsome face stretched into a mischievous smile. "Jerusha, hey. I thought I heard an elephant clomping around."

"You're the elephant. I'm the gazelle." Jerusha held her arms out and laughed as he grabbed her up and swung her around. "Put me down, you oaf. We can wrestle later."

Bobby set her down and settled his hands on her waist. "I like wrestling now. Thought we wouldn't see you 'til Thanksgiving."

Jerusha's dark eyes slid to Rebecca. "Got some stuff for Mom."

"Stuff, huh. Is that what we're calling it now?" He shook his head and eased away from her. "How come you get all the good stuff?"

Jerusha stuck her tongue in her cheek. "Maybe because you're the baby and I'm the grown up."

Rebecca plated the bacon and set it on the kitchen counter. "Children, can we please eat before the two of you launch into a full-scale war?"

"No chance," Robert muttered. "We can still make a run for it."

Rebecca tutted and shooed him and her children to the table. The meal passed in a noisy exchange of barbs between Jerusha and Bobby. When they'd run out of ammunition, the conversation turned to Jerusha's work in London at an archaeological dig and Bobby's work at his security firm.

In the middle of one of Bobby's tales of childhood pranks, Robert slid his hand over Rebecca's. "Everything ok?"

She'd never been able to fool him. No matter what was going on, he always knew when something was bothering her. "Everything's fine, darling. I'm a little distracted by some business Jerusha and I have to deal with this morning."

"If you're sure," he said, and she squeezed his hand gently.

When breakfast was done, the men took over kitchen clean-up while Rebecca and Jerusha retreated to the library. It was one of her favorite rooms, with its book-lined walls and leather furnishings. She and Robert had spent many hours in here over the years, immersed in their mutual love for the written word.

Jerusha settled onto one end of the couch across from the fireplace, one leg folded beneath her.

Rebecca took the other end, mirroring her daughter's pose. "What have you found?"

"The Shadow Enemy hasn't been dormant for the past few decades, as we thought. They've just been underground, rebuilding."

"But Alexiou was so young..." Rebecca pursed her lips together. Rumor had it, Lukas Alexiou, the Shadow Enemy's current head, had killed his father at the tender age of thirteen some twenty-five years before. All of the intelligence she'd received since then indicated that most of his energy had been devoted to keeping that organization and his family together, every single scrap. "Specifics?"

Jerusha knuckled the furrow between her eyebrows. "On the surface, Alexiou is a charming, generous man, known for his philanthropy. He runs a small auction house specializing in rare antiquities, but that's just the surface. His business connections run much deeper. He also owns antiquity dealers, an import-export business, a treasure-hunting venture, but the layers he's put between himself and those interests are deep. It took a lot of digging to find them."

"Interesting that his businesses deal primarily with antiques."

"That's not the worrying part. At the same time that Alexiou's been building his business, he's also been gathering followers to his ultimate cause, the same cause that his father pursued, destroying the People. I couldn't pin down the number of people directly associated with this aspect of the younger Alexiou's movements, but it's easily double the number his father controlled."

"By the Lady Ki, how has this slipped past us? I've personally had people following key members of the Shadow Enemy since I took over the directorship, and not a one has reported any of this to me." A slow burn twisted through Rebecca. She sucked in a breath and pinned her daughter with a hard stare. "Are you saying they've all betrayed me, and through me, the People?"

"No." Jerusha shifted and pulled a piece of paper out of her pants pocket. "I believe they're being manipulated by two or possibly three of these individuals. I just can't figure out which ones."

Rebecca took the paper with stiff fingers and examined the names. The list was headed by two members of the Council of Seven, one of whom Rebecca had always thought was a firm supporter of her leadership. Her heart thudded in her chest, booming so hard she was certain Jerusha could hear it. "This can't be right."

"I'm sorry, Mom, but everything I've learned leads me to those people."

There were more than a half dozen other names on the list, in outline form, with one to three others offset under each one, presumably allies of the main suspects. At the bottom was a list of four different individuals, separated from the others by a horizontal line. Every single name on the entire list belonged to an immortal Daughter.

"And these names at the bottom?" Rebecca asked.

"They seem to be working independently for their own purposes. None has betrayed the People that I can tell, but each one is in some way involved with the companies Alexiou controls. It could be nothing."

Or it could be something. Daughters were an independent bunch, scattered across the globe in support of the various interests of the People or in pursuit of their own agendas. Usually, those agendas centered upon education, training, or finding a mate, but not always. Sometimes, the Daughters' curiosity put their noses in business that was better left alone. At other times, it led them into situations that ultimately benefited the People. A person on the scene was usually a much better judge of a situation than a distant administrator. Rebecca had always had a firm policy of never ignoring a Daughter's innate instincts in pursuit of bureaucratic regulations. Any of the individuals on Jerusha's list could be in similar situations, simply waiting for matters to come to a head before reporting in, but how to tell?

Rebecca folded the paper in half. "Thank you, Jerusha."

Jerusha nodded. "Do you want me to pursue this?"

"No, dear. I think it best for you to return to your duties in London."

"Ok, but if you need me..."

"I'll call."

Jerusha rose, kissed her mother's cheek, and left the library.

The door snicked shut. Rebecca closed her eyes and dropped her head against the back of the sofa. All this time, the People could've been combatting the rise of the next generation of the Shadow Enemy, and instead, someone had hidden the needed information, stolen it from under her very nose. Chances were good that the one who'd done so was someone Rebecca trusted. The betrayal cut deeply, sapping her energy. What a fool she'd been. How could she not have known? Had she become so complacent in her duties that these manipulations had slipped by her?

More importantly, what was she going to do about it?

Rebecca rose and secured the list in her personal safe. She needed time to think through everything Jerusha had told her, but she didn't need the list for that. The names had already burned themselves into her memory.

THE WEEKS PASSED SLOWLY as summer hit its apex and waned toward fall. After that first date, Maya stopped resisting James and saw him as often as they both had time, usually with Dierdre in tow.

The teen's near continual presence made it impossible for them to explore a physical relationship. Maya was in no hurry, but that first kiss had kindled a longing for something deeper. As they spent more and more time together, squeezing in moments between work, family, and life, they were becoming closer, maybe even developing a solid friendship, an odd situation for her. She'd never been friends with a man she wanted the way she wanted him.

Meanwhile, James seemed determined to act the gentleman. She was equally determined that he not. Their first stolen kiss, shared in his lab with the door conspicuously locked, he backed her against the wall and kissed her so sweetly, she melted under his touch. His hands skimmed over her waist and back and shoulders, and though he nibbled gently on her neck, he made no move to go any farther.

That would never do.

Since he wouldn't, Maya took the initiative a little at a time, starting with their third kiss, in her office hidden behind the cabinet holding her supplies. She snuck her hands under his shirt and stroked his stomach, dug her nails lightly into his back, and blossomed for him, leaving herself completely open to his touch.

A few days later, he cornered her in his office and pushed her against his bookcase, exploring her mouth in a greedy kiss. She dipped a finger into the edge of his waistband, and he moaned and rocked into her, pressing his growing erection against her. He unbuttoned the top buttons of her shirt and feathered kisses along her collarbone, and his hands grew bold, grasping her bottom, fitting her against his need as he murmured encouragement, urging her into boldness. A knock on his door startled them apart. Maya glared at the door, her heart pounding, her skin deliciously tight and achy. Five more minutes and they would've been on the floor, making love. How much more could she take?

One memorable Saturday afternoon, they got a little too carried away. Dierdre ran over to a friend's house on an errand, leaving Maya and James alone. They put a movie in and settled on the sofa, both fully aware that Dierdre could be back at any moment. What started as an innocent kiss ended with him pushing her onto the couch, aligning his body on top of her, his mouth greedily devouring hers. He pushed her t-shirt up and was unhooking her bra when Dierdre came in, her mind and hands thankfully preoccupied with texting. Maya shoved her shirt down and bit back a panicked giggle, and a pink tinge crept into James' cheek beneath his hot gaze.

"Later," he whispered, and she agreed wholeheartedly. Later would be great. It was the when that was the problem.

They were more careful after that, sneaking kisses when they were alone, holding hands when they weren't, whispering promises to one another at the end of each day. It was simply a matter of time before they consummated their relationship. Only the lack of opportunity kept them from doing so.

The Friday of Labor Day weekend, James left early to pick Amelia up from Hartsfield International Airport for her week-long visit. Maya corralled Dierdre into a thorough house cleaning. Having both girls around would lessen the chance for sex. Frustrating, yes, but unavoidable. James would be with Amelia while Dierdre was on her camping trip. Maya didn't begrudge his time with his daughter, far from it, but time alone with him would be splendid, just him and her and a comfortable bed. How could she have forgotten how hard it was to have sex with children around and how deliciously frustrating the long wait was?

Maya scrubbed her bathtub, expending some of her pent up sexual energy making it shine. Other than the lack of sex, there was only one thing keeping her growing relationship with James from being perfect. She had yet to tell him the truth about herself.

After their first mutual meeting with Director Upton, James had only twice brought up the documents the IECS held that might have bearing on the artifacts recovered at Sandby borg. The first time had been directly after the meeting, when he'd confronted her and she'd asked for patience.

The last time had been a mere week ago. As the translations progressed, it was becoming clear that they formed some sort of story. James had mentioned early on that the artifacts seemed to have a pattern, and this story might be it, so he thought. The documents carried by the slain Daughter began with what Maya believed was a scene from the Legend of Beginnings, the oasis that had, according to the few historical accounts they'd found, served as a sanctuary of some sort for the Seven Sisters after they were cursed with immortality for committing a mortal sin. The narrative jumped over large periods of time as it was told from document to document. When laid out side by side from the oldest story to the newest, it was clear that there *was* a narrative of sorts, in spite of the massive gaps.

As soon as they'd begun to suspect the documents' narrative theme, James had wanted a crack at the documents he knew Maya was holding back, and he'd not been happy at all when she continued refusing access.

Maya scrubbed harder as doubt ate at her. James would inevitably learn the true nature of the People. He'd have to be brought in or he'd have to leave the project. There were no other choices. Either path would end their burgeoning relationship. With another man, it might not matter, but this man was a different story. She was beginning to care about him. No, she had to be honest. She wasn't just beginning to care about him. She was beginning to fall for him. If he learned the truth about who and what she was and rejected it, rejected her, could she handle that? A queasy uneasiness rippled through her. No, his rejection would hurt her deeply and possibly even break her heart.

James had to be told, sooner rather than later, but not just yet. Please, not yet.

ANOTHER MISERABLY HUMID DAY in the South, James thought as he waited for Amelia to debark. The air conditioning in Hartsfield International didn't quite override the sun or the heat exuded by the large number of bodies jostling from terminal to terminal.

At last, he spotted her bopping toward him to music only she could hear, and his heart melted. His little girl. Had she grown an inch over the summer or was that just his imagination?

Amelia saw him and waved, a huge smile on her elven face. They pushed their way through the crowds toward each other. James enfolded her in a fierce hug, then took her carry-on, and they braved the crowds searching for her other luggage to the accompaniment of her excited chatter.

During the two-odd hour drive from Atlanta to the IECS,

they made plans. Or rather, Amelia told him all the things she wanted to do that week and he nodded and rearranged his week in his mind. Six Flags and the Mall of Georgia were musts, as were hikes in the forests surrounding the IECS.

Because he'd promised, she reminded him.

Her phone beeped. Amelia stopped talking in mid-sentence and flipped through her phone.

"Who's that?" James asked.

Her fingers moved rapidly over the keypad, absorbing her attention. "Dee."

"Don't think I know her."

"Dee as in Dierdre, as in your girlfriend's daughter."

"Er." James' mind went blank. He couldn't say Maya wasn't his girlfriend. As seen from the outside, that's probably what their relationship looked like. He just didn't think of her that way, hardly at all unless he counted pretty much every minute he spent daydreaming about her. "How do you know Dierdre?"

"She messyed me the week after you came down here. On Facebook? And then, she introduced me to a bunch of her friends. It's, like, really cool at her school."

As Amelia chatted on about all the things she and Dierdre had talked about, concern wiggled its way through James. It's not like Dierdre had gone behind his back, though she had, or that he had a problem with the girls getting to know one another, which he didn't. That was great. But shouldn't one of them have said something to him or Maya?

On the other hand, Dierdre was a pretty independent young woman. It might not have occurred to her that she needed to ask permission or at least discuss contacting Amelia with an adult before doing so. From what he could tell, she'd been raised to be a problem solver. See the problem, find the solution, fix it. Obviously, that's what she'd done with Amelia. What bothered him were her motivations. Had Dierdre reached out to his daughter as part of her overall plan to throw him and Maya together or because she wanted to get to know Amelia, or both?

Maybe she was just being considerate. He was liable to be at the IECS for months. Hopefully, Amelia would visit him a lot during that time. She'd enjoy having friends there, enjoy having younger company than his when she was around.

He pushed the concern aside and spent the rest of the evening enjoying his daughter's company, and tried not to worry about how Amelia would react to his deepening relationship with Maya.

AMELIA'S REACTION to Maya turned out not to be a problem, thanks to Dierdre paving the way. After a while, it became apparent that she'd convinced Amelia that James and Maya would be perfect for one another. The two teens were now in cahoots, their heads bowed together more often than not, giggling about one thing or another.

They visited Six Flags and the Mall of Georgia, thankfully not on the same day. Amelia insisted they go with Maya and Dierdre, whose schedule had loosened up when the summer term ended. He and Maya rearranged their schedules, and he refused to feel guilty. They'd made a lot of progress on the artifacts, more than he could've hoped to achieve in such a short time.

He was certain progress would've been even speedier if Maya weren't holding something important back from him.

It was one of the few points of contention between them, but it was a doozy. Why did Maya continue to insist that he didn't need to see documents pertinent to their work? He suspected the Sandby borg artifacts were of life-altering importance to her. Yet, she didn't trust him enough to open up about it with him and it stung.

The week leading up to the Labor Day weekend was a happy one, in spite of his worries. In that time, James got a glimpse of what life would be like if Maya and Dierdre were part of his and Amelia's family. The two girls were joined at the hip.

Amelia had not only accepted Maya, she hung on the older woman's every word, much the way Dani and Indigo had when he'd first met them. For her part, Maya treated Amelia essentially the same way she treated Dierdre. Maybe someday, Amelia would accept a more permanent relationship between him and Maya.

The longer he knew Maya, the more frequently the idea crossed his mind.

The four of them had dinner together at Maya's house the evening before Dierdre was scheduled to leave for her two-day camping trip. Amelia hadn't asked to go, and he wasn't sure how he felt about that. He wanted to spend time with his daughter, but he was so close to losing control where Maya was concerned. One more passionate kiss and he might forget where they were and make love to her on the spot, location be damned. Considering that they had two teenagers underfoot, that might not be such a good idea. Cold showers and long hours at the gym weren't going to cut it for much longer, though.

Over dessert, Dierdre caught Amelia's gaze and waggled her eyebrows. She turned to James, eyes wide, and said, "So, we were thinking what with this camping trip and all, maybe Amelia should come along. I mean, otherwise she'd just be stuck here with you two 'cause all our friends are going camping."

A whiff of excitement shot through James. "Do you want to go, Amelia?"

"Well, sure, Dad." Amelia focused her gaze on the piece of fruit on her fork. "It'd be great, but I don't want you to be lonely or anything."

"You don't sound like you really want to go."

"Oh, yeah, I really do. It's just, you know, we're supposed to spend time together, me and you. The camping trip would be fun and all. They're going to hike and go swimming in this lake over the mountain and tell ghost stories and stuff, and Dierdre said I could share her tent, and there's lots of neat people going." She sighed and fixed a pitiful look on her face. "But I can stay here if you want me to."

Across the table, Maya covered her mouth with her napkin, her almond shaped eyes glittering. Dierdre wore the same hang-dog look as Amelia.

Oh, yeah, those two were in cahoots, all right.

He cleared his throat and laid his napkin on the table. "Yes, you're right, the camping trip would be fun."

Dierdre and Amelia glanced at each other wearing identical smiles.

"But I think you should stay here with me."

Amelia swung around, her mouth open. "Dad. Really?"

Dierdre's hands dropped into her lap. "Yeah, really, Dr. T.?"

Maya snickered, and James grinned. "Kidding. You can go, if you really want to."

Dierdre pumped her fist. "All right."

"Thanks, Dad." Amelia jumped out of her chair and hugged him tight. "You won't regret it."

The two teens raced out of the room, their excited chatter overlapping. Maya stood and stacked empty plates into a pile. "You know what this means, don't you?"

Immediately, his mind shot straight to the weekend ahead, alone with Maya, no teenagers to take into consideration. His skin tightened and his blood burned and desire pooled in his groin. "Oh, yeah."

Her mouth curled into a small smile. "It means we have to do the dishes."

"Oh, yeah. That."

He stood and helped her clear the table, but the dishes waiting to be cleaned didn't keep him from anticipating the coming weekend.

TWELVE

THE GIRLS PACKED and unpacked and repacked while Maya made the necessary calls securing a place for Amelia on the camping trip. As soon as the arrangements were made, Maya went to the attic searching for extra gear.

James followed her up the narrow stairway, close on her heels. "Amelia already knew about this camping trip."

Maya paused and peered over her shoulder. "Oh?"

"Dierdre tracked her down on Facebook not long after I got here."

"Did she really?"

"Yeah." One corner of James' mouth lifted. "She's something else."

"She's something all right." Maya pursed her lips. "Did you tell her she could?"

He shrugged. "No, but no harm, no foul, right? Besides, she was right. Amelia needs friends down here."

"Maybe," she said. And maybe Dierdre should learn to respect other people's privacy, especially where their kids were concerned. "I'll talk to her."

Maya and James dug through the attic, rounding up an extra sleeping bag and other gear Amelia might need. They dumped it in the foyer next to the front door, then Maya tracked down her errant daughter. She found Dierdre in her room lying across her bed, chatting to Amelia.

Dierdre's gaze fell on Maya. She sat straight up. "Uh-oh."

"Amelia, could you give us a few moments, please?" Maya asked.

Amelia slid off the bed. "Sure thing. I gotta talk to my dad anyhow."

Maya shut the door behind the perky teenager and speared her daughter with a stern look. "James just told me you contacted Amelia without his permission."

"Oh."

"Yes, oh. What were you thinking, Dierdre?"

Dierdre clasped her hands together in her lap. "Well, she was coming down anyhow."

"That didn't give you the right to..." Maya blew out a breath and sat on the edge of the bed. "You should've asked first."

"If I'd asked, you could've said no."

"And we could've said yes. You're a woman among the People now, Dierdre. That means acting like one, not tearing off on a wild hair whenever you feel like it."

Dierdre's eyebrows furrowed and her gaze turned hot. "That was hardly a wild hair, Mom. All I did was find Amelia and see if she wanted to be friends, and we are. She's really funny and sweet, and..."

Maya placed a hand over her daughter's. "And what, Squiggles?"

"Forget it. You wouldn't understand."

"Try me."

Dierdre shook her head, sending her braids flying around her shoulders. "You gonna ground me now?"

"That would hardly be fair to Amelia, would it? She probably wouldn't feel comfortable going on the camping trip without you."

"Probably not. She's kind of a girly girl, you know?" The mutinous set of Dierdre's mouth softened into a smile. "Thanks."

"Don't think you're getting out of it that lightly. We'll talk

155

about this later, once Amelia's gone back home." Maya stood and made her way to the door. "Almost packed?"

"Yes'm." Dierdre scrambled off the bed and bounded across the room, then threw her arms around Maya's neck. "You're the best, Mom."

"You, too, Squiggles."

They went in search of James and Amelia. Maya turned the incident over in her mind as she helped the teens finish packing, certain Dierdre's motivations for contacting James' daughter weren't nearly as pure as she'd let on.

THE NEXT MORNING dawned clear and bright. James and Amelia came by for an early breakfast. After, the four of them piled into his car with the camping gear stowed in the trunk. Dierdre and Amelia huddled together in the backseat, giggling over who knew what. Maya sat quietly in the passenger's seat listening to their chatter, mulling over the coming weekend.

From the moment James had given permission for Amelia to go on the camping trip, Maya's thoughts had lingered on what would happen when she was finally alone with him. Was she ready to be with him that way? Surely after all these weeks she must be, but instead of the calm excitement she'd expected to feel, butterflies danced in her stomach and molten heat slid through her blood, consuming her.

Half an hour after leaving her house, they arrived at the campers' meeting point, the head of a local, well-known trail. Maya helped Dierdre and Amelia with a final check of their camping gear while James filled out Amelia's paperwork. After hugs and goodbyes, the group set out, Johnny Linton between Dierdre and Amelia, one long arm slung around each of their shoulders.

James leaned against the hood of his car, his eyes narrowed on the departing group. Maya lingered with some of the other parents, watching the camping party until they disappeared around the first curve of the trail. She inhaled slowly and stuffed her fingers into the pockets of her shorts. Making sure the girls got off to a good start wasn't procrastinating, was it? And besides, she didn't want to seem overeager.

The last stragglers rounded the curve and the other parents drifted to their cars and left. Maya slipped into the passenger's seat of James' car and buckled in as he started the car and eased out into the string of departing vehicles.

The drive back to her house was made in near silence. Maya clasped her hands together in her lap and watched the passing scenery. Her heart skipped and the butterflies in her stomach tangled into a knot, and her mind twisted over the possibilities. Would he want to stay? Leave? Go out? None of the above?

James pulled into her drive and turned off the car. He twisted his hands around the steering wheel. "Dinner tonight?"

"Sure."

"Six ok?"

"Anytime's fine." She drew in a slow breath and blurted, "Do you want to come in?"

The corners of his mouth tilted up in a soft smile. He faced her, and his eyes were hot, greedy, and so beautiful, her heart skittered to a stop. "Yeah. I'd like that."

They got out of the car and walked into the house together, shoulder to shoulder. James waited patiently as she unlocked the door, then slipped inside behind her. She shut it and rested her forehead on the cool, wooden door.

"You ok?" he asked.

She turned, putting her back to the door. He was standing at the foot of the stairs with his hands stuffed into the pockets of his shorts and his shoulders hunched. The butterflies dissipated, leaving only the heat, and she held her hand out. "Can you do something for me?"

He stepped closer and slipped his hand into hers. "Anything."

"Kiss me," she breathed. "I want to feel you, all of you."

157

James tugged her into his arms and lowered his mouth to hers, claiming her in a soft kiss. She opened for him and wound her arms around his back, clinging to him as he deepened the kiss, tasting her in slow sweeps of his tongue and gentle nips of his teeth.

It wasn't enough.

She eased her hands under his t-shirt and caressed his bare skin. It was smooth and warm, his muscles firm under her touch, and she wanted so much more, the fierce burn of passion, the eager touch of his hands roaming over her bare skin, him inside her, stroking them both past pleasure into ecstasy. She wanted all of that, craved it, and she wouldn't settle for anything less.

She broke the kiss and panted, "James, please."

"Yeah," he said. "Me, too."

His hands fumbled with the hem of her shirt, yanking it up and over her head. He pulled his shirt off and dropped it on top of hers, then pressed her back against the door, holding her there with the weight of his body. His skin skidded across hers, creating a sweet, sweet friction. "Better?"

"Much."

He slid an open-mouthed kiss down the side of her neck, trailing beautiful heat. It rebounded inside her, pinging through her blood, and settled between her thighs, intense, liquid fire. She moaned and dug her fingers into his back, reveling in his bare skin melding with hers, the moist heat of his mouth, the delicious feel of his erection pushing against her core through their clothing.

His mouth met hers again. She fumbled with the fastening on his shorts, aching to feel him. Her fingers were too clumsy, her need impatient. She delved a hand into the waistband, following the silky line of hair trailing from his navel downward.

His hand gripped hers, holding it in place inches from where she wanted to be, and he tore his mouth away from hers. "Bed," he said, his voice gruff.

"Here."

"Bed, now." He gritted the word out and ground his erection into her. "Please, Maya. Don't make me wait any more."

She caught his earlobe between her lips, sucking gently. He shuddered and moaned, and she rubbed her face against his neck, hiding her satisfied smile. "Upstairs."

He glanced over his shoulder at the stairs, then dropped his forehead to the door. "Jesus."

She laughed, low and husky, and pushed him gently away from her. Urgency drove them up the stairs as fast as they could manage, trailing shoes and clothes as they went. They tumbled onto her bed, rolling together, landing with him stretched out on top of her, their hands joined, her arms pinned above her head. She rolled her hips upward, urging him to take her.

"Wait." His hand skimmed down her side and rested on her hip, pushing it into the mattress. "Let me..."

She laughed and shifted beneath him, and his erection prodded at her core.

"Oh, God," he moaned, and slid into her, filling her completely. He flexed his hips, seating himself within her, and a wave of something close to ecstasy tore through her. She gasped and lifted her knees, pulling him in deeper.

He buried his face in her neck and murmured, "That's it."

He moved against her, slowly finding a steady rhythm, deepening his thrusts, the pleasure building with each sharp push of his hips. She raised her hips in counterpoint to his and tightened her hold on his hands, and the heat building within her peaked sharply and erupted into a million shattering pieces. He thrust into her a final time and came, spilling into her on a low, shuddering moan.

They lay like that for a long while, their breaths slowing from gasps to sighs, their bodies cooling in slow increments. James slipped out of her, rolled onto his back, and tucked her tightly against his side. Maya snuggled into him, draping herself over him, and laughed. They were lying catty-corner on the bed, the duvet wrinkled and bunched beneath them, but what a beautiful, delicious rush it had been.

He kissed the top of her head and relaxed under her.

"Don't go to sleep," she said.

"I'm not," he promised, his voice soft and sleepy.

She huffed out a sigh. "Under the covers with you."

"In a minute."

The air conditioning kicked on, blowing a stream of cold air into the room. James sucked in a breath and shifted onto his side, facing her. "That's really cold."

"I tried to get you under the covers."

"Next time I'll listen." He smoothed a hand up and down her back. "You ok?"

"Mmm." Ok was probably not the word. More like smug, satisfied, womanly. Content.

"Not too rough?"

The concern in his voice tickled her. He hadn't been rough at all. She ran a leg over his, enjoying the crisp hairs scratching against her skin. "Just right."

"We, ah, got a little carried away." His cheeks flushed and his eyes closed, crinkling the laugh lines at their corners. "Actually, we got a lot carried away."

"It's ok."

"I'm clean, promise. I haven't had sex, er..." He cleared his throat. "It's been a long time."

"Me, too."

His mouth opened, closed. He blinked and cleared his throat again, and she bit her lip, containing a laugh. She kissed his nose and rubbed her fingertips through the spattering of hair on his chest. "There's nothing to worry about, really. It's a no harm, no foul situation."

Emotions flickered across his lean face, hope, relief, and something indefinable. "Really?"

"Cross my heart."

It was the closest she could come to saying, *Hey, James, I can't get pregnant right now because I'm immortal and only ovulate about once a year, twice if I'm lucky.* She wasn't ready for that conversation and neither was he. Maybe they never would be.

She pushed the gloomy thought away and kissed him lightly. "Shower?"

"Together?"

"Sure."

A slow grin stretched across his mouth. "Well, if you insist."

And she did.

THAT NIGHT, after a quick supper in her kitchen, Maya put in a movie and cuddled with James on the couch. Without Dierdre around, they could hold hands and share intimate caresses and long kisses as the movie played, a quiet background to their passion.

Maya felt no guilt whatsoever in taking advantage of her daughter's absence.

And since Dierdre was gone, Maya didn't hesitate to squeeze in as much time as she could with James, making up for the time they'd miss when Dierdre and Amelia came back from the camping trip. "Stay with me tonight."

His hand paused in mid-caress on her thigh. "Are you sure?"

"I am." She settled against him, rubbing her temple across his shoulder. "You don't have to."

"I want to. You have no idea how much. I just want you to be sure."

"I'm sure."

She cupped his cheek and kissed him, and they forgot about the rest of the world for a while.

After the movie, James made a quick trip to his on-campus apartment for clothes and toiletries. Maya slipped into the shower. As the water sluiced over her, her mind lingered on their shower together earlier, after the first time they'd made love.

He'd taken the soap and run it over her, exploring her as he hadn't done before, and she'd done the same, touching him, kissing him, molding herself to him. The water was cold by the time they got out and continued their explorations in her bed under the warmth of the duvet.

Now, she hurried through her ablutions. He'd be back soon and she wanted to be ready for him. She chose her outfit carefully, a black lace bra and panty set covered by a short kimono-style robe, and did a quick mirror check of her hair, smoothing the frizz out with her fingers. Satisfied, she dimmed the lights in her room and turned down the duvet.

Downstairs, the front door creaked open. Maya's heart leapt into her throat. He was back. Her eyelids fluttered closed and the heat, sated during their earlier interlude, rocketed through her, coalescing into a greedy, eager yearning. How could she want him again so soon?

She shook the thought off and forced herself into a measured step out of her bedroom and down the stairs toward the foyer.

James glanced up and fumbled the bag he was carrying, dropping it. "Um. Wow."

She rested her fingers along the stair railing and smiled. "Ready?"

"Oh, yeah," he breathed. He bounded up the stairs behind her, his bag forgotten, and followed her into the bedroom. His hands slid around her, spreading warmth under the slow, steady touch. "That is a spectacular outfit."

She snagged his hands and pushed them away, holding them against his thighs. "My turn."

He grinned. "If you insist."

She tugged his t-shirt off and dropped it on the floor. His bare chest gleamed in the dim light. She raked her nails lightly across his stomach, and he sucked in a breath, tightening the muscles under her fingertips. She flattened her palms against him and explored him slowly, learning the feel of smooth, warm skin

162

stretched over hard muscle, memorizing every curve and bump and dip of his lean body.

He'd apparently vented his sexual frustration at the gym, and she couldn't complain a bit.

His hands grasped her hips, digging into the skin there. "Maya, come on. Let me touch you."

She dragged hot, open-mouthed kisses down his neck and over his chest as her fingers unfastened his shorts. "Bed," she said, deliberately echoing his earlier plea.

"Ok." He sat down on its edge and pulled off his socks and shoes as he watched her, a small smile curving his mouth.

Maya shrugged her robe off. It slithered to a heap on the floor. James' eyes followed it down, then slid upward along the long length of her legs. She stepped out of the robe and strolled toward him, slow and easy, and a hot glow sparked in his gray eyes.

She pushed him back onto the bed and straddled his hips, lowered her head and kissed him gently, and he kissed her back, teasing, nipping kisses, beautiful and light, setting off a cascade of molten need within her. She rubbed herself over his rigid length. His hips jerked upward, meeting hers in a bold thrust, and she smiled. This was what it meant to be a woman, to revel in the way a man reacted to her, to savor his hitching breaths and shuddering sighs and the desperate need twining between them.

She broke the kiss and trailed hot kisses down his lean form, nuzzling her nose into the silky hair covering his chest, dipping her tongue into his navel, grazing her teeth along his skin above the waistband of his shorts. She shoved them down, taking his boxers with them.

James lifted his hips and wiggled out of his clothes. "I should've let you do this the first time."

"I liked our first time exactly the way it was."

His expression softened. "Yeah, me, too. It was perfect."

She unfastened her bra and slid it off her shoulders, baring herself to him. "Maybe we can reach perfection again."

He propped himself up on his elbows, his warm, gray eyes running over her nearly nude body. "I think we already have. Why don't you come over here and let me test that hypothesis?"

"Only if I can touch you, all night, everywhere." She shimmied out of her panties and dropped them on top of her robe. "Over and over again, any way I want."

"Yeah, I think I can handle that. Come here."

She crawled onto the bed, skimming her stomach over the tip of his erection, sliding her skin across his, aligning their bodies. "You rang?"

He moaned and dropped back against the bed. "I take it back. Much more of that and I'm going to come before we ever get started."

"That would be a shame." She rubbed herself along his length in long, easy strokes. "There's so much more waiting for you."

"Tease," he said gently, and she tilted her hips back, taking him into her in one smooth rush.

She undulated her hips in slow circles, her eyes on his, her palms flat against his chest. "You feel so good, James, so right."

"God, Maya."

He pushed his head into the bed and arched into her, and his hands roamed over her body, cupping her breasts, brushing her nipples, gripping her hips, urging her to move faster, harder, and she did, working her body against his, their gasps overlapping in a wanton symphony. He thrust into her and came, and his release throbbed through her, pushing her over the edge into her own release.

"James," she cried, and he slid a thumb over her clit, sending her high again.

Maya leaned over him, panting as her heart slowed. His eyes were closed, his chest sheened with sweat. A pulse beat furiously at the base of his neck. She dipped her head and sucked lightly, tasting the salt of his skin. Would they ever get around to having leisurely sex or would their need would always be so demanding, so consuming, so blissfully unrepentant?

"Mmm," he moaned. "You're insatiable."

"Complaining?"

"What?" His eyes popped open. He flipped her onto her back and braced himself on his elbows above her. "No. Are you kidding? No."

She laughed and trailed her fingers through the moisture on his skin. "Positive?"

"Absolutely no complaints here." He brushed his lips against hers. "In fact, if you give me about five minutes, I think we can go again."

He made good on his word, loving her with the patience of a man with all the time in the world. Afterward, they showered and fell back into bed, holding one another as sleep pulled them into its insistent grasp.

THIRTEEN

D ANI SAT in the living room of Dave's apartment, her gaze glued to Godzilla stomping around Tokyo on Dave's TV, eating a bowl of popcorn she'd popped in Dave's microwave while she waited for the man himself to make an appearance.

It had been a month and a half since she'd blackmailed him into this little bargain. He'd held up his end of the deal, to an extent, but now, just when his information was getting good, he'd gone walk-about on her. It was time for a little come to Jesus talk with him, just to remind him of the way things stood.

After all, her patience only went so far.

A scratching noise sounded at the door, followed by a click, and it slid quietly open. A moment later, Dave's shadow fell across her. Ten to one, he had his gun drawn. Big guy was a bit paranoid.

"What are you doing here?" he asked, enunciating each word carefully.

She took her time selecting a piece of popcorn, picking through the popped kernels in search of just the right one. "The mountain didn't come to Mohammed, so Mohammed picked the lock on the mountain's door and helped herself to some popcorn. You should get a better lock."

He grunted, set his gun on the coffee table, and dropped onto the couch beside her. He closed his eyes and dropped his head back against the sofa's plush leather.

"You look tired, Davy boy." She shook the bowl in his general direction. "Have some popcorn."

He opened one eye and peered at her, then dipped a hand into the bowl.

They munched in silence, riveted to the movie. Beside her, Dave relaxed, his body gradually sinking into the cushions. He was sitting close enough for the heat radiating off his body to warm her, a not unpleasant feeling. He was at least two hubbas, more if he'd smile every once in a while, but not Mr. G-Man. He took himself way too seriously.

She, of course, had no such problem. Why be serious when there was so much fun out there, waiting to be had?

The movie came to its inevitable end and the credits rolled. Dani set the bowl of popcorn on the coffee table and stretched her legs out, mimicking Dave's sprawling posture. "So, Davy boy. Any news on the artifact front?"

He sat up and rubbed a tired hand over his close-cropped hair. "You are one persistent lady."

"Hey, you're lucky I let you watch the rest of the movie."

He shook his head, a half smile flirting at one corner of his mouth. "Very generous."

She arched one eyebrow. "Was that an actual joke? I didn't know you had it in you."

He grunted again, closed his eyes, and slumped into the sofa. "I know where all the artifacts are."

"Well, why didn't you say so?" Dani sat up, bouncing around on the sofa, facing him. "Tell Dani all."

"Mmm." He yawned, snuggled deeper into the cushions, and crossed his arms over his broad chest. "Maybe tomorrow."

Dani gaped. Tomorrow? What did he mean, tomorrow? This wasn't friggin' *Annie*. She narrowed her eyes and ran through her options. What could she do to get Stoic Dave to talk tonight?

"Don't." His voice was flat, uncompromising, and sounded

an awful lot like a warning.

"Don't what?"

"Don't do whatever you were about to do." He yawned again and sat up, rubbing his eyes with the fingers of one hand as he stood. "I'm beat."

"So you're, what, going to bed?"

"For a blonde, you're pretty bright." He pointed to the door set into the wall behind and to the left of the TV. "Spare bedroom. It's yours, if you want it."

"I know what's in there. You were gone a long time and I got bored." Dani sat back on the sofa and eyed him. "Aren't you worried I'll get mad and, I don't know, tell somebody you're double dipping?"

He shrugged out of his t-shirt, scratching his chest in a half-hearted stretch, his well-formed muscles stretching and flexing. "If you were gonna do that, you'd've done it by now."

Dani's heart flipped in her chest and her mouth went dry. Her eyes dropped to the smooth muscle and the line of blonde hair leading from his navel downward. It disappeared into the low-slung waistband of his jeans, and she bit the inside of her cheek, holding back a sigh. Dave out of his clothes was a sight to behold, shooting him to at least a two point five on the Hubba Meter. That was all this was. She couldn't be attracted to him, not to straight-laced, by-the-book Dave Winstead. No way.

"I could still do it," she said, and hid a wince. Where had that quaver in her voice come from?

"Good night, Dani."

He strolled into his bedroom and shut the door.

Dani sat back on the couch, flummoxed. She'd totally intended to rat Dave out if he didn't get her the information she'd requested, right up until the moment he took off his t-shirt and her heart went thumpity-thump.

A soft snore drifted to her from behind the closed door and Dani shook her head. She cut the TV off, slipped into the spare bedroom, and readied herself for bed, amused in spite of herself.

A well-muscled chest had thwarted her blackmail scheme. She must be getting soft in her old age, that or going barmy. She smiled, slipped into the guest bed, and snuggled under the covers. Well, at least she could enjoy the view on the way to Crazyville.

THE WEEKEND'S IDYLL couldn't last no matter how much James wanted it to. He spent nearly every minute with Maya, talking about everything, laughing at the silliest things, making love with her over and over again. He watched her practice with her short staff, joined her at the gym to lift weights, and went with her to the grocery store.

The sly, knowing glances following them when they were out in public didn't bother him as much as they would've before his arrival in Tellowee. Now, he played along, holding Maya's hand, standing a little too close to her, stealing soft kisses in the produce aisle.

She dug her elbow lightly into his ribs. "Cut it out."

"Hey, we gotta feed the rumor mill." He draped an arm around her shoulders and brushed a kiss across her temple. "If they're talking about us, they're giving somebody else a break, right?"

She shot him a disgruntled stare, but she didn't shrug his arm off or shy away from his touch.

Part of him hoped that by firmly entwining his name with Maya's in the public sphere, it would help cement their private bonds. She was still holding something back, something that might be important. She didn't trust him, either, but he took the long view more and more often. Someday, she might feel free to open up to him. He could wait, if that's what it took, though he hoped he wouldn't have to for much longer.

Work took a back seat to their time together. That bothered him less the more time he spent with her. He'd been in the middle of translating a frustratingly difficult passage before

Amelia's visit. Maybe the break would give him a fresh perspective.

That night was his last night with Maya. Tomorrow morning, they'd leave her home and pick up the girls, and their idyll would come to an end. Even after Amelia went back to Connecticut the day after the Labor Day festivities, Dierdre would be there. With her around, there'd be no more hot kisses whenever the mood struck, no more long, intimate caresses, no more sex.

He was beginning to think he couldn't do without Maya's touch for long. At the rate they were going, he was pretty sure *long* was less than a day.

Maybe they could sneak off campus for nooners.

Naw. Nothing got by this crowd, and eventually it would get back to Dierdre. Much as he liked the teenager and wanted her to accept him, she had no business poking her nose into her mother's sex life. Dierdre being who she was, though, he was pretty sure she'd try. That was a line they'd have to draw. God willing, they'd have to draw it soon.

He and Maya went out for supper that night in Clayton, winding their way along the sidewalks through tourists up for the long weekend, enjoying the local bands playing on the square. Afterward, when they made it back to her home, he pulled her up the stairs, undressed her slowly, and made love to her to the rhythm of a thunderstorm breaking over the neighborhood. They fell asleep wrapped around each other with rain pinging against the tin roof overhead.

JAMES WOKE UP curled around Maya, his stomach to her back, an arm thrown across her waist. It was still dark outside, the sun not yet above the mountains. He snuggled closer to her, marveling over the perfect fit of her body against his.

He dozed, his mind drifting from Maya to the camping trip to the translations. A scene flashed before him in a dreamy sequence, of seven women, a grove of trees, a horse-like animal, the scene from the cylinder seal, one he'd never really understood. There wasn't enough context, and not nearly a large enough sample for a solid interpretation. He'd talked himself hoarse trying to convince Maya to open up and share what she knew, and her continual refusals were frustrating as hell. Whatever she hid from him could hold the answers they needed. Why didn't she see that?

He murmured and shifted, still half asleep. The scene blurred, shifting into an oasis he'd visited before Amelia's birth. The strong equatorial sun glimmered off the water trapped in a pond. Trees shaded the banks, offering respite from the heat to the sparse vegetation below. Travelers through that area visited the sanctuary often, refilling water bottles, sharing a light meal at the midpoint of their journey.

A section of the translation he was working on popped into his mind, rousing him from sleep. He tried to push it away. God, it was too early for that, way too early for work and sanctuaries and...

His eyes popped open and he sat straight up in bed, wide awake. Why hadn't he made the connection before? He scrambled out of bed, jostling Maya in the process.

She rolled over and peered blearily at him. "What are you doing at," she squinted at the clock and grimaced, "five forty-eight in the morning on our day off?"

"Gotta go." He yanked on clothes and stuffed his bare feet into running shoes. "Be back soon."

He kissed her soundly, ignoring her sleepy protest, and raced out of the bedroom. He'd found the key. Holy cow, he'd really done it. If he was right, and it felt so, so right, he'd just found a way to unlock the document he was working on, and maybe something that would help them understand the entire collection taken from the anomalous grave at Sandby borg.

FOURTEEN

WHEN MAYA WOKE AGAIN, James was still gone. She snuggled into his pillow, breathing in the clean, woodsy scent of his shampoo. Something tender shifted and slid through her, filling her with an aching need.

Her stomach clenched into a knot. She hadn't been able to tell him about the Daughters or herself, about the long, lonely years she'd waited to find someone, and now it might be too late. Her heart was on the precipice, ready to make the fall into love. Would he despise her when he found out the truth or would he forgive her for holding back so long?

No more fear.

She inhaled his scent one more time, making it part of herself, then got out of bed and readied for the long day ahead.

He came in an hour later while she was on the phone with Director Upton, several hours after he'd left their warm bed. His grin was triumphant and a tad smug. She eyed that grin as the director issued instructions. What had he been up to?

He wrapped his arms around her waist and drew her tightly against him, her back to his stomach. Her eyes widened and she clutched the phone to her ear.

Paper rattled on the other end of the line. "Will tomorrow morning be too soon?" Rebecca asked.

"Ah, mmm-hmm," Maya murmured.

James pushed aside her hair and scraped his teeth along the

side of her neck, and she gasped.

"Maya," Rebecca said. "Are you still there?"

Maya cleared her throat. "Ah, yes, Director. Sorry. I'm a little...distracted."

James tugged her more firmly against him, rubbing his erection against her bottom through the thin layers of their clothing. "Hurry up," he whispered. "I need you."

"Tomorrow's fine, then," Rebecca said.

James yanked Maya's shirt up and cupped her stomach, skimming his fingers along her skin, teasing her with his light strokes. Her eyes slid shut. "Of course, Director. We'll be there."

"I'll see you then." Rebecca's voice took on a sly edge of humor. "Oh, and Maya? Tell James I said hello, would you?"

"I'll do that." Maya hung up the phone and clucked her tongue. "That was naughty."

His breath feathered over the side of her neck. "You liked it."

"Well, yes, but that's not the point."

He tugged her around and captured her mouth with his, and every coherent thought drained out of her head, everything but him. He seduced her slowly, pushing her a little higher with his mouth and his hands, and made love to her there in the kitchen, in the bright light shining through the windows into the heart of her home.

Later, after her breaths calmed and her heart found a sane rhythm, she said, "The director called."

They were still leaning against the wall, his body holding hers upright, his hands circling in lazy strokes along her sides. He buried his face in her throat and nipped at her pulse. "I gathered."

"She wants to see us tomorrow as soon as you get back from taking Amelia to the airport."

"Any idea why?"

"Something important came up and she wants to brief us on

it. She didn't say what."

"Tomorrow's fine." He eased away and smoothed her hair back. "How much longer do we have?"

She glanced at her watch. "Maybe an hour. Why?"

"Shower," he said, and the low flame burning within her jumped and writhed and ached.

An little before lunch, they dressed and drove out to the trailhead. A few minutes after they arrived, the group straggled into the parking area, Dierdre and Amelia near the rear. The girls pushed their way through the crowd, Johnny Linton close on their heels, and stowed their gear in the trunk of James' car, chattering in excited bursts about the weekend's events.

Johnny kissed them both on the cheek before heading off, and James frowned. "That boy just kissed my daughter."

Maya pursed her lips, hiding a smile. "He's been known to do that."

"You don't say." James narrowed his gaze on the departing teenager. "I think it might be time for the *you're not old enough to have a boyfriend* talk."

Maya snorted. "Good luck with that."

"Hey, Amelia listens to me." The frown softened and a small smile tugged at his mouth. "Sometimes, when she wants something."

The four of them stopped by Maya's house so Dierdre and Amelia could clean up. After, they wandered through Tellowee, eating lunch at the café, walking the streets with the other residents, enjoying the mid-day parade. Johnny Linton tracked them down and draped a casual arm around Dierdre and Amelia's shoulders.

James stuffed his hands in his shorts and scowled. "Does he have to do that?"

Maya tucked her arm through his elbow. "Do you really want an answer or are you just grumping because your daughter has male friends?"

"He's not looking at her like he wants to be friends, exactly."

"Relax, James." Maya rested her head on his shoulder and skimmed her hand up and down his arm. "He won't do anything she doesn't want him to."

"That's what I'm afraid of," he muttered, and Maya laughed, tickled by the gruff honesty.

At suppertime, James cornered Johnny at the grill while Amelia and Dierdre helped Maya prepare side dishes. She listened with one ear while the girls gossiped and giggled. They'd become such fast friends and seemed so close, no doubt thanks to Dierdre's meddling. Maya couldn't complain. It had eased Amelia's path toward accepting her father's relationship with a woman other than the teen's mother, hadn't it? And maybe everything would work out there, if Maya could find the courage to tell him the truth about herself.

If he could accept that truth without coming to hate her for it.

They watched the annual Labor Day fireworks from Maya's backyard, Johnny sitting on a blanket between Dierdre and Amelia, Maya and James behind them in folding lawn chairs. She threaded her fingers through his, enjoying his warmth, giving him her own in return.

The fireworks ended in a dazzling display of light and sound. Johnny said his goodbyes and, much to James' disgust, kissed both of the girls goodbye before shaking James' hand and dropping a kiss to Maya's cheek.

"Affectionate booger, isn't he?" James asked.

"It's our way," Maya said gently.

Dierdre skidded to a stop in front of them, Amelia not far behind. "So, like, me and Meely had an idea."

Maya huffed out a laugh. "Oh, you did, did you?"

Amelia nodded, her gray-green eyes wide in her pretty face. "We don't have to leave until in the morning, you know?"

"I did know," Maya said, matching the teen's solemn tone. "And?"

"Well, see." Dierdre pursed her lips and rocked back on

her heels. "We kinda wanted to stay together tonight."

James shook his head. "We really need to get back to the apartment so Amelia can pack and rest for the trip."

"Come on, Dad," Amelia said, her expression melting into a plea. "It'll be months before I can come back. I bet Maya will let us both stay the night. Please?"

"You can use the spare bedroom, James," Maya offered. "The girls can bunk together in Dierdre's room. There's plenty of room for both of you here."

Dierdre clasped her hands together under her chin, her expression a twin to Amelia's. "You wouldn't want to deprive your only daughter of friendship, would you, Dr. T.?"

He laughed. "All right, all right. I guess it won't hurt, as long as it's ok with Maya."

His gaze slid to hers, and the hot gleam burning there sparked an answering call within her. They wouldn't spend the night together, not with Dierdre and Amelia in the house, but there was nothing keeping him from sneaking into her bed after the girls were safely asleep, and back into his own after making love to her one last time.

And that's exactly what he did. As he moved over her, rocking them both into sweet oblivion, Maya clung to him, desire tangling with a bone deep fear that it would be the last time she'd ever hold him that way.

JAMES AND AMELIA left for the airport early the next morning, not long after the sun peeked over the hills.

Maya rose and showered, dressed in casual work clothes, then stripped and remade her bed. It would be a long, long time before he made an appearance there again, if ever, once he learned what she was. Better to make a clean break of it rather than wallowing in what might've been.

Dierdre loped downstairs just as Maya took her first sip of coffee. The teenager rubbed her flat stomach under the sweatshirt she'd pulled on over ragged shorts, stretching and yawning her way to the refrigerator. "Mornin', Mom."

"Morning, Squiggles. Did you and Amelia have fun last night?"

"Yeah. She's coming back for Thanksgiving. We're kinda making plans to hang out together then." Dierdre sat down at the kitchen table and bit into a strawberry, chewing it slowly. Her gaze dropped to the plate of fruit and cheese she'd scrounged. "Johnny's got a crush on her."

Maya set her mug on the table. "I thought he had a crush on you."

"He did, but that was ages ago. He wasn't for me 'cause, you know." Dierdre hunched her shoulders and her lips trembled once, then firmed. "I just knew."

Maya reached across the table and squeezed Dierdre's hand with her own, inwardly cursing the fate awaiting any immortal Daughter. To search forever hoping to find love, only for it to crumble under the weight of the passing years and the fickle nature of the human heart. "I'm sorry."

"No biggie. We were too young anyhow, but now that Amelia's gonna be coming down, it'd be cool if they hooked up."

"I wouldn't count on her coming down again, honey."

Dierdre glanced sharply up. "You didn't tell him."

Maya sighed and skimmed a finger around the top of her mug. "I couldn't, not yet. I just wanted some time with him as a normal couple before all that got in the way."

They sat in silence, Dierdre picking at the food on her plate, Maya running her fingers over the ceramic mug.

Dierdre screwed her face into a frown and pushed her plate away. "D'you think he's the one?"

"I don't know. He might be."

"You love him?"

Maya sipped her coffee, grimacing as the lukewarm liquid hit her tongue. "Yes, I think so."

"But you don't trust him."

"We've not been together very long, but maybe, in time."

"You didn't trust my Dad."

"Oh, honey."

A helpless fury rose in Maya. Dierdre's father had been so special, so warm and loving, and Maya had hoped he'd be the one. She'd clung to that hope for years, right up until a Marine chaplain had shown up on her doorstep the week before Dierdre's fourth birthday with the news that Eddie had been killed by friendly fire. He'd died a long time before Dierdre should've formed an attachment to him, but she'd always missed him, and it tore at Maya every single day.

"I loved your father very much, Squiggles, but he just wasn't the one. I'd change that if I could."

Dierdre nodded, her expression glum, so different from her normal demeanor. "Sometimes I hate being a Daughter."

"I know."

"It sucks having this stupid curse hanging over you." Dierdre's eyes filled with tears. She blinked up at the ceiling and swiped the cuff of her sweatshirt across her face. "I liked Johnny, too."

"Me, too. I'm sorry he's not the one."

"Yeah. But if I can't have him, I guess Amelia going out with him's the next best thing." Dierdre's eyes dropped, meeting Maya's, and her lips twitched. "That sounded horrible."

Maya bit her lip, trying to contain her humor. "Maybe just a little."

"No, a lot. I can't believe I said that."

Dierdre she snorted out a laugh. Maya's own laughter escaped, and they burst into giggles, laughing hard in the early morning sunlight, accompanied by the occasional car whizzing along the street outside.

Dierdre sighed out her last laugh and swiped her face again. "Sorry, Mom. I guess the whole thing bothered me more than I thought."

"It's ok, Squiggles. Love is hard no matter how old you are."

"Yeah, I guess. I'm glad Johnny's still my friend, though, and if he had to fall for another girl, at least Amelia's, you know, sweet and everything."

"That she is," Maya agreed, and she breathed a silent prayer to the Lady Ki, thanking Her for giving her daughter a resilient spirit.

AMELIA BUBBLED enthusiastically about her time in Tellowee all the way from Maya's house to the airport, right up until she kissed James goodbye and boarded her plane. Any other time, he would've loved listening to her, but after two nights of little sleep and an early morning drive through rush hour traffic, his mind was muddled and his nerves were frayed.

The lack of sleep was his fault, and time well spent. Maybe there'd even be a repeat in the near future. Surely Dierdre had sleepovers.

Or did teenagers still do that?

Traffic was heavy on the drive back up. Was it ever not in the Atlanta area?

He tuned his radio to a local blues station and let his mind drift, to Amelia and her new-found friendship with Dierdre, to Maya and his deepening feelings (Did she feel the same?), to work and the translation he'd finished early the day before after an epiphany brought on by the intimate company of a good woman.

Hmm. Maybe he'd have to try that again the next time he was stuck. Him and Maya in bed for a weekend, skin on skin, breaths mingling, bodies joined so intimately, he couldn't tell where he ended and she began. He grinned and tapped his fingers against the steering wheel in time to Steve Ray Vaughn. Well, it was worth a try, anyway.

When he was ten minutes out, he called Maya with a heads up on his arrival time. Not long after, he eased into his parking spot outside his apartment, then ambled to her office, whistling tunelessly. Her door was open, so he went in, closing it softly behind himself.

She was seated at her desk, seemingly immersed in a report. Her hair was twisted into some sort of knot at her nape. Stray curls had escaped, framing her face, softening the strong lines of her cheekbones. She hardly ever wore make-up, not that he cared. With or without it, she was one of the most beautiful women he'd ever met.

Maybe that didn't have anything to do with make-up or clothing or the radiant glow of good health she exuded, but with the woman he'd come to know over the past few months. Under her reserve, he'd discovered a warm, wickedly humorous woman with a deep love of family. Her work wasn't just a job. It really mattered to her, and he admired that about her. No, he admired all of her, every single aspect, the lover he'd come to know, her steady relationship with her daughter, the woman who'd brought down a skilled fighter calmly and with a deliberation few could match. If he wasn't careful, that admiration would morph into something deeper, something stronger, maybe something lasting and true.

He stepped around her desk and kissed her cheek. "Hey, gorgeous."

She put the report down, stood, and edged away from him.

He closed the distance between them, slid his hands around her waist. "What's wrong? Morning after jitters?"

"Hardly." She placed a chaste kiss on his cheek. "How was the trip?"

"Driving through Atlanta is like racing the Indy 500 on a bicycle with flat tires."

She smiled, relaxed, fiddled with his collar. "It's not that bad."

"Mm-hmm. Keep telling yourself that."

He bent to kiss her, and she turned her head slightly away. A shaft of worry speared into him. "Are you sure everything's ok? No second thoughts?"

"Everything's fine." Her gaze drifted over his left shoulder and pinned itself there. "Really."

He eased back and studied her. This didn't feel right, but other than pushing her, and he was pretty sure that would piss her off, what could he do? "Ready to meet the director?"

"Sure."

They walked together to Director Upton's office, a foot of space between them. Over the weekend, they'd gone hand in hand everywhere. Now, she seemed reluctant to touch him.

He shoved his free hand into the pocket of his slacks, tightened his grip on his briefcase, and forced himself to follow her lead. Maybe if she weren't so cold, the distance wouldn't bother him. They were at work, and if there was any place for circumspection, it was there, but this... This wasn't like Maya at all, and hadn't been the entire time he'd known her. Even that first day, she'd been warm, open, receptive. The woman beside him had hardened herself, shutting him out as surely as if she'd shut a door in his face. What was going on?

He opened the door for her and followed her through. After the meeting, he'd get to the bottom of her sudden about-face. He had other things he wanted to talk over with her, but they'd start with the distance she'd deliberately put between them.

Director Upton was ready to see them when they arrived. She met them at the door to her office and directed them to the sitting area on one side, waving them onto the settee. "I have good news. Dani called. She's located all of the missing artifacts and is putting together teams to retrieve them."

"Er," James interrupted. "By retrieve you mean...?"

Rebecca's gaze remained steady. "Some things you may not wish to know, Dr. Terhune."

"Ah. The police won't be involved?"

Maya crossed her legs and folded her hands together in her lap. "Law enforcement agencies tend to be inefficient when dealing with stolen artifacts."

He'd had first-hand experience with that, but shouldn't they at least be consulted?

"In this case, there's a real danger that the artifacts might be sold or removed to a place where we can't track them," Rebecca added. "Specifically, they may have fallen into the hands of our, ah, rival."

James' eyebrows shot up. "The IECS has a rival?"

Maya's lovely mouth turned down at one corner. "So to speak. This rival hasn't been active in a while. Has something changed?"

Rebecca hesitated. She and Maya shared a look James couldn't interpret, but worry grew in the pit of his stomach. He'd only known Maya a short time, true, but he'd never known her to show fear, not until that moment. If anybody had asked, he'd've said she wasn't capable of fear.

A cold chill shivered down his spine. What kind of rival generated fear in the fearless?

"Possibly," Rebecca hedged. "That's not something we need to worry about for the moment. Right now, we should all concentrate on translating and interpreting as many of the artifacts from the Daughter's grave as we can, and quickly. If you need my help or the help of anyone else, please use it. These artifacts are our top priority."

James stared at her. "Er, Daughter?"

Maya ignored him. "Of course, Director."

"I'll let you know when Dani has retrieved the artifacts."

Not if, but when. Wasn't the director placing too much confidence in the effervescent Dani? She seemed capable, but she was young, maybe too young for the job she'd been given.

Which he wasn't going to think about. The whole thing was illegal from start to finish. He didn't have a problem with that. The artifacts had been stolen and should be returned, but was it really necessary to steal them back?

Rebecca's reclined in her chair. "Oh, and Maya? Please bring James up to date, today if possible."

It wasn't a request. He glanced between the two women, noting the cool command of one and the weary resignation of the other. What the hell was going on?

Maya nodded. "That was the next item on our agenda, Director."

"Good. Please keep me updated on your progress."

They chatted for a few minutes more, then left. James pulled Maya aside in the hallway as soon as they were out of earshot. "What was that about?"

"I have a few things to show you. It won't take long."

She led him to the IECS museum, housed in the same building as his office. He'd only visited it once, and that briefly. Between the translations, his burgeoning relationship with Maya, and his personal project, his time for explorations of the campus at large had been limited. Now, he admired the displays of ancient amphorae, weapons, armor, and ephemera, including some documents carefully enclosed in hermetically sealed cases.

Maya jerked her chin toward the back. "This way."

They threaded through a maze of artifacts, some dating back millennia according to the description plates James studied as they went past. She stopped in front of a door with biometric security and pressed her thumb to the pad, then entered a code, waiting for the lock to click before entering.

A small room spread out before them, maybe ten feet long on each side. In the middle stood a glass case containing several fragments of ancient documents in a variety of media, much like the collection they'd found in the Sandby borg grave. A plaque was mounted to a stand next to the case.

Maya lifted a hand toward the case and plaque. "Go ahead."

James placed himself squarely between the two objects and bent down, peering intently at the fragments through the protective glass. "What are these?"

"Pieces of an origin myth. We call it the Legend of Beginnings. It describes seven sisters who were cursed with immortality for slaying the men of their tribe."

"Fascinating." He shifted his stance and skimmed over the plaque's text. "Who were the sisters?"

"You'd know them as forerunners of the Amazons."

"No kidding." He straightened abruptly. "Wait. Why have I never heard this before?"

Maya gazed steadily at him, her face a stony mask. "Because we've done everything we could to erase it from history."

James gaped at her. "Why? If you have proof the Amazons were real, it would turn history on its collective ear."

"Yes, it could, but it would also open the path to knowledge, a knowledge of the Daughters who sprang from the Sisters, who shared the curse of the Sisters, and who live today with that curse."

"What are you saying?"

"The Seven Sisters were real, James, and so is the curse."

James ran a hand over his hair, ruffling it. "So the Sisters, what? Became immortal and had children who were immortal, too, and these people survived to modern times?"

"Not the Sisters, no. They all died millennia ago, but yes, their children still live and many of them are immortal."

The blood drained from his head and he swayed. Either Maya was crazy or she was...crazy. What other explanation could there be?

He'd been sleeping with a crazy woman who believed immortal Amazons roamed the streets of America. A short, harsh laugh burst from him. Jesus. "Come on, Maya. You don't expect me to believe that."

Her shoulders tensed, hunching slightly. "Believe what you want, but it's true."

"What proof do you have?"

"Do you need proof?"

"Yeah, maybe I do."

"The proof is here. It's been here all along. Haven't you noticed the unusual number of young, athletic women at the IECS?"

Yeah, he had. Tom had brought up that very thing the first night they'd met. His heart dropped like a stone in his chest. Then the exhibition, the gymnastics, the graduated displays of combat. The unusually focused nature of the students, their physical discipline, and, sweet God above, survival and weapons training.

And the weapons in Director Upton's office. Rebecca the Blade, her husband had called her.

Was it true? Were these women really immortal descendants of the Amazons?

He paced away and back again, facing Maya and the improbable tale she'd spun head on. "Are you one, an immortal?"

"I am."

"And Dierdre?"

"The sins of the mother, James," she said softly, and the sadness in her voice echoed through the room and straight into his heart.

"Dani and Indigo and..."

"All of them, yes, though a handful of the Daughters you've met are mortal."

"My God."

"No, James. It is to a goddess that we owe our salvation. For every curse, there is a path to redemption. The Lady Goddess offered the Sisters such a path and their descendants have the same choice."

He waited, his muscles tense, hoping she'd tell him, and praying equally hard that she wouldn't.

"All we have to do is trust a man, submit our will to him." She laughed, the short sound bitter and entirely humorless. "Sounds easy, doesn't it?"

Not so much. Their time together was beginning to make an awful lot of sense to him, and not just the lack of trust. "You've never trusted me."

"I've never trusted any man, James," she said, her voice

barely louder than a whisper. "But I've come the closest with you."

"And if you did trust me? What then?"

"I'd become mortal and live my life as a normal human."

"What about Dierdre?"

"Each individual must break her own curse."

"So you used me to try to break the curse."

Her face paled beneath its natural brown. "It wasn't like that."

He barked out a laugh. "Right."

"I swear, James, it was never like that. I knew there was a chance, but I also wanted to get to know you, just because," she shrugged and glanced away. "I was attracted to you from the start."

"And you enticed me here to, what? Test my mettle? See if I measured up?"

"You were invited here solely to work on the artifacts and assist with translations of other collections. The attraction between us was an unexpected bonus, for my part, anyway, but it played no role in your being here."

He shook his head and rubbed the nape of his neck. How could he ever believe that after she'd hidden so much from him?

"If you believe I'm immortal, that the Sisters existed and their Daughters still live, why is it so hard to believe I wasn't using you?"

"I'm not so sure I believe any of this." Everything she'd told him, everything that had ever happened between them, spun around and around in his head, and it was just too much. He needed to be alone, needed to be away from her and the secrets she'd kept. "I need to think."

"James, please."

She reached toward him, and he drew back, stepping out of her reach, her flinch no more than a tickle along his numb heart. One touch and he might just say to hell with it, to hell with everything, and fall back into bed with her. That wouldn't solve anything. She'd still cling to her tale, and he'd still have to deal with it.

She threaded her fingers together in front of her. "You'll have the time you need, but please don't take too long."

"Sure," he agreed, though how could he possibly know how long it would take to deal with the load she'd just slung at him? Hell, he didn't even know if half of what she'd said was true, and he hadn't even begun to sort out his feelings for her. A sharp pain set up residence in his left temple. Any way he went, he was sc-sc-screwed.

Maya's grip tightened and the skin over her knuckles whitened. "Until you've come to terms with this, please don't leave the campus."

He opened his mouth, closed it again. Where would he go? Who would he tell? He finally croaked out a shaky, "Why?"

"You're a security risk. We can't have you wandering around unaccompanied until we know you can be trusted."

"Jesus, Maya. Isn't that taking the trust issue a little far?"

"Unfortunately, we've learned this the hard way."

"And if I can't be trusted?"

"That's not a situation you need to worry about."

"Yeah, I think it is, since it concerns me," he shot back. "What would you do?"

She hesitated, then admitted, "You'd be taken care of."

"Taken care of. As in eliminated? Killed? Wiped from the face of the planet?"

"Don't be melodramatic," she said, her voice sharp and impatient.

"Then don't jerk me around."

She gazed at him for long moments. "I care about you, James."

He searched her face, looking for signs of duplicity, and saw only sincerity in the tense paleness of her skin, in the worry clouding her warm, golden-brown eyes. It was hard to believe this woman, sweet Maya with her gentle laughter and beautiful touch, could be a cold, deadly killer. On the other hand, he'd witnessed her fight with India. Maya had controlled the outcome, a sign of her skill and resolve, and a warning to anybody foolish enough to cross her.

"That wouldn't stop you from *taking care* of me, would it," he said slowly.

"Please don't put me in that position."

"Ok." He inhaled deeply, exhaled on a huff. God, he needed to think, needed some space, needed time to sort through everything. "I'm going now."

"Take care of yourself, James," she said softly.

"Yeah, sure."

He stumbled to the room's entrance, too overwhelmed to care how he must appear to her. What did it matter? She was old, immortal, implacable, and he was just a man. He opened the door, slipped through it, and glanced back. Maya skimmed her fingers along the edge of the glass case. A lone tear streaked down her face and her lips trembled, and God help him, he wanted to go back in there, pull her into his arms, and tell her everything was going to be ok. He closed the door and walked away, leaving her to her secrets and him to the task of mending the dent she'd made in his heart.

FIFTEEN

A BLESSED NUMBNESS settled over James during the walk to his apartment. He slipped inside, grabbed a beer out of the fridge, and slumped into the sofa, one hand on his stomach, the other holding the beer.

The sun dropped behind the hills and the security lights came on. The beer grew warm in his hand. Moisture leaked down the sides, pooling unnoticed on his skin. His conversation with Maya played over and over again in his head, a never-ending loop of revelation and disbelief.

Questions battered him into exhaustion, about Maya's veracity, her sanity, the implications of a millennia-old culture existing in modern times, virtually hidden from the rest of the world, and about the implications to himself and Amelia, to his personal work, and to the work he was doing for the IECS.

Which had probably been founded as a shelter for these women, a sort of sanctuary, not unlike the one he'd found referenced in the Sandby borg artifacts. He scowled at the darkened TV across the coffee table. He'd forgotten to tell Maya about it. He'd forgotten to tell her a lot of things.

He lifted the beer to his mouth and sipped, then grimaced. Damn it. It was too warm to drink. He peeked at his watch and sighed. It was after midnight by a long shot and he still hadn't sorted out all the questions rattling around in his head. He needed to get it out, maybe talk to somebody else, but who?

Phil and George were out of the question. They were just too young and they probably had no clue they were living among immortal Amazon-type women. Phil would probably love that. He loved being at the center of the local singles scene, and that scene suddenly made an awful sort of sense. The guys had been right. It was kind of like a meat market.

Tom might be a good sounding board, but he probably didn't know about the Daughters, either, and without him, James was stuck with too many questions and no way to resolve them.

A light bulb went off in his brain. Robert Upton. Of course. James glanced at his watch again and cursed under his breath. Still a long way 'til a decent hour. First thing after the workday started, he'd go to Dr. Upton's office and quiz the older man. Maybe *he* had the answers James needed.

He spent a restless night staring at the ceiling in his bedroom, out the window, at the closet door, and finally fell asleep in the predawn hours of morning. He awoke groggy and irritable, shivered through a quick, cold shower, and dressed, then set out in search of Dr. Upton.

The campus came to life as he walked along the paths winding between the buildings. Dew clung to the grass, carrying the chill of late summer. Fall would be there soon. He could already smell it in the air, a comforting scent that triggered a wave of nostalgia for his own days as a student.

Dr. Upton's office was located in the same building as his. James had discovered that not long after Maya's fight with India when he'd consulted with Dr. Upton on some hard to read documents. He hadn't been back since, but the building was well laid out, not that large in the scheme of things, and virtually impossible to get lost in.

He jogged the last few feet to Dr. Upton's office and groaned. The other man's office hours didn't start until later that morning. He leaned against the wall and scrambled for a way to fill his time, anything to keep his mind busy while he waited.

The museum. Right. He could go there and do what he

should've insisted on doing the day before, attempt to authenticate the fragments of the origin myth.

The museum was open, the air hushed, as if no one were in. He wandered through the exhibits, rereading the posted descriptions. Several of the artifacts were ancient, others equally as rare, and still others were displayed for no apparent reason. There was no overt theme to the items on display. Maybe they'd all been owned by Daughters or pertained to them in some way, or maybe some of them even dated back to the time of the Seven Sisters Maya had told him about.

He found the door to the room housing the origin myth, scowled at the security system, and backtracked to the museum's entrance.

A guard was strolling through the first row of exhibits, her sable hair coiled into a bun at the nape of her neck, her all black uniform sharply pressed. She smiled. "Dr. T, hello. Maetyrm Maya said you might stop by."

He shuffled to a halt. One of these days, maybe he'd get used to everybody in Tellowee knowing who he was, even when he hadn't met them. "Er, she did?"

"Of course. Director Upton, too. They said you might want to study the Legend of Beginnings up close." The guard swept her hand toward the back. "If you'll come with me, I'll show you how to access it and key in a password for you."

"Ah, thank you," he said, and followed her toward the rear of the museum, listening attentively as she walked him through the procedures for entering the room. She opened the door for him, nodded once, then closed it, leaving him alone.

He inhaled slowly and moved to the display case. The plaque he'd paid scarce attention to the day before contained a summary of the myth. Seven Sisters lived with their parents in peaceful coexistence with the People, a band of Neolithic, nomadic hunter-gatherers that included the sisters and their parents. The men of the People murdered the girls' parents and enslaved the women of the People. The sisters fled and wandered the land for many days, finally coming to rest in an oasis known as Sanctuary where they lived and trained for seven years.

The eldest daughter, Kiya, dreamed of a way to free the women of the People. The sisters set out, hoping to right the wrongs done by their fellow tribesmen. They located their former tribesmen and slaughtered the men, then freed the women and children. Upon seeing the blood of the men, the god An cursed the sisters to immortality, never to bear sons, never to know peace. The goddess Ki saw that An had been unjust and used all of her strength and power to modify the curse, giving the sisters a way out.

Redemption, Maya had said.

The myth ended with a warning to remember the past. A small offset section contained a note about rumors of a lost prophecy detailing how the curse might be broken for good.

James rubbed his eyes wearily. If Maya had shown him this from the start, it would've helped him tremendously. He'd suspected as much, but now with the proof laid in front of him, a slow burn roiled in his stomach. By holding this information back, she'd deliberately jeopardized their work. His gaze fell on one of the smaller fragments, on the symbol it had taken him so long to understand, vivid proof of the harm she'd inflicted on their work. *Sanctuary.* Now he knew exactly what kind of sanctuary the translation referred to.

But why? This work was vitally important to her, so why not tell him from the start?

James thanked the guard and left the museum, trudging toward Dr. Upton's office, his mood no better than it had been before he'd studied the legend. He knocked on the door, tried the doorknob, and stuck his head inside.

Robert took one look at James and sighed. "So, now you know, do you?"

James dropped into one of the chairs in front of Dr. Upton's desk. "Oh, yeah."

"You're wondering if it's all true or if there are a bunch of crazy women running around pretending to be Amazons."

James stared, then scrubbed his hands across his face. Right. The other man had probably had a very similar reaction to his own. He'd forgotten for a minute who Robert was married to. "Is it true?"

"Oh, yes. Took me a while to get my mind around it, too, but eventually I realized that Rebecca is one of the sanest, most stable women I've ever met. And then, of course, there's the fact that I've known her immortal daughters for decades, and they've never aged a single day in all that time."

"Jesus," James breathed. "Really?"

"I wouldn't lie." Robert threaded his fingers together over his chest and leaned back in his chair. "Look, I know you have questions, but the best place for you to find those is with Maya. It'll be better coming from her because she's lived it. I just married into it."

"No, I mean, yes." James slouched in his chair, regarding the older man carefully. The questions humming through his mind were coalescing into a simple handful, and with that narrowing came an uneasy acceptance. Maybe Maya was telling the truth after all. Maybe she wasn't as crazy as he'd thought she was, and maybe he'd been wrong to jump on her the way he had. "I guess I just needed to hear somebody else say it."

"That helps," Robert said, grinning. "It also helps to get drunk. Nothing like seeing the bottom of a cup to help a man make sense of things."

James scowled. He'd tried drinking and ended up pouring it down the sink. "Couldn't go off campus last night."

"Maya put you on lockdown, did she? Well, you should've called me. I'd've taken you out myself and we could've gotten drunk with style."

James hunched his shoulders. "I didn't think of you until the middle of the night."

Robert's chuckle boomed through the small office. "Better

late than never."

James attempted a smile. His mouth made it halfway, wobbled, and collapsed into a frown. "Did Director Upton threaten to kill you when she first told you?"

Robert's bushy eyebrows shot toward his thinning hairline. "What? Surely Maya didn't say that. That's not how the Daughters deal with men, I assure you."

"Er, actually, she said she'd have me *taken care of.*"

Robert's expression cleared and he threw back his head, laughing in earnest. "She's really got you by the short hairs, doesn't she? Normally, if a man doesn't fall in line, the Daughters simply remind him of the consequences. A good thrashing usually does the trick. Humiliating, yes. Life threatening, no. It's been centuries since they've actually killed a man for not falling in love with them."

Heat spread up James' cheeks and his shoulders hitched an inch higher. How was he supposed to know that? "So, she won't actually kill me, then."

"Son, if you're stupid enough to let a woman like Maya Bellegarde slip through your fingers, dying is the least of your problems."

They chatted for a few minutes more before James left. Dr. Upton had set James' mind at ease in a way only a man could. Ok, so it had been embarrassing, but he was a little more grounded now. His mind was settling, and he was beginning to believe that Maya had told him the truth, about the Seven Sisters, about herself.

The question that stuck out to him the most, the one that really worried him now that he'd stepped onto the long road to belief, was what this meant to him and Maya. How could he continue a relationship with her, knowing that at least part of her was in it for some sort of mystical cure? Or had she been truthful when she'd insisted she was with him out of an honest attraction? Could he ever be sure? Did certainty really matter?

He stuffed his hands in his pockets and shambled along the

path outside his office building, head down, feet aimless. He'd done most of the pursuing. She'd been the reluctant one and had only warmed up to the idea of being with him after spending a lot of time around him. Maybe she really had been telling the truth, about that part anyway.

All of that aside, he wasn't ready to forgive her and he couldn't quite face her yet. His stomach rumbled, reminding him of the time, and James veered off toward the cafeteria. Food first, then translations, then lots and lots of sleep. Tomorrow was soon enough to deal with Maya.

THE HOURS TICKED BY. Maya took her work home to avoid even a sight of James and vowed not to cry. It was her own fault for not telling him sooner, before they'd started dating. At the very least, she should've told him before they'd made love the first time.

Dierdre had the week off from school, so they had movie night, Dierdre's choice. Naturally, she picked the sappiest love story in their DVD collection. Maya's vow not to cry lasted right up until the part where it looked like the leading couple would never get together. Tears trickled down her cheeks and she sniffed, trying to hold them back. Dierdre laid her head on Maya's shoulder, and they finished watching the movie together, each silently considering a bleak, loveless future.

Sleep eluded Maya. She rested in bed, her eyes following the light the moon cast into her room as it moved through the shadows. James had every right to be angry and no reason to believe her. She'd left instructions for him to have access to the Legend and to any documents in the Archives he needed. He was a man of science and he'd want something other than her word as proof. It shouldn't bother her, but it did. All his talk of her trusting him, and then he scoffed when she finally told him the truth. Trust was a two-way street. Why couldn't he see that?

She avoided dwelling on their relationship as much as

possible and threw herself into work and training, driving herself to physical exhaustion. Still, the hours bled slowly by, sleep eluded her, and the dull ache in her heart refused to soften.

Two days after Maya showed James the Legend of Beginnings, Director Upton called. Her voice was terse and to the point. "We have a serious problem, Maya. Do you know where Dr. Terhune is?"

"He should be on the compound. Why?"

"We can't find him. The guards don't remember him leaving, and he's not in his office, his lab, or his apartment."

Uneasiness pinched at Maya. Surely James wouldn't have left the IECS, not after her warning. "Have you tried the gym? Or maybe the running paths. He likes to run."

"I'll send someone out to check. It's of vital importance that I speak with him as soon as possible."

Dread joined the uneasiness, mixing queasily in Maya's stomach. She placed a hand there and inhaled a shaky breath. "What's wrong?"

"It's Dr. Terhune's daughter. She's been kidnapped."

"Blessed Ki," Maya breathed. "I'll be right there."

She hung up and yelled for Dierdre, racing through the house searching for her daughter.

Dierdre poked her head over the rail at the top of the stairs. "What's wrong, Mom?"

Maya took the stairs two at a time and bustled her daughter into her bedroom. "Amelia's been kidnapped."

"Oh, no." The color leached from Dierdre's face. She staggered to her bed and dropped onto its edge. "When? Who? *Why?*"

"I don't know, Squiggles. I don't know anything yet." Maya brushed her hair back, tugging on the strands. "I want you to pack, enough for a week at least. I may have to leave and I want you safe while I'm gone."

"Ok. I..." Dierdre's expression crumpled. "You'll get her back, won't you? I mean, she's just a mortal and she's a girly girl and she doesn't know how to protect herself."

Maya sat down beside Dierdre and draped an arm around the teen's shoulders. "Don't worry. We'll get her back."

And Maya would, no matter what it took.

She helped Dierdre pack and half an hour later, dropped her daughter off at her dorm. As soon as her daughter disappeared up the stairwell to her room, she jogged to Director Upton's office. The director's receptionist waved her through. Maya shoved open the door and came to a full stop. Rebecca was alone in her office.

Maya shut the door and strode to the director's desk. "Have you found James?"

"He's being brought up now."

The door opened and James was pushed inside, an irritated scowl fixed on his face. He wore running shorts and a ragged t-shirt with the arms and neck cut out, both soaked with sweat. His gaze zeroed in on Maya. "What the hell? Can't a man enjoy a damn run without being man-handled? I was still on campus."

"That was my doing, Dr. Terhune," Rebecca said, "and I apologize for the rough treatment. A matter of some urgency requires your presence, and I'm afraid security got a little carried away bringing you here."

"Next time, just ask," he grouched.

"Of course. Would you like to sit?"

"I'd rather get back to running, if you don't mind. It helps me think, and suddenly, I find myself with a lot on my mind."

Maya glanced away and crossed her arms over the ding in her heart.

Rebecca sighed and sank gracefully into the chair behind her desk. "All right, then, to the point. Dani called in a couple of hours ago. Your ex-wife was found dead in her home. I'm sorry to have to break the news to you like this. "

"Oh, my God. What happened?"

"The police are still investigating, but she may have been murdered."

James' skin paled. "Where's Amelia? She wasn't home, was she? Is she all right?"

"We don't know exactly where she is, but we're certain she's alive. We've received a ransom demand."

"A ransom..." He staggered to a chair and sank down, his elbows on his knees, his head hanging. "For what? I don't have the kind of money a kidnapper would demand."

"Not money," Maya said. "Artifacts. Specifically, the artifacts from the Sandby borg grave."

"You're kidding."

"We believe the person behind this is the same one who had the other artifacts stolen in the first place," Rebecca said. "It seems he'd like the complete set."

James swiped a hand through his hair and sat back in the chair. "Why Amelia? I have no authority over the artifacts."

"She was vulnerable," Maya said flatly. "That's why we have this compound, James, because we're hunted. It helps us protect ourselves and our families."

James turned furious eyes on her. "You let her leave knowing she might be in danger."

Maya returned his glare. "If I thought she was in danger, I would never have allowed her to leave. How can you think otherwise?"

Rebecca raised her hands. "Getting angry won't help."

Maya sucked in a breath, forcing her frustration aside. "Sorry, Director."

"Our enemy has been silent for decades, James," Rebecca said. "We had no reason to believe Amelia was in any danger. This is simply not something we could've predicted."

He cleared his throat and fixed his gaze on his knees. "What can we do to get her back?"

"We're going to hand over the artifacts. More specifically, you and Maya will hand them over." Rebecca placed her hands flat on her desk, her expression as calm and even as her voice. "Once you have Amelia and return to the IECS, you may continue working on the translations using the images we've made, just until we can get the artifacts back. In the meantime, you and your daughter will be protected. On this, you have my word."

James ran a hand over the wet strands of his hair, ruffling them into a tangle of dark spikes. "Fine."

Maya breathed a small sigh of relief. Having his cooperation would smooth their way considerably, though it wasn't as necessary as he probably believed. "When do we leave?"

"As soon as you can pack. Dani is trying to track Amelia's location as we speak. We've been given a time and place to meet, but it would be nice to have another option."

"I'll call the airfield and have the plane fueled."

"No need. I did that as soon as I tracked the two of you down. I also took the liberty of having the artifacts in our possession packed for transport. You'll be escorted to the airfield. We're putting security on alert here and sending word out to as many of the People as we can reach. The Shadow Enemy is back. Best be wary."

Maya bowed. "Of course, Director."

She grasped James elbow, tugging gently, and he stood, following her without question. Outside, his steps gradually slowed, then stopped. "Does anything good ever come from meeting with her?"

"Sometimes."

"Hunh." He ran a hand over his hair, shaking some of the moisture out of it. "What time do you want to leave?"

"Will forty-five minutes give you enough time?"

"Yeah, sure."

He stood there, staring out into space, his shoulders slumped, dark circles marring the skin under his eyes. "Will you get her back?"

Maya curled her fingers into fists. She wanted to touch him, to hold him, to comfort him in any way she could. He wasn't ready for that. Maybe he'd never want that from her again. "I will."

"Ok." His gaze met hers, and the desperate fear burning out of his gray eyes tore at her. "Is Dierdre safe?"

"She's on campus now and won't leave until we return with Amelia."

"That's good, then."

He made no move to leave. As gently as she could, she said, "We need to go soon."

"Yeah. Sorry."

"I'll meet you at your apartment."

"Sure."

Still, it took a moment for him to leave. Maya watched him long enough to make sure he was headed toward his apartment, then jogged to Dierdre's dorm and outlined the plan to her daughter.

Dierdre's eyes were red and puffy. She wrapped herself in Maya's embrace and cried into her mother's throat. "You have to get her back, Mom. You just have to."

Maya smoothed Dierdre's hair back and rocked her gently. "We will, Squiggles. I promise."

She stayed as long as she dared, then said her goodbyes, promising to call with news as often as she could. On her way out, she tracked down the dorm mother and filled her in. Dierdre would need people around her, friends and people who cared about her, and until Maya returned, that would have to do.

She ran back to her house, redressed in comfortable travel clothes, and grabbed her bug-out bags, one holding enough clothing and toiletries for three days, the other containing a small weapons cache. After a call to check on the plane's status, Maya locked her home tight and strode back onto campus, determination marking every stride she took.

JAMES STEPPED into his apartment. The door snicked shut behind him, jerking him out of the daze he'd slid into. Too much had happened over the past week, too many shocks, too many surprises. He stood there a minute, sorting through everything, and settled on the one thing he could do something about. He had to save his daughter, and then, somehow, he had to find a way to tell her about Linda.

Dear God. How on earth could he possibly tell Amelia her mother had died, that the woman who'd given birth to her, sheltered her, loved her in her own absent-minded, full-hearted way, would no longer be a part of her life?

He flinched away from it. Maybe by the time they'd found Amelia, he'd have the words she'd need from him, and if not, at least she'd know she still had him.

He stripped and stepped into the shower, allowing the water to wash everything away. Amelia kidnapped, forcibly taken for a purpose beyond his control or doing, her mother dead, him embroiled in a generations-old struggle between immortal Amazons and a deadly enemy. He shuddered and stepped out, dried off quickly, and threw on the first set of clothes his hands fell on.

He dragged out his suitcase and randomly tossed items inside. Clothes, toiletries, the book on his nightstand. A knock at the front door interrupted him. He hustled through the apartment and jerked it open. Dierdre stood on the other side, her tear-stained face pale. James opened his arms and she stepped into them, clinging to him.

"Shh, now," he murmured. "We'll get her back."

"I know, Dr. T." Dierdre sniffled into his chest. "Mom's the best at this kind of thing. You'll see."

James wasn't so sure. Maya was all he had, though, so he'd just have to trust her, wouldn't he? "Come on back. We can talk while I finish packing."

Dierdre followed him to the bedroom, took one look at his suitcase, and managed a shaky laugh. "Good thing I'm here, Dr. T. You'll never survive New York like that."

She repacked his suitcase, taking out the shorts he'd thrown in, pretty much all he'd packed, and adding in sturdy jeans, t-shirts, and a couple of sweatshirts. "Ok, undies and toiletries now. You're gonna need more than toothpaste and a razor, Dr. T."

James huffed out a laugh. "Bossy."

"Somebody's gotta keep you in line." She waited while he gathered toiletries and stuffed them into his suitcase, then closed and zipped it. "I heard Mom told you about the People."

"Yeah?"

She shrugged. "We don't keep many secrets."

"Right. Well, that was a pretty damn big secret."

"You don't understand, Dr. T." The skin around her eyes tightened and her mouth pursed, and she looked so much like Maya, James' heart thumped hard against his sternum. "It's our way of life, our *whole* way of life. That's what's on the line every time an outsider learns about the People. They got Amelia and she's just a mortal, not even blood kin. All they're doing is holding her for ransom. What do you think they'd do to us?"

Clearly something bad, judging by the tone of her voice. He apparently had a lot of history to learn and no time to absorb it all.

"They took Mom once, when she was little." Her voice dropped to a harsh whisper and her hands curled into fists against her thighs. "The Shadow Enemy killed her parents while she watched. If the servants hadn't helped her escape, Mom would've died, too. We're blood enemies, Dr. T., and they won't stop until we're all dead, all of us."

The blood drained out of his face. "Jesus."

Dierdre's hand wrapped around his forearm. Her fingers dug into his skin, bruising him, and her hard eyes searched his face. "You have to protect her, Dr. T. My Mom. You have to bring her *and* Amelia back. Promise me."

He pulled Dierdre into a hug, rocking her in a futile stab at comforting her. If Maya was in a danger so great she couldn't protect herself, what could he possibly do to keep the promise

Dierdre wanted him to make? He couldn't fight or wield a staff or shoot a gun, thanks to his parents' pacifist objections and his own complacency. By God, if he made it out of this situation in one piece, he was going to learn how to protect himself and Amelia and the two Daughters he had somehow grown to love. Never again would he be in this situation, no matter what he had to do, even if it killed him in the doing.

SIXTEEN

ANI FIT binoculars to her eyes and studied the scene below. After tracking down the artifacts, with a lot of help from her favorite undercover Feebi, she'd assembled teams to retrieve them, then been foiled when Dr. Terhune's daughter was kidnapped and a ransom demand issued. Amelia had been brought here, to a warehouse not far from the docks. It was too much to hope that the missing artifacts had been moved here as well, but a girl could wish, couldn't she?

Once she'd checked in, Dani had been given strict instructions to *observe only* while Maya and James made their way north to the Big Apple. The same teams that had been intended for artifact retrieval would now be used to provide backup for Maya.

It was a shame, too. Kicking butt and taking names was a lot more fun than waiting in the wings surveilling.

Of course, if things turned bad here, she'd go in, orders be damned. A kid had been taken and was being held by some very bad people. No way would Dani leave her in there alone, not for long.

A footfall scuffed on the roof behind her. Dani glanced over her shoulder. Two men were behind her, one lanky and lean, the other a couple of inches taller than her and stocky, hired thugs from Dave's crew. The Blessed Mother knew she'd observed them often enough. They ambled slowly toward her, spreading out in a futile attempt to flank her, and satisfaction burst through her. Wasn't it just her luck that they were spoiling for a fight, just when she felt like fighting?

She stood and bestowed her best come-hither smile on them. "Howdy, boys. What brings two nice men like you to a dump like this?"

They glanced at one another. Lanky's eyebrows shot toward his crew cut.

Stocky shrugged. "Boss said not to pay no mind to the broad's yapping."

Dave, that rat bastard.

"Hey," Dani snapped. "The only yapping anybody's doing is on your end, you lily-livered, speckle-sided son of a goat farmer."

Stocky grinned and waggled his fingers at her. "Put your money where your mouth is, sweetheart."

Dani grinned back. Fight it was.

Lanky leapt toward her, arms open. She slapped her palms over his ears, and down he went, screaming. She nudged him with one booted foot, satisfied he'd be down for a while. Nobody ever saw that one coming.

Stocky grabbed her from behind, locking his arms around her chest, pinning her arms in place. Dani admired the firm steel of his arms and the flat, muscled planes of his chest (A girl had to take her pleasure where she found it, didn't she?), then threw her head back sharply into his face. He dropped her and staggered backward, blood streaming from a cut on his lip.

Well, damn. She'd missed his nose.

Lanky was on his hands and knees, struggling to his feet. She kicked upwards, catching him in the stomach, and he collapsed onto the rooftop with a muttered, "Oomph."

Dani hitched her hands on her hips. "Come on, guys. Y'all are making this way too easy."

A small pinch in her arm startled her. She looked down. A tranquilizer dart protruded from her clothing. She whirled around, staggering, and glared at Dave. He lowered a small tranquilizer gun and tucked it into the back of his jeans as he walked toward her, one corner of his mouth quirked up in that almost smile of his.

Her vision blurred, taking the world with it. He'd shot her with a tranquilizer. He'd really shot her. "Son of a...," she said, and sank into oblivion.

She woke slowly, groggy from whatever Dave had shot into her. She lifted one eyelid, had her eye burned by a shaft of too-bright light for her trouble, and shut it again. Son of a bitch. Where had he taken her?

She calmed her breathing and listened. Shoes scuffed against concrete. Water dripped, pinging metallically in an irregular rhythm. Something clicked nearby, maybe a light switch. Somebody's breath hitched, a near sob, as if he or she had been crying.

Dani shifted as subtly as possible, testing her arms and legs. They were nearly immobile, her arms bound behind her at her wrists, her ankles wrapped tightly together. She clenched one hand into a fist and wiggled her arm back and forth, trying to get a feel for the material holding her. It felt a little sticky. Duct tape maybe?

She opened her eyes a slit, allowing them to slowly become accustomed to the light. The room spun once, then snapped into focus. A rectangular folding table had been erected about fifteen feet in front of her and to the side. A lamp sat on its surface, along with water, packaged food, and what looked like a first aid kit. Dave stood in front of the table watching her, his blunt features a hard mask.

Another man was beside him, dressed in a fashionable black suit with a red tie. He appeared to be in his late thirties, and was trim and clean-cut with black hair and vivid blue eyes. He might've been handsome if not for the cold amusement etched into his features.

This one she didn't know, in spite of the weeks of recon she'd done. Ol' Dave had been hiding things from her. She narrowed her eyes in his direction. That's ok, 'cause she knew where he lived. He had to sleep sometime, didn't he?

Other people were spread around what looked like the interior of the warehouse she'd been casing before that rat bastard tranqed her. She counted two, four, blinked as her vision blurred, and estimated instead. At least twenty just in her line of sight and probably more she couldn't see, both inside and out. Great.

The hitched breathing came again to her right. Dani shifted her head slowly, avoiding sudden movements. The tranq would filter out of her system soon. Until then, she'd take it nice and slow.

She finally turned her head far enough to the right to locate the source of the breathing. A pretty, young girl with deep reddish-brown hair was tied to a chair some eight feet away. Her face was tear-stained and too pale, and her lips were pressed tightly together. Dr. Terhune's daughter, had to be. Dani examined the girl from head to toe, searching for any signs of injury, but could find none other than some redness around the girl's wrists where she'd likely been straining against the ropes.

The kid got ropes and she got duct tape. Go figure.

"She's unharmed," the man in the suit said. His voice was low and smooth. The toney accent held an undertone of the Mediterranean.

"And I should believe you, why?" Dani asked.

He bowed slightly, almost mockingly, in her direction. "Forgive me. We haven't been introduced. My name is Lukas Alexiou. You would know me better as the leader of the Shadow Enemy."

A chill raced along Dani's skin. *This* was the famed Shadow, the leader of the People's mortal enemy? He looked like he should be watching an opera, not cutting down innocents left and right.

"My word is my bond, Miss Nehring," he continued. "In fact, I believe now that we've met, we have a little business to attend to." To Dave, he said, "Please bring me the man who killed this child's mother."

Two men pulled a twenty-something man forward. His clothes were torn and blood-stained, and his face was so bruised and battered, he would've been hard to identify even for kin and friends.

Lukas studied the man coldly. "I gave very specific orders for this mission. What were those orders, John?"

The beaten man mumbled something too low for Dani to hear. Amelia sobbed once, cutting it off with a sharp inhale.

"Correct," Lukas said. "The woman was not to be harmed. Retrieve the girl, do no harm. A very simple request, John, yet you disobeyed me and killed a woman, leaving a mess that must now be cleaned up. What do you have to say for yourself?"

John shook his head slowly and whispered, "She came at me with a cast iron skillet."

"I don't care if she came at you with a shotgun," Lukas screamed, startling everybody except Dave. "She was not to be harmed!"

The man broke into helpless sobs. Dani's lip curled into a sneer. Why did men always resort to blubbering when faced with retribution?

Lukas cleared his throat and smoothed a hand over his hair. "My apologies, ladies. Incompetence brings out the worst in me. Mr. Winstead, if you please."

Dave stepped forward and, with a blank expression, backhanded John, knocking the bound man to the ground. John's blubbering came to an abrupt halt.

Lukas sighed and straightened his cufflinks. "Much better. Now, on to business. Miss Terhune, I realize you are not a Daughter, but given your father's situation with Maya the Protector, I think it fair to say that you will soon be adopted by the People as one of their own."

Dani sucked in a quick breath. How could the leader of the People's enemy possibly know something as intimate as Maya's relationship with James Terhune?

"Because of this," Lukas continued, "I am willing to follow the People's tradition and allow you the right to kill this man for what he did to your mother."

"No." Amelia closed her eyes and turned her face away. "I don't want to."

"Oh, but I insist. It is the People's way, is it not, Miss Nehring, vengeance in the face of injustice?"

Lukas' tone was light, playful even, and he smiled, a vacantly pleasant expression. Dani shivered. The man was about as sane as an escapee from the loony bin. She had to find a way to deal with him, though, and fast. She glanced at Amelia, young, mortal Amelia. "She's not old enough. Fourteen is the age of decision."

"But in these circumstances, with her mother murdered before her very eyes, surely we can waive a few months and allow her to avenge that death."

"No," Dani insisted. "In that case, her nearest relative would step in for her. Since she doesn't have a relative here, exacting vengeance falls to me."

Lukas threw his head back and laughed, the sound grating across Dani's nerves. "I was told you were a canny warrior, Miss Nehring, and now I can see how very true that is. Of course, I cannot let you kill my man here. Why, we would have to untie you for that, and then you would try to kill us all. What a shame that would be."

Dani gritted her teeth. Crazy he might be, but Lukas Alexiou wasn't dumb, more's the pity.

"No, we shall wait for Miss Terhune's father. He and Dr. Bellegarde should be here bright and early tomorrow morning. I regret that we shall have to leave you tied to that chair. I've been told you could create quite a bit of mischief for us if we allowed you to roam freely."

Dani shot a killing glance at Dave. He returned her gaze with a stony one of his own.

Lukas glanced between the two of them and folded his

hands together at his waist. "Why, is this a love match in the making? Will yet another Daughter succumb to frail mortality through her love of a mere man?"

Dani rolled her eyes skyward. "Oh, yeah, that's exactly what it is."

"Mr. Winstead does seem rather fond of you. Perhaps I shall give you to him once this unpleasant situation is resolved. On the contingency that he not harm you, of course. Can't have one of the Daughters bruised, can we?"

Dave grunted.

Dani smiled sweetly. "Sure, give me to him. I'll make sure he suffers for it."

Lukas clucked his tongue. "Now, Miss Nehring, that is not the way one treats a lover."

"We're not lovers, ergo..."

"I know what it's like to love a Daughter," Lukas murmured. He walked over and bent down, putting himself on eye level with her, and brushed a loose curl away from her face.

Dani swore he did it with tenderness, but still, his fingers brushing against her bare skin repulsed her. She quashed a flinch as his hand withdrew. "Who did you love?"

He eased upright, his gaze fixed on a scene only he could see. "I have loved her for an eternity, and always will. She betrayed me, yet love her I do. Can you believe that?"

She scrambled through the tales she'd heard of doomed alliances between Daughters and members of the Shadow Enemy. None matched with this man. "If she betrayed you, why do you still love her?"

"I have no idea," he said, and it struck Dani as the most honest thing he'd said.

"No matter." He shook his head and returned to Dave's side. "She and I shall be together again soon. It has been foretold."

"Care to share that foretelling with me?"

Lukas laughed again, this one softer, almost genuine. "What

do you think this little scenario is about but the Prophecy? Surely Dr. Terhune has gotten that far along with his translations."

Dani's lips thinned. She was just a soldier in the war between their peoples. Her knowledge of those kinds of things was limited to what she needed to know for the missions she undertook, and only that.

"I have only come across it once before, you know. That's why I had to have these artifacts. My father destroyed the first mention of it when he learned..." Lukas' voice trailed off and his eyes glittered, cold, ruthless, determined. "Well, that's a story for another time. He paid for what he did, and I have searched since then for another version in the hopes of finding *her*, the woman I am meant to love. She and I will be together, Miss Nehring."

"Ok, well, if you'll tell me who she is, I'll be sure to warn her."

He smiled. "Oh, my sweet, you are a breath of fresh air and I have thoroughly enjoyed our conversation."

That made one of them. For her part, the whole incident had confused the hell out of her. The only thing she was sure of was that Lukas Alexiou was as mad as the Hatter.

"But, we must be going. I have instructed my colleagues not to harm you. Unless you want me to kill one of them for doing so, please do not antagonize them." He walked over and, bizarrely, pressed a kiss to the top of Dani's head. "They will be forced to retaliate and the whole thing will spiral downward from there. Be a good girl, will you?"

"Sure," she said, though she had no intention of doing any such thing. Staying where kidnappers put her wasn't in her nature, and it wasn't a lot of fun either. She glanced around, tallying the number of men around her with a clearer eye. There was a lot of fun to be had inside that warehouse and she didn't want to miss a minute of it.

Lukas patted her head, smoothing her hair back. "There, now. That wasn't so hard was it?"

He pivoted and left. Dave speared Dani with a long, intense

glare, a warning unless she was sadly mistaken, then followed the Shadow Enemy's leader out of the warehouse.

Dani turned and met Amelia's fearful gaze evenly. The sight of the girl tied to a chair pissed Dani off good. She inhaled through her nose and pushed it aside. Anger didn't make for a clear head, and she needed every wit she could scrape together if she was going to get them out of this mess. "You ok, kid?"

Amelia jerked her head up once, then down. "Yeah. You?"

"Never better. Give me a few minutes to get out of this duct tape and we'll be on our way."

A man wandered over, Stocky from the rooftop. His lip had been cleaned, though it was still cracked. Maybe he'd have a nice scar as a reminder not to mess with Daughters. He pointed to two other men and gave them instructions to drag John out of the way, then turned a murderous stare on Dani.

She cocked an eyebrow and smiled coyly, suppressing a weary sigh. It was gonna be a long night.

AN ESCORT met Maya at James' apartment nearly an hour after they'd parted ways outside Director Upton's office. Maya stowed her gear in the trunk of one of the luxury SUVs the IECS maintained for just such occasions. The sturdy vehicle was equipped with bulletproof glass, armor plating, and other security upgrades. The gas mileage was horrible, but it was one of the safest vehicles available to them.

James yanked the door open as Maya was raising her hand to knock. He held a small carry-on bag and a slightly larger suitcase. She grabbed the suitcase and waited while he locked his apartment door, studying him from under lowered eyelashes. The skin under his eyes was still too dark and there were lines on his face she'd never noticed before. He moved slowly, deliberately, nothing like the steady, energetic man she'd come to know. Everything that had happened since Labor Day flashed through her mind, the last time they'd made love, telling him about the People, Amelia's kidnapping and the death of his ex-wife. She bit her lip and followed him down the stairs and outside. He probably hadn't slept well since then, and at least part of it was her fault.

The air in the back of the SUV was uncomfortably tense during the ride to the airfield in Gainesville and the airplane the IECS kept there for dignitaries and to provide emergency travel. Maya and James were driven straight to the hangar, and from there escorted out to the waiting plane.

Four other people were already on board, all immortal Daughters renowned for their skills as warriors. Alafair originally hailed from the Anglo-Saxon kingdom of Wessex. Brigid was also from what had become the British Isles. She smiled politely at Maya and James as they approached. Hawthorne's fiery temper had led to more than one unfaithful man losing his head, and probably good riddance. The fourth Daughter, Greta, had immigrated to the Midwest with her immigrant grandchildren some hundred years before and had settled in the South after their deaths. Maya greeted each of them with a nod. Thank the Blessed Mother the director had been able to gather such a good group on what amounted to a moment's notice.

James settled into a seat next to a window, to the rear of the four women seated together near the front of the passenger area.

The plane was too small for privacy, as much as Maya would've liked it. She sat down across from him, relaxing into the seat. "You should get some rest. We're not liable to get much once we arrive in New York."

He scraped a hand across his face and yawned. "Don't think I could."

"At least close your eyes for a while."

He did, drifting into sleep a few minutes later, likely lulled by the steady thrum of the plane's engines. Maya found a light blanket and draped it over him, then took a pillow from the overhead storage and tucked it gently under his head.

He was too pale. Poor man. To have his ex-wife murdered

and his daughter kidnapped on top of everything else. Even with her strength, there were things Maya couldn't protect him from. She slumped into her seat, arms crossed over her stomach, her legs stretched out in front of her. The darkest side of the curse she lived under wasn't the continual fighting, the ever-present prickle of knowing someone was coming after you. It was being unable to protect those that meant the most from the life she and the other immortal Daughters were doomed to live.

Maya deliberately emptied her mind and closed her eyes, dozing off and on during the short jump to New York. A few minutes before they landed, she woke James, giving him time to pull his thoughts together while the pilots went through their landing routine.

Not long after, Maya, James, and the four Daughters loaded themselves and their gear into two vehicles and headed for the home of a mortal Daughter who'd agreed to house them overnight. Night had fallen while they were in the air. Maya fixed her gaze on the streetlights whizzing by as they made their way along the crowded causeways. James sat beside her, staring out the opposite window.

So much distance separated them, physical, emotional. It might as well have been a mile as the length of the backseat. Sharp regret roiled through her. Damn it, she should've told him sooner, should've given him a chance to come to terms with it before they made love. Maybe they could've avoided the distance that had sprung up between them. Maybe if she'd told him before, he wouldn't have reacted the way he had and they could face this threat together.

When their vehicles rolled to a stop along the sidewalk outside Ella Deyton's home, the lights in every room of the house seemed to be on. Ella had only been mortal for three years. She and her now husband had met while Ella was in New York on vacation, taking a break between one duty and the next. They'd fallen in love and married, and though Ella was a Southerner by birth, she'd opted to live with her husband near his family.

Ella's husband, Greg, opened the door and invited them in, leading them through the house into the kitchen. Ella was sitting at a small table, nursing her infant son. Upon seeing the child, Hawthorne, Greta, Alafair, and Brigid instantly melted from battle hardened warriors into cooing admirers, all crowding around the infant as if he were the next Messiah.

Maya lowered her head, hiding a smile. In a way, he was. The birth of a Son was always heralded, not least because it was preceded by the breaking of a curse.

Ella and Greg had prepared a meal for them, so they sat and ate and talked, sharing and gathering news. James sat quietly, eating his fill, his attention apparently on the discussion bandied back and forth around him. Maya leaned close and whispered, "You ok?"

He nodded and jerked his gaze away from hers.

Ella put Maya and James in a bedroom together, apologizing for the lack of space as she paired the four Daughters off and led the immortal women to other rooms. Maya followed her through the house, noting where the other Daughters would bed down and making sure they had what they needed.

A short while later, she returned to the bedroom she and James had been assigned. He was staring blankly at the double bed, his hands stuffed into the pockets of his jeans, his shoulders slouched.

Maya closed the door and cleared her throat. "Ella doesn't know we're, ah, not together. I can sleep somewhere else, if you'd rather."

"We're both adults," he said flatly. "I think we can handle sleeping in the same bed for one night."

They took turns getting ready for bed in the room's bathroom, then turned the lights out and settled down on opposite sides of the mattress, not touching, not speaking.

An odd pressure filled Maya's chest and climbed into her throat. She turned on her side away from James and buried her face in the pillow, determined not to regret the past. She couldn't undo it no matter how often she second-guessed herself, and it was futile to try.

The mattress shifted. A warm arm slid around her waist as James curled around her. "Don't cry."

She placed a hand over his, holding him to her. "I'm not."

"You're sniffling."

She sighed. Busted. "Not on purpose. Go to sleep. You need the rest."

His arm tightened around her. After a long moment, he said, "I haven't forgiven you."

"I know."

"I probably will, though."

The pressure in her chest eased slightly. "Really? You're not still mad?"

He huffed out a short laugh. "I'm pissed about the whole thing, you hiding things from me, my daughter getting mixed up in this blood feud, and Linda being killed. She was a good woman, Maya. She didn't deserve to die."

There was nothing she could say to that, nothing at all. She stroked her fingers over his hand, comforting him as much as she could.

His breath feathered across her shoulder. "Will you tell me about your life?"

She turned over, facing him, tangling her legs with his. "Someday."

"Dierdre told me a little."

"Oh?"

"She came by while I was packing and we talked."

"Hmm. Dierdre breaking the rules to talk to you about my past. Now, there's a surprise."

He laughed softly. "She loves you."

"I know."

"Don't ever hold anything back from me again."

"Only if I have to," she promised.

216

He blew out a breath, then kissed the tip of her nose. "I guess I can live with that."

Maya snuggled into him, breathing in his woodsy scent, so grateful for his touch, she ignored the uneasiness continuing to ping through her gut.

SEVENTEEN

THE HOUSEHOLD woke early. Daughters streamed up and down the stairs and in and out of rooms, comparing weapons, discussing possible scenarios, rehashing plans. Once dressed, Maya riffled through her weapons bag while James brushed his teeth and shaved. She sorted them into two piles, those she could possibly conceal and the ones she'd carry in specifically so they'd be taken.

James came out of the bathroom and let out a low whistle. "Are those really necessary?"

"Yes." She perused him from head to toe. "How comfortable are you wearing an ankle holster?"

He shoved his hands in his pockets and fixed his gaze on the mini-arsenal she'd assembled. "No idea. Never worn one before."

"Please tell me you've at least shot a gun."

"Er, well, no."

Maya pressed the heels of her hands to her eyes. "When we get back to the IECS, you're learning how to shoot."

"Ok."

She opened her eyes wide. "Ok?"

"Yeah." He hunched his shoulders, let them fall. "We need to learn how to handle ourselves better, me and Amelia, especially if we're going to be..."

"Going to be what?"

He rubbed a finger over the tip of his nose and his lips twitched. "You know. You and me."

She definitely wanted a you and me with him, later, when they'd sorted out Amelia and the artifacts and went home to Tellowee.

"Right." She selected her Keltec .380 from one of the piles. "Ready for a crash course in guns?"

He accepted the gun gingerly. "Ready as I'll ever be."

She ran him through the basics of holding and shooting the gun, and exchanging clips. He was a fast learner, but still fumbled with its unfamiliar feel.

The third time he bobbled it, she said, "Just relax."

"It's really light." He brought the gun up again, attempted a two-handed hold, and dropped his hands. "This isn't as easy it looks on TV."

"No, it's not. Try not to put both hands up when you're shooting." She pulled his arm up and adjusted his one-handed grip. "The pistol is too small for that. If you're not careful, you could take a finger off."

He paled. "Er, gotcha."

"Point the gun as if it were your finger, ok? And remember. Aim small, miss small. The range for this gun is short, so wait until your target is within about ten feet and aim at the torso. Otherwise, you'll probably miss and piss somebody off."

"That would be bad," he said mildly.

The ankle holster gave him a little trouble. Maya made him walk around the room with the holster on, both with and without the gun inserted. Eventually, he walked naturally, casually. She helped him put a clip holder on the inside of the opposite ankle and had him walk some more. When she was certain he was as comfortable as he could be, she chambered a round in the Keltec, ejected the clip, loaded another bullet, then slipped the magazine back into place, inserting the gun and the extra clip firmly into their respective hiding spots.

"Ok, you're set," she said. "All you have to do now is draw, point, and shoot."

James peered down at his ankles. "Ah, what about the safety?"

She nodded. At least he knew that much about guns. "This gun has no safety. The first time you fire it, you'll have to pull back firmly on the trigger, about an inch. After that, shooting will be a lot easier."

"If it's that easy, how do I keep from blowing a hole in my foot?"

"It won't go off until you pull the trigger," she assured him. "Just make sure that if the police come, you take the gun off and kick it away from yourself before you can be seen holding it. Carrying a gun in New York without a permit is a felony. Better to get rid of the gun before you're caught with it, ok?"

Maya sorted through the remaining weapons and handed him a wickedly sharp folding knife. "Carry this in your coat."

He slipped it into the inside pocket of his jacket and eyed her as she tucked weapons of all shapes and sizes in every location they'd go, ending by strapping her short staff to her back.

"Won't they search us?" James asked.

"I'm counting on it." She smiled as she adjusted the fit and angle of the staff. "I'll be heavily searched. That's why I'm carrying all these weapons. Chances are good they'll miss one."

"Right."

"You, on the other hand, will probably get off lightly, since you're a man."

"Is that some kind of reverse discrimination?" He cocked his head, a small smile lifting the corners of his mouth. "I think I'm offended."

"Discrimination is discrimination, no matter whom it's perpetuated on," she said lightly. "These people are far more scared of Daughters than they are of a mortal language expert."

"Ah. Ok. I won't take offense then."

"Good." She stood on tiptoe and kissed him. "I'd hate for

you to be offended because I'm a better fighter."

"What can I say? I'm really secure in my manhood."

She patted his cheek. "You should be."

THEY LEFT ELLA'S HOUSE a short time later, James, Maya, and the four Daughters they'd traveled north with all crowded into one vehicle, an SUV outfitted exactly the way the one in Tellowee had been. Maya sat on James' lap, creating just enough room in the backseat for Hawthorne and Brigid. The closer they came to the meeting point, the more his body tensed and the harder his fingers dug into her hips.

Three blocks away from the meet, Alafair stopped the SUV and everybody piled out. She and Greta jogged off in one direction, Hawthorne and Brigid in another, each pair heading toward the teams already in place. As long as Maya, James, and Amelia were in no danger, those teams would hold back. If the situation turned deadly or if an opportunity arose to regain the artifacts, they'd move in with the fury and ferocity of their warrior ancestors.

Maya slipped into the driver's seat, James into the seat beside her. His hands were unsteady on the seatbelt. It slipped out of his fingers and he grimaced. "Sorry."

"Don't be. Everyone's nervous their first time out."

He cut a side-eyed glance at her. "It's that obvious, huh."

She smiled and tucked her hand into his. "Only to someone who's been through it before. Ready?"

He jammed the seatbelt in place and stared out the windshield. "As I'll ever be."

She started the SUV and eased onto the road, driving carefully, her eyes scanning the road ahead and the area around them. They reached the meet a few minutes later. The abandoned warehouse was situated in a block of outdated industrial buildings. Some of the upper windows of the warehouse were broken and the tin roof had a huge dent in it.

Weeds grew through cracks in the pavement and along the sides of the buildings, catching trash as the wind blew through the alleys and along the roads. Half a dozen burly men gathered at the main entrance, guns holstered at their sides.

Maya parked fifty feet away and cut the engine. "Remember, I'm your security. Don't go in if I can't go with you. That's not part of the deal, ok?"

James scrubbed his hands down his thighs. "Sure."

"Follow my lead and try to stay behind me if things go south. Only use your gun if we're separated."

He hunched his shoulders around his ears. "I'd already forgotten about it."

"That's ok," she said, her voice calm and even. "You'll move more naturally if you forget it's there and that'll deflect suspicion away from you. As long as you remember it's there if you need it, you'll be fine."

James inhaled slowly, releasing the breath on a huff. "I'll remember."

"Ideally, you'll never have to use it. That's what I'm here for."

Two men separated from the group and walked toward them, one waving his hand at Maya and James. She opened her door and yelled, "Stand back. We're getting out now."

The men stopped and waited as Maya and James exited the vehicle and retrieved the three cases of securely packed artifacts from the SUV's cargo area. As Maya suspected, she was thoroughly searched with a surprising professionalism. Sometimes, the Shadow Enemy hired mercenaries and thugs to do their dirty work, and they weren't always concerned about how well they did the job.

Nearly all of her weapons were located and confiscated. The only two she had left were a small knife she'd tucked into the front waistband of her jeans and the staff. One man pointed at it. "Boss says we should take everything."

Another man snorted and waved the first man off. "It's just a stick. She can't do nothing with a stick."

Maya smiled sweetly. Oh, the naïveté.

The men were much less thorough with James, catching the knife, but not the gun. Maya trained her eyes on the men, well away from James' ankle and the weapon hidden there. Hopefully, he wouldn't have to use it, and neither would she.

The artifacts were inspected last. Maya refused to hand them over, instead opening each one herself, displaying the artifacts for the man apparently in charge. At last, he nodded and waved toward the door. Two men escorted Maya and James inside, walking to the side and slightly behind them.

The brightness of early morning dimmed inside the warehouse. The poor condition of the exterior belied its sturdiness. Boxes stacked on pallets were located at regular intervals throughout the front half and the concrete floor was clear of dust and debris.

The back half of the warehouse was full of people. Maya counted eighteen men scattered across the room, plus two men standing near two people secured to chairs. The older man was dressed in a fashionably tailored suit, solid black. The younger wore jeans and a t-shirt under a light jacket. Like the other men, the casually dressed one had a handgun holstered at his hip, while the man wearing a suit appeared to be weaponless

The occupants of the chairs captured Maya's attention. As expected, Amelia was one, but what was Dani doing there? Director Upton had issued strict instructions for the younger Daughter to hold back, orders Dani wouldn't have broken without good reason. Had something unexpected happened?

Maya snagged James' elbow and halted twenty-five feet away from Amelia and Dani.

The sharply dressed gentleman stepped forward and held his hands out, palms up. "Welcome, friends. You're right on time."

"We have the artifacts," Maya said. "Release the girl and we'll turn them over."

"What? No time for a little chat?" His mouth twisted into a mocking smile. "Let's at least exchange introductions. I shall go first because, well, it's my party. Lukas Alexiou, and this is my right-hand man, David Winstead."

Maya assumed a bored expression and bit her tongue.

"And you are Maya the Protector, I presume, accompanied by the talented James Terhune. It is a pleasure to meet you both. Mr. Winstead, would you please cut Miss Terhune loose? Careful now."

Winstead pulled a pocket knife out of his jeans and cut the ropes securing Amelia to the chair. She rubbed her wrists and allowed the man to pull her up by the elbow without protest.

Lukas cleared his throat and adjusted the knot in his tie. "Before we begin, I must take a moment to express my deepest condolences to you, Dr. Terhune, on the death of your ex-wife. It was never my intention that she be harmed. The gentleman responsible will be dealt with appropriately, I assure you."

James sucked in a breath, and Maya cringed inwardly.

"Thank you," he said, and Maya sighed. At least he'd stuck to a tactful response.

"I see my men left you your staff, Dr. Bellegarde. I tried to impress upon them the importance of removing all your weapons, but they simply could not believe a woman wielding a stick could be dangerous. Would you care to give a small demonstration for their benefit?"

"Perhaps another time," Maya said.

"Of course. I trust you'll not feel the need to use your staff while under my protection." Lukas' gaze dropped to the cases James held. "And now, for business. Mr. Winstead, would you be so kind?"

Winstead murmured to Amelia and she stepped forward hesitantly, walking slowly across the concrete floor until she stood in front of her father. The teenager partially blocked Maya's view of Alexiou and Winstead. Maya shifted subtly to the side, positioning herself with a clearer path to them.

"Dad," Amelia said, her voice trembling. "Mr. Winstead told me to take two of the cases back to him."

James tensed. "Can't you stay here and let me take them back?"

"No," she whispered. "He told me to do it."

"Give them to her," Maya said softly.

James' lips thinned. "You better know what you're doing, Maya."

He gave Amelia the two cases he held. She gripped the handles tightly, walked slowly toward Dani, and handed the cases to Winstead. He set them on a table set off to the side, then nudged Amelia and murmured to her. She nodded and retraced her steps, taking Maya's case, returning with it to Winstead's side, and giving it to him without a fuss. He caught her arm and held her in place beside the table.

Lukas opened the cases, inspecting the contents carefully, his eyes wide. "Lovely," he murmured. "Thank you for bringing these. They'll make a beautiful addition to my collection." He glanced at Winstead and shut the cases, one by one. "Alas, we seem to have a small problem. This is not the complete set."

Maya stiffened. "That's everything the IECS holds except the skeleton."

"Please do not lie to me, Dr. Bellegarde," Lukas said, a chill underlying the pleasant tone of his voice. "Where is the armband?"

"Sweden," she said promptly. "If you want it, you'll have to negotiate with Dr. Lindberg and his team."

Lukas drew the handgun smoothly from Winstead's holster and pointed it at Amelia's head. James gasped and stepped forward, and Maya grabbed his arm, stopping him cold.

"No more games," Lukas said. "Give me the armband now."

Maya's jaws snapped shut. "I don't have the armband. If I did, I'd give it to you."

"Would you?" Lukas asked softly. "Would you really?

Perhaps with a little more incentive."

He shifted and pointed the gun at James and his finger tightened on the trigger. Winstead jerked Amelia away from Lukas. Maya shoved James with her left hand, hard, and with her right, she unsheathed her staff and threw it in one fluid motion.

The staff sailed through the air, tumbling end over end.

The gun went off, its loud bark echoing in the warehouse.

The bullet hit below her left clavicle, pinching Maya's skin, the force of the impact pivoting her around.

Time slowed. Her gaze fell on James sprawled across the cold concrete floor. He scrambled to his knees, shouting at her. Winstead covered Amelia's head with a large hand and shoved her face into his chest. Dani screamed, her face contorting as she struggled against her bonds.

And Lukas Alexiou, the man of the hour, gaped at Maya, his expression so full of sorrow and shock, it wrenched her heart.

She staggered to the side and blackness crowded around the edge of her vision.

Daughters poured into the warehouse from every entrance, avenging angels hell bent on loosing their fury on the unsuspecting Shadow, and Maya sagged to the floor, energy draining from her in a dizzying rush.

JAMES SCRAMBLED UPRIGHT, stumbling to Maya's side as she staggered sideways. He caught her, eased her onto her hands and knees, and knelt beside her.

"Amelia," she said, her voice strained.

James swiveled around, scanning the room in frantic bursts. Amelia was huddled beneath the table not fifteen feet away, hands over her head. Winstead was hustling Lukas Alexiou toward a rear exit. He stopped and scooped up a screaming Dani, threw her over one broad shoulder, and grabbed Alexiou's elbow, nearly dragging the older man in his wake. Dani kicked and twisted, her screams unintelligible over the sounds of

Daughters flooding into the building, engaging the men Winstead and Alexiou left behind. Winstead smacked her bottom hard, and Dani squawked. A moment later, the three slipped outside and were gone.

James shifted his attention to his daughter. "Amelia!"

She glanced up and began crawling toward him, dragging Maya's staff in one hand and a small box in the other. By the time she reached them, Maya was lying flat on her back, her skin unnaturally pale, her breathing shallow. James pressed his hands against the bullet wound. Blood seeped through his fingers, coating everything in its path in a sticky, red mess.

Amelia reached him and opened the box, a first aid kit. She sifted through it, tossing aside items willy-nilly. She ripped open the packaging on a large piece of gauze, nudged his hand aside, and slapped it over Maya's wound.

Maya moaned. Her eyes fluttered open and she swiped weakly at Amelia's hands. "Need to get up."

James placed a restraining hand on her unwounded shoulder, holding her in place. "We're taking care of you, Maya. Just hold still, ok?"

"Protect you," she wheezed out. Amelia removed one piece of gauze and exchanged it for another, pushing firmly against the wound. Maya grimaced and gritted her teeth. "Let me up."

"You're bleeding too much," he said flatly. "There's a hole in your shoulder, and I don't care what you say, I'm not letting you get up."

"Right arm...still good."

Amelia sat back abruptly, her young face nearly as colorless as Maya's. "We're out of gauze and she's still bleeding."

"Here." James yanked his jacket off, then his t-shirt, the cool dampness of the warehouse chill against his bare skin. He folded the t-shirt in a rough square and handed it to Amelia. "Use this. If that doesn't work, I'll look for something else."

Amelia glanced over his shoulder and squealed, and James whirled around. One of Alexiou's goons was heading their way, eyebrows lowered, his mouth a thin line. James' heart dropped like a lead weight into his stomach. They were defenseless with Maya wounded and flat on her back.

The gun. He mentally smacked himself in the forehead and fumbled with the ankle holster, trying to remember Maya's instructions as he pulled the tiny gun out from under his pants leg.

"Aim small, miss small," James muttered. He aimed and pulled the trigger, and pulled. The goon was almost on top of them and closing fast. James squeezed harder, praying the gun would go off in time. After a small eternity, it fired, recoiling against his hand with a loud bang. The goon staggered sideways and blood spread across his torso in a dark patch. James squeezed the trigger again. Almost immediately, it went off, the sharp report carrying across the warehouse.

The goon dropped to the floor with a thud. Behind him, another goon was running toward them. James fired the tiny gun and missed. Damn. The gun had a really short range. He'd forgotten all about that.

"Small gun, small range," he mumbled, then laughed shakily. His life was becoming a litany of catch phrases for handling weapons.

Maya coughed, drawing his attention away from the second goon. "Get out."

"I'm not leaving you here, Maya."

"Go," she insisted.

"I'm staying here until we can move you. You have to trust me."

"Do," she said, and passed out.

Pain exploded through James' jaw and he dropped the gun. The momentum of a punch carried him backwards across Maya's body, jostling Amelia in the process.

For the love of God. They were in the middle of a mini-war zone. How could he have forgotten that other goon?

Amelia scrambled for the staff with bloody hands while the

goon hoisted James up by two beefy fists clasped in a punishing grip around his upper arms. She swung the staff like a baseball bat, connecting with the goon's back. The goon loosened his hold on James. She arched back for another swing, and James wiggled, struggling to get free. She swung again, solidly connecting with the goon's back. He dropped James and rounded on Amelia. She shuffled slowly backward, staff cocked on her shoulder, her mouth set in a hard line.

James scrambled along the ground for the gun, both eyes fixed on Amelia. Where was it, where was it? His hand connected with metal and the gun skidded sideways. Damn it. He glanced down, swiped it up, and launched himself across Maya's prone form, jabbing the gun into the other man's back. The goon froze in mid-reach. Amelia swung, hitting the hefty man in the jaw. His head popped around and he swayed. James shoved his shoulder into the goon's side, and the man fell, thumping into the concrete floor.

James braced his hands on his knees. "Good swing, honey. Maybe you should try out for softball next year."

Amelia wheezed out a breath and her eyes went wide. "Dad, geez."

"It's just a suggestion." He held out his hand. "Give me the staff. I'll hold off the goon squad while you take care of Maya."

He laid the gun on the floor beside Amelia as she leaned over Maya, then stood guard over the two of them with the staff cocked back over his shoulder in a two-handed grip.

Bodies littered the floor, more than James remembered seeing as they walked in. Most were men, though a few Daughters had fallen. At least a dozen conflicts were still raging through the warehouse. Very few of the men had their guns out. James studied them as he turned in slow circles. Empty holsters, guns well out of reach. Right. They'd been disarmed.

A cold chill slithered down his spine. He swung around and glimpsed a woman he'd never seen before standing beside the table. She was small and delicate. Her hair hung past her shoulders in a straight, black waterfall. She wore a knee-length emerald lamé jacket over an incredibly short black sheath paired with black, thigh-high boots. Her hands gently stroked the artifacts in the still-open cases. She closed one of the cases and picked it up, then pivoted toward the back entrance.

"Hey!" he said.

She stopped and peered over her shoulder, a small smile on her beautiful mouth. She blew him a kiss, and in two blinks, she was gone.

James dropped his guard and stared at the spot where she'd been. She couldn't have just disappeared. Maybe he was hallucinating. He rubbed his eyes with the heel of one palm and glanced around. Maya on the floor, Amelia hovering over her, Daughters gleefully hacking at men with staffs and assorted weaponry. Nope, not hallucinating, yet only two cases lay on the table.

Another goon broke free from a Daughter and loped toward them. James swung the staff in a circle, testing its weight. Time to make good on his promise to Maya.

EIGHTEEN

P EOPLE BUZZED in and out of the waiting room, doctors and nurses, police officers, those waiting on loved ones. James, Amelia, and several Daughters huddled together out of the way, waiting for Maya to come out of surgery. They'd brought her to the Emergency Room on the pretext that she'd been mugged. Two officers had come by not long after and taken statements. James had given them some totally made up malarkey. Nobody would've believed the truth anyway.

And now they waited as a surgeon attempted to remove the bullet where it had lodged against Maya's shoulder blade.

Daughters trickled in and out of the waiting room, some sporting bruises and cuts, others bandages or stitches. James had long ago lost track of their names. One brought James coffee and Amelia juice, another brought sandwiches, still another brought clean clothes. They'd both been grateful, especially Amelia. Maya's blood had soaked through her pants and part of her t-shirt, and had nearly dried by the time they made it to the ER.

A number of Daughters also brought updates. Lukas Alexiou and his man, Winstead, had escaped with Dani to parts unknown. A team had been sent after them, primarily to recover Dani. Director Upton had been updated and was apparently already on her way to New York. Two cases of artifacts had been recovered at the warehouse and securely stored in an unknown location.

James didn't mention the woman in the green coat. He still wasn't sure he hadn't imagined her, but if he hadn't, the director was probably the first person who needed to know about her.

They'd been waiting two hours when a Daughter walked in and sat down beside James. She was athletically slender with auburn hair and hazel-green eyes, and was dressed as many of the other Daughters were in comfortable casual clothing. "Hello."

God. Another Daughter to remember. "Hi."

"I'm Annette. You must be James."

James nodded, hitching his thumb at his daughter. "Amelia."

"Nice to meet you.'

"Likewise."

Slow humor spread across her oval face. "You don't know who I am."

"Ah, no. So many people have come in and out."

She snickered. "She must not've told you. I'm Maya's eldest daughter."

"Her eldest..." James heart sank into his stomach. Maya had *promised* not to hold anything else back from him. "Just how many of you are there?"

"Just me and Dee."

"Are you sure? Because Maya's surprises keep popping out of the damn closet with surprising regularity."

Annette patted his arm. "She probably hasn't had time to explain everything yet."

James inhaled sharply and rubbed his forehead. "Yeah, probably. A lot's happened over the last few days."

They passed the hours chatting, waiting for an update on Maya's progress through surgery, post-op, and then in recovery, no visitors allowed. James called his family, letting them know Amelia was safe. Annette took a quick break to update Dierdre on Maya's condition. Amelia fell asleep, curled into a chair beside James with her head propped on his shoulder. A familiar looking Daughter (Greta maybe?) pulled out a deck of cards and started a game of no-stakes poker with several others.

Talking with Annette and watching the impromptu card game absorbed James' attention, pushing out the day's events. Amelia's tear-stained face as she took the cases of artifacts from him. Dani tied to a chair, helpless. Maya shoving him out of the way and taking a bullet for him, then lying in a pool of her own blood.

So much blood.

His stomach twisted into a sick knot. She'd come so close to dying. He was sure, or as sure as he was of anything, that the only thing separating Maya from death was the curse.

The surgeon pushed his way through the waiting crowd and discussed Maya's prognosis with them. Annette, as her official next of kin, took the lead, though she included James and Amelia in the conversation. The surgeon emphasized Maya's needed for recovery time. A hysterical laugh bubbled up from James' gut. Maya was immortal. She had all the time she needed.

That night, she slipped into a coma. The days passed slowly and her wound began to heal, but she didn't wake up. James and Amelia stayed at the hospital during the day, leaving only to eat, sleep, clean up, and pass regular updates along to Dierdre. They took turns reading to Maya or talked softly in the waiting room when the hospital staff chased them out of her room. Annette slipped in and out frequently, as often as duty allowed. Getting to know her had made their wait slightly more bearable.

A rotating team of Daughters stayed with James and Amelia, acting as security while another team protected Maya. Director Upton had expressed her deep concern that James and Amelia were vulnerable, and he'd put up no resistance to the security detail. He didn't think he could stand having Amelia taken again.

A week after Maya had been shot, James and Amelia sat at her bedside, Amelia reading, James watching her. She'd closed herself off since the kidnapping. That couldn't be good. Didn't she need to talk about it, maybe start coming to terms with what had happened with her mom and everything else?

He crossed his arms over his chest and cleared his throat. "Can we talk?"

Amelia glanced up, smiling. "Sure. What's up?"

"I thought maybe we could talk about your mom."

Her smile faded. She marked her place in the book and tucked it into her lap. "Can't we talk about something else?"

"I know it's hard, sweetheart." He reached across Maya's body, holding his hand out to her. "I know you miss her. It's not good to bottle it all up inside."

"I just don't wanna talk about it. I just don't..." She sniffed and turned away. "I can't."

He sighed and withdrew his hand. "Ok. I'm here if you need me, if you want to talk. I'll listen."

She nodded and closed her eyes. "Can I finish my book now?"

"Sure, sweetheart."

He slumped into his chair and scrubbed a hand over his nape. Maybe she just needed more time. Maybe when they had Linda's funeral, Amelia would gain some kind of closure or something, or maybe being back in Tellowee with Dierdre and her new friends would help. At least she knew he was there for her, and that's the only way he could figure out to help her.

One day slipped into the next with no real change in Maya's condition. The hope James held that she'd wake up began to fade. Sitting at her bedside gave him too much time to think, about the things she'd told him, about that day at the warehouse. Was there anything he could've done differently? If he'd known how to fight, would Maya have pushed him out of the way and taken a bullet for him or would he be the one lying there? If he'd accepted everything she'd told him, the People, the curse, her own immortality, would that have changed the outcome?

Two weeks after Maya's injury, Director Upton had Maya transferred to a hospital near the IECS under the care of a doctor with a broad experience in the People's peculiar physiology.

James, Amelia, and Annette accompanied Maya back, along with a small staff of nurses and the cadre of Daughters acting as security.

As soon as the IECS' private plane touched down in Gainesville's airfield, James relaxed. They were almost home. Here, he and Amelia could rebuild their lives in a safe environment where nobody could get to them, and here, Maya would find the help she needed. At least, he hoped she would.

REBECCA SAT behind her desk, waiting for the arrival of Dani's FBI agent. The past few weeks had been an uproar of activity and uncomfortable revelations. Important artifacts had been found and then stolen. The Shadow Enemy had resurfaced, headed by a man about whom the People knew very little. And a traitor lay in their midst.

The latter had occupied Rebecca's thoughts through an uncounted number of sleepless nights, draining her energy and sapping her strength. Still, she had to find a way to deal with those events and the ones yet to come. Through it all, the People must survive. That had always been her driving concern.

Her secretary buzzed with the message that David Winstead had arrived. Rebecca studied him as he entered, the broad shoulders and tall frame, the no-nonsense haircut, the stony expression. He looked like a thug, moved like a dancer, and, from what she could tell, had the strategic skills of a chess grandmaster.

A smile touched her mouth. Yes, he would do nicely.

"Mr. Winstead." Rebecca stood and held out her hand, measuring his grip as he shook it. "Welcome to the IECS. I trust you had a pleasant trip."

"Pleasant enough," he said, his voice low and rough.

"Please, won't you sit?" She perched on the edge of her chair. "I appreciate your coming on such short notice and breaking your former engagements to assist us."

He dropped into a chair in front of her desk. "Not like I had a choice."

"Hopefully, our business won't take much of your time. I presume you're still undercover with Alexiou?" He nodded once, and she continued. "I'm curious. What excuse did you give him for coming here?"

"Told him I was coming after the girl." He shrugged and one corner of his mouth tilted up in a half smile. "Alexiou has a soft spot for women. Took a shine to Dani in particular."

Rebecca tamped down her concern. Having the leader of the Shadow Enemy *take a shine* to a Daughter could never be good.

A ruckus sounded outside her door, and Rebecca sighed. Voices raised in anger, something banged against the wall, and the doors to her office flew open, revealing a furious Dani. Her gaze zeroed in on Dave and she froze. "You low-down steaming pile of goat feces."

"Dani!" Rebecca said. "Mr. Winstead is a guest here."

Dani inhaled a long, slow breath and her hands unclenched. Her green eyes were bright, though, and bored holes into the hapless agent's broad shoulders.

"Please have a seat, Dani. We have much work to do."

Dani stalked to a chair and flopped into it, her glare steady. Rebecca bit back a sigh. At least her youngest hadn't killed the poor man. What a public relations nightmare that would be, and it would forever ruin the relationship Rebecca had carefully cultivated with the director of the FBI.

She flattened her palms on the surface of her desk. "I have several reports from Daughters who were at the warehouse last week during the exchange. Only two cases of artifacts were recovered. Mr. Winstead, by any chance is the third case in Alexiou's possession?"

"No, ma'am," he said flatly. "I left all three cases on the table when I took Dani and Lukas out of harm's way."

"I would've been better off if you'd left me there, you

Neanderthal," Dani hissed.

Rebecca sighed. "Dani, please."

"He threw me over his shoulder and spanked me!"

Rebecca pursed her lips, hiding a smile.

"And then he let me 'escape' through a sewer. It ruined my favorite pair of boots." She rounded on Dave. "You'll be paying for those, Ape Man."

Dave's stony expression remained unchanged.

Dani slouched into her chair, her pretty face set in a scowl. "My hair still smells like sewage."

And that was the sticking point. Dani could be called many things, but vain she was not, except when it came to her hair. Rebecca eyed the lustrous, golden curls. If it were her, she'd be upset about the smell, too. That didn't help the situation they were in now, though.

"Let bygones be bygones, daughter. We need to focus on tracking down the missing artifacts." Again. Would they never be able to hold all of them in one place? "Now, several Daughters reported seeing a woman at the warehouse during the fight. One Daughter thought this woman took the case."

"No one recognized her?" Dani asked, her voice almost calm.

"Unfortunately, no. I was hoping Alexiou had electronic surveillance installed in the warehouse."

Dave nodded. "He does. Shouldn't be hard to gain access."

"Thank you. All I ask is that you not mention our involvement in your investigation."

"If I can. Alexiou wants the artifacts as much as you do. Pretty sure he'll do what he has to to get them back."

"Of course," Rebecca said. "Any idea why?"

He lifted one shoulder in a quick shrug. "Something about the Prophecy of Light."

Rebecca sucked in a breath. "What did he say about it?"

"He was never really coherent when he talked about the prophecy," Dave admitted. "Kept mentioning a woman, though, and I got the feeling she was somehow tied to it."

"Someone he loved who betrayed him." Dani shot a glare in Dave's direction. "Alexiou talked about that after Mr. Caveman here drugged me and tied me to a chair. Sadly, I now know how it feels to be betrayed."

"It was duct tape," Dave said evenly, "and I was protecting you."

"Do I look like I need your protection?" Dani snapped.

"As a matter of fact..."

Rebecca tapped one palm against the top of her desk. "Children, could we please stay on task?"

"Sorry, Maetyrm," Dani muttered. "Alexiou got a little weird about this woman. I couldn't figure out who he was talking about, except that he believed she was a Daughter."

"Did he ever mention a name?" Rebecca asked.

Dave leaned forward and braced his forearms on his thighs. "No, never, but he dreamed about her a lot. Sometimes, he'd wake up screaming in the middle of the night, but he never called out a name, that I know."

Rebecca sighed. "A name would be incredibly helpful."

"To be honest, I'm not sure he ever met this woman in real life. Until the artifacts were found in Sweden, I thought she was all in his head."

"I'd appreciate it if you'd pass any additional information you learn on this woman, her relationship to Alexiou, and the Prophecy of Light back to me."

"If I can," he said.

"Good. Now, I would very much like it if the two of you could put aside your differences long enough to track down the missing case of artifacts. Start with the woman in the warehouse. The resources of the IECS and the People are at your disposal."

Rebecca stood, signaling the end of the meeting. Dani and Dave rose as well.

"Got a few things to clear up before we start," he said.

"If you could stay here a day or so before you clear those

‌‍‍‌‌

things up, I'd consider it a personal favor," Rebecca said. "We have a great deal of background material available that may assist with your efforts to recover the artifacts. Dani will fill you in. And, of course, my husband and I would enjoy having you over for dinner tonight, if you have the time."

"Appreciate the offer," he said. "If you'll excuse me, I need to make a phone call."

"Of course."

He nodded to Dani and left. As soon as the door swung shut behind him, Rebecca came around the desk and gathered Dani in a tight hug. "I was so worried about you, daughter."

"I was ok. The big lug really was trying to protect me, more's the pity."

"Don't be so hard on him, then."

"Oh, don't worry. He can take it."

They chatted for a few moments more, as much so that Rebecca could take the time to assess Dani's condition as anything. Dani wasn't her child by birth, but the younger Daughter was still hers in all the ways that mattered. A mother's worries never ended, not when a child was placed in her care, and not when that child was a woman fully grown.

Rebecca cupped Dani's shoulders. "Don't forget dinner tonight, darling. The boys will be so excited to see you."

"We'll be there."

"Try to be polite to Mr. Winstead in front of Robert. Otherwise, he'll get ideas and you'll never hear the end of it."

Dani rolled her eyes skyward. "Don't I know it."

"Would you rather take Mr. Winstead to the Archives or the museum to fill him in?"

"The museum. He'll like all the weapons. They're about his speed."

"Dani," Rebecca chided gently. "He's our best lead on the artifacts. Try to be nice to him."

"All right," Dani said, her mouth twisted into something between a smile and a grimace.

"Oh, and darling, if he betrays the People, don't hesitate to do what must be done."

Dani's expression hardened. "Of course, Maetyrm."

Rebecca shooed her daughter out, then put her hand on her abdomen over a growing knot of unease. Something unpleasant was about to happen, something holding the potential to cause a great deal of harm. She was certain the days ahead would be brutally unkind to her daughter, and equally certain there was nothing anyone could do to stop it.

MAYA'S TRANSFER between hospitals went off like clockwork. The new hospital, located half an hour outside of Tellowee, was staffed with medical personnel who understood the slightly different physiologies of immortal Daughters. Unfortunately, they were of little help.

Ethan Phillips, a well-built doctor in his early thirties with auburn hair and light green eyes, took over Maya's care. He introduced himself to James as a member of the People, a son of a Daughter whose curse had been broken when she'd fallen in love with Ethan's father. The young doctor relayed the information as casually as most stated their name, unknowingly corroborating Maya's story. James tucked the knowledge and Ethan's ease with it away for future reference.

On the third day after Maya's arrival, Ethan tracked James down and asked him to step outside Maya's room for a brief update. "There's really nothing physiological keeping Maya in a coma. The bullet caused relatively little damage and the wound is healing rapidly."

James sighed and scrubbed a weary hand over his face. "So, what's keeping her in a coma if not her injuries?"

"There are a few possibilities. Do you mind if I ask you a personal question?"

"Sure."

"How deep is your relationship with Maya?"

Heat rushed into James' cheeks. "Er, pretty deep."

"Hmm." Ethan cleared his throat and tapped Maya's chart against his thigh. "It's possible your relationship with her somehow triggered her change from immortal to mortal."

"She's broken the curse?"

"Maybe," Ethan hedged. "The curse and everything associated with it is mystical in nature, not physiological, including an individual's removal from the curse's influence. If the curse is a factor here, there's nothing medical we can do for Maya except keep her comfortable and hope for the best."

The sit-and-wait policy did not a thing to ease James' concern for Maya, but his conversation with Dr. Phillips did give him a lot to think over. If Maya had somehow broken the curse, did that mean she trusted him or maybe even that she loved him?

He tried not to get his hopes up, but the thought eased some of his doubts about their relationship.

Amelia settled in at the on-campus school better than James could've hoped, thanks in large part to Dierdre's influence. He took the two of them shopping to replace the clothes Amelia had left behind in Connecticut, thrilling them no end in spite of the gloom of Linda's death and the lingering concern over Maya. As soon as the police cleared Linda's house from investigation as a crime scene, James planned to have a moving company go through it and store everything until he and Amelia found a more permanent home. He'd never allow her to go through that house again, not after she'd watched her mother die there.

The police were still investigating Linda's murder and pressing James for any information he could give. Director Upton had advised him not to reveal his knowledge of the killer's identity and whereabouts. Doing so would focus attention unnecessarily on James. The police would want to know how he knew who Linda's killer was, potentially opening up a can of worms he just didn't have the energy to deal with, not then, maybe not ever, so he held his tongue. When Linda's body was released, he and Amelia would go back to Connecticut for the funeral, but that might not be for a long while.

After Maya's first week at the new hospital, Annette returned to work, promising to come back as soon as Maya woke up, and as often before then as she could manage. She kissed James on the cheek and told him how glad she was her mother had someone so good in her life. He hadn't known what to say to that.

With Annette gone, he, Amelia, and Dierdre fell into a routine. While the girls were in school, James worked at Maya's bedside, occasionally taking breaks to talk to her about his progress. The girls came to the hospital once school was out, accompanied by a protective escort. After a good visit, he drove them to his on-campus apartment, fed them supper, and helped with homework.

As often as not, Dierdre spent the night, sharing Amelia's bed. The two of them talked until they fell asleep, and when James checked, they were usually facing one another in the double bed, holding hands as if they needed the comfort even in sleep. James spoke with Director Upton and Dierdre's dorm mother about Dierdre's continual presence. Both women assured him that she was far better off in his and Amelia's company than alone while Maya was in the hospital.

Everybody seemed so accepting of his role in Maya's life, as if when she woke up, everything would magically be ok between them. Even he was beginning to believe it.

The girls settled in, his work on the artifacts progressed to the point of near-completion, and Maya remained in a coma. Summer turned to fall. The nights grew chilly enough for coats and tourists came out in droves on the weekends to see the turning leaves.

One night three weeks after their return to Georgia, while James was making supper and listening with half his attention to Amelia and Dierdre gossip about boys, Dr. Phillips called. Maya had come of the coma and was asking for them.

NINETEEN

MAYA SHIFTED on the hospital bed. She was groggy and stiff, and her shoulder twinged every time she moved. It had nearly healed while she was unconscious, so Doc Phillips said, but she was still oddly aware of it.

As soon as she'd regained consciousness and buzzed a nurse, he'd slipped into her room and examined her from head to toe. She'd been lucky the bullet had hit as high as it had, he'd said. A little lower and closer to the center of her body and it would've punctured a lung. A hit in the other direction would've shattered her arm socket. She could've lost the use of her arm or, worse, the arm itself.

"So I'm lucky to be in one piece," she'd murmured, earning a sharp glance and a sharper retort.

"You're lucky somebody was there to stop the flow of blood and watch over you," he'd said. "A few more minutes and you would've died."

Maya's eyes slid shut. The curse didn't really grant immortality. It just made Daughters really hard to kill. That hardiness aside, when somebody tried to kill you and kept trying, sooner or later, it would catch. She'd trusted James to watch over her when she was too weak to do it herself, trusted him to do what he had to in order to protect him and her and Amelia. For the first time in her life, it had felt right trusting a man. Her faith had apparently been well placed.

The door to her room burst open and Dierdre tumbled inside, followed closely by Amelia and James. Maya grinned. Here they were. She held out her arms and caught Dierdre as she leapt onto the bed, accepted a prim hug from Amelia, and finally, James' kiss on her forehead.

He settled into a worn chair at the side of the bed. "It's about time you joined us."

Dierdre slid off Maya and sat on the side of her bed. "Yeah, Mom. You need to come home real quick. Dr. T. is a terrible cook. He's about starved us to death."

Amelia hid a giggle behind her hand and James sputtered out an aggrieved, "I am not."

They filled her in on the events of the past few weeks. Amelia had enrolled in Tellowee's high school one grade behind Dierdre and was taking her first ever martial arts class.

Maya cut a side-eyed glance at James. How could she tell him that Amelia learning how to defend herself wouldn't have kept her from being kidnapped? He might change his mind, and Amelia really *did* need to learn defensive skills, at the very least. So did he, something she'd take care of as soon as she was able-bodied.

Dierdre shared the news that she wasn't playing volleyball. "Mom, it's, like, ninth grade. I've got three more years to play. Besides," she said, her eyes wide, "you needed me more."

Maya squeezed her hand. "My sweet Squiggles."

James propped an elbow on the chair's arm and rubbed a finger over his smile. He was quiet while the girls rambled about everything from shopping to school to boys, heavy on the boys. They'd have to talk soon. She had so much to tell him, but not here. Not in front of the girls.

The doctor kept her overnight for observation, then released her into James' care with the warning to take it easy and report back if she had any problems.

James bypassed her house and took her straight to his

apartment, settling her onto the couch with the solicitude of someone looking after the terminally ill. After the third time he asked if she needed anything, she finally snapped. "I'm fine, James, really. Please quit hovering."

He slumped onto the sofa beside her and took her hand in his, chafing warmth into her skin. "You were in a coma for more than a month. I think I can be forgiven for hovering."

Maya rested her head on his shoulder. "You can stop now. I'll be fine."

"Promise?"

"Yes."

Maya closed her eyes, content to rest on the sofa beside him. The injury had sapped her strength more than she'd expected it to.

James brushed his cheek across the top of her hair. "Dr. Phillips said you might be mortal now. Any chance you might've broken the curse?"

Maya sighed and buried her face in his throat. "When I was lying there, after Alexiou shot me, I tried so hard to get up and protect you and Amelia."

"I know, sweetheart. Shh. Don't think about that now."

"No, it's... You leaned over me and asked me to trust you, and I realized right then that I did. I trusted you, so I stopped fighting and I believed in you, and it was like this huge weight lifted off of me." She clutched his hand, holding him to her, allowing his strength to bolster her own. "I've never felt that free before."

"And you think that was the curse breaking?"

"Maybe," she said softly. "Maybe I'm scared of hoping too hard."

"Maybe you shouldn't be so afraid of what hope can do." He cupped her jaw and tilted her face toward his, his eyes soft and warm. "I love you, so much. I want to try to work things out with you."

"Ok."

"Just ok?"

She smiled and draped her legs over his lap and curled her fingers into the smooth cotton of his shirt. His arm around her back was hard and strong and comforting. Three hundred years she'd waited to find him, or nearly so, and now, here he was at last. "Yup, just ok."

"Not, 'Of course, James, I'm madly in love with you and want to be with you forever'?"

"Sure."

"Sure, what?"

Her smile widened into a grin. "Sure, I'm madly in love with you."

"Really?"

"Really."

"What about the forever part?"

"If you insist," she teased.

He kissed her then, slowly and gently and with much more patience than she probably deserved, and she kissed him back, showing him in the best way she could how much he meant to her. After, she told him about Annette and about Dierdre's father, and about her parents.

He hugged her close, surrounding her with his gentleness. "Dierdre said you watched them die."

"I was very young, maybe four or five. It's hard to remember that far back."

"It's ok." He cleared his throat, and when he spoke again, his voice was softer, hesitant. "Ah, I just realized I don't even know how old you are."

"Two hundred and ninety seven on my last birthday. I was born in 1716 in New Orleans."

"Wow. You're a real cradle robber."

She laughed. Her shoulder twinged and she winced. Being mortal wasn't all it was cracked up to be.

James smoothed his hand up and down her arm. "What happened to your parents?"

"My mother was a young Daughter out on her first real mission alone. She was sent to investigate my father, a Frenchman in New Orleans on business. He was suspected of aiding our enemy."

"The Shadow Enemy?"

"Right. Mámá entered his household as a slave. She was a mulatress, so it wasn't hard for her to blend in, but she was educated and beautiful and charming. From what I've pieced together of that part of her life, it was relatively easy for her to gain Pápá's trust. He took her as his mistress and she became pregnant."

"With you."

Maya nodded. "They fell in love. The Shadow Enemy discovered their liaison and came after them in the middle of the night."

"Dierdre said the servants protected you?"

"They did. Some of them died trying to smuggle me out, but not before I watched my parents being killed. I can still remember my mother drawing a sword and challenging her attackers even as they cut her down."

"That's an awful thing for a young girl to have to live with."

It was, but it wasn't the most horrible story she'd ever heard. Other Daughters had pasts so tragic, none dared speak on them. And at least Maya had survived to pass down what little she knew of her mother to her own children, preserving the memory for generations to come. "It's the price we pay for our heritage."

"I'm sorry."

His words surprised her. "Why?"

"Because you've had to live with this for so long."

She pressed a kiss to his cheek, lingering with her lips against his skin, repaying a measure of his kindness. "There's nothing anybody could've done to change that."

"I know." He threaded his fingers through hers and stroked his thumb across her skin. "But there might be a way to stop this war between the People and the Shadow Enemy."

"What?" She jerked upright and stared at him. "How?"

"Labor Day morning, when I raced out of here so early. Do you remember?"

Maya narrowed her eyes. "I was enjoying that early morning cuddle before you woke me up."

He kissed her forehead. "That morning, I had an epiphany of sorts that's helped me translate the remainder of the Sandby borg texts."

She opened her mouth, and he touched his finger to her lips, silencing her.

"Even the Linear A tablet," he continued. "Sanctuary. That was the symbol I needed. It brought everything else into context, and from there, it was just a matter of time until I figured all of it out."

Her breath whooshed out of her. "Sanctuary as in where the Seven Sisters sought refuge?"

He pressed his lips together. "I think so."

"Does Director Upton know?"

"I've told her some, but not all," he admitted. "I wanted to share this with you first."

"James," she chided. "She needs to know this."

"She knows enough to get started," he assured her. "But there's more."

"I love it when you say that."

He grinned and brushed the tip of his nose across hers. "The rest of the tablet contained a prophecy. I've been studying the fragments in the museum, about the origin myth? And I think the Linear A tablet might contain the Lost Prophecy."

She jumped into his lap, ignoring the pain in her shoulder. "You are a language god."

She kissed him soundly and coaxed him into taking her to bed, and showered him with enough affection to last him a lifetime.

SUPPER THAT NIGHT was a madhouse. Amelia and Dierdre insisted on cooking. The menu was a little creative and they talked over each other as they turned the efficiency kitchen into a disaster area.

James supervised from the relative safety of the table. It was good to see Amelia regaining some of her natural effervescence, though she refused to talk about her ordeal. It had been a month since her mother's death and her own kidnapping. How long did it take for somebody to heal from that kind of trauma? He slouched into the hard backed chair and scowled. Surely healing meant talking about it, at least a little.

A few minutes after the four of them sat down to eat, Maya said, "I called Director Upton earlier and made an appointment for us to see her in the morning so we can discuss the rest of your work."

James passed a plate of lopsided pancakes to Amelia. "What time?"

"As soon as the girls get off to school. I hope that's not too early."

"Not a bit. Besides, it's nice to start the day with positive news for a change."

Dierdre bit her lower lip and gazed at him with wide, hope-filled eyes. "What kind of news, Dr. T.?"

Maya winked at him. "James is nearly finished working with some documents, the ones he came here to translate and study. He thinks he's found a reference to the Lost Prophecy."

Dierdre gaped. "No way!"

Amelia's fork clattered to her plate and her already-pale skin whitened. "The Prophecy of Light?"

James and Maya exchanged a glance. "How did you know about that, honey?" James asked.

"Mr. Alexiou talked about it when he kidnapped me. Well, he didn't kidnap me personally but, you know, after."

Maya laid a comforting hand on Amelia's arm. "At the warehouse?"

"Yeah, then," Amelia said. "He was kinda crazy, but he wasn't mean to me or anything, except for, you know, tying me up and stuff. And even then, he got mad about Mom..." Tears welled up in her eyes. She sniffed them back and glanced down at her plate. "He wanted me to hurt the man who killed Mom."

A slow heat burned through James' veins. Goddamn Alexiou. He'd managed to pack a lot of harm into a few days. James inhaled a sharp breath and managed a calmly spoken, "What did you do?"

A tear slipped down Amelia's cheek. "I told him no, then Dani said she'd do it, and Mr. Alexiou laughed and told her he couldn't untie her."

"What did he say about the Prophecy, Amelia?" Maya asked gently. "Do you remember?"

"I don't remember all of it. I was really scared, you know?" Amelia shifted toward him, her brows furrowed, and grasped James' hand. Her fingers dug into his skin, biting through flesh into bone. "But he went on and on about it. Something about loving somebody for a long time and how she betrayed him, but he still loved her, and how they'd be together again."

James cupped her hand. "Did he say who?"

"No. He just said he'd been looking for the Prophecy and something about his dad. I think something bad happened. You know, to make Mr. Alexiou crazy."

"Why didn't you tell me this before?"

"I didn't want you to be mad at me." Amelia's face crumpled and a sob escaped her throat. "Mom was trying to protect me when that guy killed her. It was my fault she died."

"No, honey." James rose and pulled her into a hug. "It's not your fault. You had nothing to do with that, ok?"

Maya and Dierdre slipped out of the room, tears trickling down Dierdre's furious face. She and Amelia had grown so close, and from Dierdre's expression, it appeared she'd taken Amelia under her protective wing, much the way her mother had done with him.

He held Amelia through a storm of tears and quiet sobs, murmuring softly to her, reassuring her that everything would be ok, even if it never was again. How could it be when her mother was gone? Linda might not have been the best parent when it came to remembering the little things, but she'd loved Amelia so much. She'd been a good mother, and he hated that Amelia had lost her, that Linda's life had been wasted on the whim of a madman.

Amelia's tears wound down. James dried her tears and, when he was sure she was ok, encouraged her to get ready for bed. As soon as she'd scooted off toward the safety of Dierdre's friendship, he began cleaning dishes off the table. Maya joined him a few minutes later.

"Dierdre ok?" he asked.

"Yes. Amelia?"

"She will be." Somehow, some way, his daughter would be fine, no matter what he had to do to help her get to that point.

Maya helped him load the dishwasher, and after, he sent her off to rest on the couch while he finished. Somehow, the girls had managed to strew flour from one end of the little kitchenette to the other, and had dirtied what looked like every pot, pan, and cooking utensil while they were at it.

James scowled at a gooey egg beater and dunked it under running water. He'd been lumping Dierdre with Amelia as if she weren't just his daughter's friend and the child of his lover, but part of his family. He and Maya hadn't quite settled things that afternoon, but they would, and soon. He loved Maya and he knew she loved him, too, but they couldn't keep playing at being together. If they were going to act like a family, they should *be* a family.

He was just old-fashioned enough to want to be married to the woman sleeping in his bed while his daughter was under the same roof. If he had his way, that's exactly where Maya would be later on that night, and exactly where he wanted her to be for the rest of their lives.

He stuffed the last dirty dish into the dishwasher, turned it on, and padded into the living area. Maya was curled up on the couch fast asleep, her face half buried in the pillow. She'd overdone it. Hadn't he told her to take it easy for a while?

He scrubbed a hand over his hair, ruffling it into an untidy mess. Ok, there were only two beds in the apartment. The girls were in one, and it might be manly, but he wasn't sleeping on the couch, not on Maya's first night home. He strode into his bedroom and turned down the covers on his bed, then crept into the living room and carried her through the apartment. After everything they'd been through, he couldn't stand not having her near. Tomorrow they'd settle the issue of family, and soon, maybe they'd be one.

THE NEXT MORNING, Maya and James dropped Dierdre and Amelia off at school. Maya stared through the passenger's side window of James' car, following their progress through the school grounds as they mingled with their friends and disappeared into the school's entrance.

James had insisted on driving, though the entire IECS campus was scarcely a mile across. Hardly a difficult walk on a bad day, let alone a bright, fall morning like that one. Maya hadn't argued nearly as hard as she should've. She was still a little weak and her shoulder wasn't healing nearly as quickly as she was used to her body healing. She sighed and rested her forehead on the window. Maybe it would never heal properly, but it was a small price to pay, all things considered.

"She'll be ok, won't she?" James asked.

"She will be, once she's had time to adjust." Maya shifted in the seat, facing him. "Kids are more resilient than we give them credit for being."

"Yeah, I guess." He glanced away and ruffled his fingers through the hair at his nape. "Are we in a hurry?"

"We don't have a set time we need to see the director, if

that's what you mean. Why?"

His mouth thinned. "This isn't how I wanted to do this."

"Do what?"

"Ask you to marry me. We never really got around to that yesterday."

"Hmm."

"I mean, I thought I might ask you to dinner and give you a ring or something." He huffed out a short laugh and shook his head. "Lame, I know, but it's traditional, right? But here we are in a car watching our daughters walk to school together and..."

Maya laid a hand gently on his forearm. "Here's fine, especially if you'll just go ahead and ask."

"Yeah?" A slow grin curled the corners of his mouth and crinkled the corners of his eyes into a smile. "I love you. Marry me."

Her own lips twitched into a grin. "Ok. When?"

"Today would be great, maybe tomorrow. A week, tops."

She laughed and kissed him, savoring the slow press of his mouth against hers, the warmth of his skin, the quiet love they'd found. Her heart turned over and something beautiful and light bubbled through her, spilling over into their kiss.

"Mmm." She pulled back, breaking their embrace before they got carried away. "Director Upton's waiting."

He groaned. "You had to remind me."

He started the car and eased into the road, and a few minutes later, parked outside the building housing the director's office. Rebecca was waiting for them and sat quietly through James' update on his recent findings, her hand palm down on the report he'd given her, covering his translation of the Prophecy of Light.

"Thank you, Dr. Terhune," she said. "I hope you'll consider continuing your work with the IECS."

He leaned back in his chair and glanced at Maya. "Actually, my work with the Sandy borg artifacts is nearly finished. I've even managed to piece together a loose narrative based on them."

Rebecca arched an elegant blonde eyebrow. "So you'll be leaving us then?"

Maya smiled. "I've almost convinced him to stay on permanently, Director. James has asked me to marry him."

"And you said yes. Congratulations to the both of you. Will you be holding a traditional ceremony?"

"A traditional ceremony?" James asked.

Maya groaned. "She means a traditional wedding of the People."

"And that's different from a regular ceremony, how?"

"You don't want to know," she said firmly. To Rebecca, she said, "We haven't gotten that far yet."

Rebecca tilted her seat back. "You will, of course, take him to see the Oracle."

Maya nodded. There were some traditions worth keeping, and that was one. "Of course, Director."

"Good then. Dr. Terhune, please let me know what I can do to assist with any additional work you do regarding the Sandby borg artifacts."

"There is one thing. I understand Tom Fairfax has been updating the Archives' cataloging system and adding better inventory lists." James leaned forward and met Rebecca's gaze evenly. "I thought we might want to search the Archives for documents related to Sanctuary, anything that might help us understand the records from the Sandby borg site better. Would it be possible for him to do that while I work my way through the rest of the Sandby borg items? He probably has the best grasp on how to find things at the moment, and we could really use some help."

"Yes, of course," Director Upton agreed. "I also have another recommendation, someone who assisted heavily when we first began building the Archives here. I can't guarantee she'll come, but I'll try to persuade her of the importance of the work being done here."

James rose and shook Rebecca's hand. "I appreciate that."

"Anything to assist with your work, particularly if it helps us locate Sanctuary," Rebecca said.

Maya and James left not long after. As soon as they were in the car, he said, "Ok, I know you guys have a long history together, but sometimes I feel like you're speaking a different language. What is the Oracle?"

"If you'll drive to the Archives, I'll show you."

"The Oracle is in the Archives."

"Yes and no. I promise I'll explain, but it's better if you see this with your own eyes." She gripped his hand, a silent plea for understanding. "Much like the origin myth."

"Ah. Ok."

He drove them to the Archives' parking area and helped her out of the car, his hands gentle. She let him, not necessarily out of a need for assistance. She enjoyed his touch, enjoyed having him near, and she was beginning to rely on his strength as much as her own.

Maya signed out a golf cart and showed James around the Archives. He'd never been beyond the reading room before. As they traveled deeper and deeper into the mountain housing some of the People's most valuable items, she outlined its history.

"Members of the People who originally settled here came because it was a frontier, a place where they were free to live as they chose. They befriended the local tribes, including the Cherokees, and eventually founded the town of Tellowee."

"So Tellowee is a Cherokee name?" James asked. "I wondered."

"It means 'white oak grove,' and yes, it's Cherokee. The People discovered a system of caves here and eventually expanded and modified them into the Archives, as technology improved and necessity demanded. The mountain is solid granite, but the caves could be humid."

"Hence the need for technology."

"Right. More importantly, the People could fall back here in an emergency, and they often did."

He gazed around them, his eyes roaming over the concrete-lined halls and the doors spaced at irregular intervals. "I can imagine. This place is huge on the inside."

Maya turned into one of the older, narrower tunnels and slowed their speed. "We've added to it over time. The area we're in now is part of the original cave system, whereas the Archives is housed in the newer sections. Technology," she reminded him. "And because we have the room and the security, many of the other settlements of the People have opted to send some of their holdings here."

He jerked around, facing her. "Wait. Tellowee isn't the only one?"

She shook her head, sending a mass of kinky curls flying around the sides of her face. "There are a handful of places like Tellowee around the world, places where the People can live in relative peace."

"How many of you are there? Surely not that many."

"There are nearly three thousand immortal Daughters at the moment, more or less, and more mortal Daughters and Sons. We stop counting the number of mortals after the second generation from immortality."

Maya eased the golf cart to a stop outside the entrance to the Oracle's chamber and nodded to the two Handmaidens flanking a large, heavy door. "Here we are."

One handmaiden entered information into a keypad affixed to one side of the door, then waited while Maya pressed her thumb to the scanner plate and entered a second code. The door's lock released, and the Handmaidens pulled the door open, allowing James and Maya to enter.

Here, the tunnel was even narrower, wide enough for just two people to walk side by side. The light fixtures were recessed into the walls and gave off a scant glow. The dim lighting combined with the close quarters and a damp chill turned the tunnel slightly spooky. In spite of the creep factor, younger Daughters somewhat irreverently called it the Tunnel of Love.

After twenty feet, the tunnel widened into a roughly round room with concrete walls, floor, and ceiling. Seven alcoves were evenly spaced around the room, each containing an artifact lit by a small spotlight, each one believed to have been a possession of one of the Seven Sisters. Two Handmaidens guarded the tunnel's terminus. Two others stood at attention in the center of the room at the foot of a rolling gurney draped with cloth. A fifth Handmaiden sat in a chair next to the bed, book in hand. She glanced up when Maya and James entered and smiled sweetly at them.

On the platform, a woman lay prone. She was dressed warmly and covered from head to toe by a transparent veil. A quiet reverence filled Maya. This woman had come to play a central role in the People's rituals, binding them together as surely as any legend or prophecy or shared history.

James stood stock still at the entrance, his avid gaze cataloging every detail of the room, from the alcoves to the Handmaidens to the woman at its center. "The Oracle?" he asked quietly.

"Yes." The reading Handmaiden marked her place in the book and moved out the way. Maya twined her fingers with James' and led him to the Oracle's side. "This is her."

"Did she give the People the Prophecy?"

"Nobody knows where the Prophecy came from." Maya shrugged and considered the sleeping woman. "It's possible she did, but it would've had to have been a very long time ago, before our written records begin."

James tilted his head to the side. "She doesn't issue prophecies, but you call her the Oracle?"

Maya pursed her lips, stifling a laugh. His confusion was natural, and so very endearing. "She was found in a cave, a grotto, really. I think it was somebody's idea of a joke. You know, mysterious woman in a cave, the mystical elements of the curse and the People's origins?"

"Gotcha. So who is she?"

"We don't really know. She's been this way for as long as anyone can remember, and we have some very old Daughters."

James dipped toward the Oracle and exhaled sharply. "She's not breathing."

Maya snagged his arm and tugged him backward. "Relax. She doesn't breathe. In fact, she doesn't move at all, not that anyone can see. We think she's in some sort of mystical stasis."

"So you just put her here and what?"

"Protect her. Watch over her." Maya lifted the veil away from the Oracle's face and torso and folded it carefully below her waist. "Hope she wakes up so we know who she is."

James cleared his throat. "Er, should you be doing that?"

"It's ok. This is part of the tradition. When a Daughter breaks her curse, she comes here with the one she trusts to pay homage to the Oracle."

"So you trust me, then? Your curse is broken?"

She smiled up at him, this man who meant so much to her. He'd earned her trust and ensnared her heart, and managed to save her in the process. "Yes and yes."

He slid an arm around her shoulders, and she leaned into him, thankful for his presence, grateful he'd taken a chance on her and had the patience to wait for her trust to grow. After a while, she took one of the Oracle's hands in her own and explained quietly how she'd met James and what he meant to her. When she'd emptied her heart and run out of words, she pressed a kiss to the Oracle's hand, surprised as she always was that the sleeping woman's skin was warm and soft, kept so by some force beyond Maya's reckoning.

"Can I touch her?" James asked.

Maya arched a single eyebrow. "You really do like older women, don't you."

James shot her an exasperated look. "One at a time is more than enough for me, sweetheart. I wanted to thank her, like you did. Can I do that?"

"I don't see why not."

James lifted the Oracle's hand and bent down to whisper softly, as if she really were asleep and he didn't want to wake her. Then he kissed her hand as Maya had done and stepped back.

Maya reached forward to draw the veil back across the Oracle's body.

The Oracle gasped and arched upwards. Her eyes shot open. "Gulnar?" she rasped. "Gulnar nadji?" She collapsed against the gurney and her body jerked, her limbs flailing against its metal sides. Maya snagged James' elbow and pulled him out of the way as five Handmaidens raced to the Oracle and braced themselves on either side of her, containing her on the gurney.

Maya's hand tightened on James' arm. "What did you do?"

"I talked to her, just like you did," James said, his voice shaking.

"What did you tell her?"

"I told her what you did, how we met and how I love you, and then I told her we'd found the Prophecy of Light and that we hoped to use it to break the curse."

The Oracle sagged and stilled. One of the Handmaidens radioed out. Another ripped the cloth away from the gurney's edge. Two others unlocked the wheels and rolled the Oracle carefully out of the cave. In a few moments they were gone. The remaining Handmaiden escorted them out past the two Handmaidens standing guard and left them at the golf cart.

Maya and James navigated their way to the Archives' entrance in silence. When Maya turned in the golf cart, the guard on duty relayed the information that the Oracle was on her way to the hospital near Tellowee.

James walked beside Maya to the car, head down, his expression pinched. "I'm so sorry, Maya. If I would've known she'd react to me..." He shuffled to a stop and stared at the sky above them, clear blue and cloudless. "Has no man ever spoken to her before?"

She threaded her arm through his and rested her head on his shoulder. "She has a lot of visitors, James, Sons and men like you who've become part of the People. It almost certainly wasn't your presence that triggered her seizures."

"Still, maybe I shouldn't have told her about the Prophecy. Maybe it would've been better if I hadn't said anything at all."

"I think you did exactly the right thing."

The Oracle had awakened, if only for a moment. James couldn't know what that might mean. He had no idea of her importance or of the significance of what he'd said. Maya turned the possibilities over, studying them carefully. Could the Oracle be connected to the Prophecy somehow? Is that why she'd woken now or had it simply been her time to wake up? And what was it she'd said? *Gulnar nadji.* Nothing Maya recognized, but maybe someone else would know the phrase.

All of that would be resolved in time. The Oracle would be cared for and maybe she'd even wake up for good. The curse would be broken, their enemy defeated, and the People saved. The hope that these things would come to pass was greater now than it ever had been before. Maya tucked the worry and hope away. For now, she had more pressing matters to think about, a family to build, a life to live, and a love to bind it all together.

She took James' hand and kissed him softly, absorbing his heat into her own, and with it some of his worry. He relaxed against her and she knew he'd be ok, that he'd go on to fulfill his promise to the Oracle. He'd help the People break the curse, and he'd love Maya forever. That was what she'd waited for her whole life, a man she could love without reservation, someone who loved her just as fiercely.

She intended to enjoy every moment with him.

The Prophecy of Light

In the days of Shadow
The Light will awaken
Daughters and Sons will gather
Where the bones of the Sisters shall lie
The storm will rise, but
The bow of the Enemy will unbend
And the Light of the People
Shall see into the darkest Shadow
Two paths lie before the People
Strength brings victory
Weakness is death
Only the Light can decide
Which one to follow

Acknowledgments:

Many thanks to Richard E. Hopkins, Jr., whose knowledge of weapons proved incredibly useful to the creation of the fight scenes. Richard also served as the "alpha" reader, the hole finder, the grammar check, and the final editor for both the first and second editions. Without him, this story would have floundered from the first word.

A huge thank you to my son, who provided invaluable feedback on the deeper story line. Muchas lovas!

Finally, thank you to Autumn's End Designs, Clayton, Georgia, for providing props for the photo for the original cover; to Deb's Cats N Quilts, Franklin, North Carolina, for help in selecting appropriate fabrics for the costume; and to the cover model for her patience during the chilly photo shoot.

About the Author:

Lucy Varna lives in Georgia, surrounded by her large, extended family. Visit her online at:

www.lucyvarna.com
www.daughtersofthepeople.com

The People's adventure continues...

Sanctuary (Daughters of the People, Book 5)
Jerusha Mankiller and Drew Martin continue the People's search
for Sanctuary and the Bones of the Just.

Coming soon!

Don't miss the first Sons of the People novel!

Single mom Sera Noland wasn't looking for love the day Levi
Ewart walked into her life, especially when her heart, and her
son's, had already endured enough hurt to last a lifetime.

Look for *Say Yes* (A Sons of the People Novel)
coming in April 2015.